STEFFANIE EDWARD

THIS
OTHER
ISLAND

bookouture

Published by Bookouture in 2021

An imprint of Storyfire Ltd.
Carmelite House
50 Victoria Embankment
London EC4Y 0DZ

www.bookouture.com

ISBN: 978-1-80019-362-8
eBook ISBN: 978-1-80019-361-1

To my mother, Patricia Edward, for your love and everything

Chapter One

Joe

2000

October. Not even deep into autumn, but the outside temperature was close to freezing and the wind was shuffling dirt and leaves everywhere.

Stepping out of the lift and out through the main doors of his block of flats, Joe sniffed the cold air, then turned his face away from the stench of sour food coming from the huge bins to his left. Joe was no fan of the cold. The shivering, the runny nose. The thing got right inside of your bones. He shuddered, adjusting his scarf to make sure it covered more of the back of his head and fitted tighter around his neck.

Already, he couldn't wait to get back inside, but buying his daily newspaper at seven in the morning had become part of his ritual. Gave him a reason for getting dressed. Today he needed to get fresh milk – sugar as well, for the coffee he'd need once back inside.

Out of the entrance and into the street, Joe pushed down on his trilby and lowered his head to avoid a head-on with the flying bits in the air, then shoved his hands in his pockets.

A force stopped him in his tracks. An arm was around his neck, pressing against his windpipe. He struggled to breathe.

'Who...?' He tried to speak, but the pressure on his neck got tighter.

'Shut it, old man,' the person behind him said, his voice vicious, direct, and so close, Joe felt hot breath touch his ear. 'Don't say a word.'

Joe was being dragged backwards on his heels, down the side alley that drunks and the like used as a toilet.

'What de—?' he started.

'Keep your mouth quiet, or you'll be meeting your maker.'

'What de—? What you think you doing? Let me—' Joe said loudly.

'What did I tell you?' the voice said.

Something like a fist was pressing into his back. Joe turned to get a glimpse of his attacker.

The fire in the young man's honey-coloured eyes took Joe by surprise. For a moment he forgot about the imminent danger he was in. He wasn't in a pissy alley, headlocked by a stranger with too much strength for this old Joe to match. He was somewhere else: forty years into his past, on the top deck of the ship making its way to England. The man tackling him wasn't a stranger, either. It was a rival. Ian.

'Keep moving,' the voice said.

It's him or me, Joe told himself, and jabbed his attacker with his bony elbow, hoping to destabilise him.

'I said—'

The sharp burn from a thrust in Joe's side sent his thoughts crashing into pain. Raw. Stinging. Scorching pain. He was falling, voices mumbling, feet were running. A warmth ran down his right side.

He was bleeding.

Chapter Two

Me and Pattie were playing outside when Auntie Agnes called us in and announced that I was going to England. My parents wanted me – the six-month-old child they'd sent to St Lucia, five years ago, returned to them.

'But why?' I asked.

'I would rather you didn't go too,' Auntie Agnes said, looking over my head, blinking like something was troubling her eyes.

'And what about Pattie? She can come too?'

Me and Pattie were only months apart in age. We were like sisters and shared everything, except knickers and a birthday. If one of us got into a fight, the other one jumped in to defend her. When a box came from England, neither of us could wait to see what sugary treats, toys and nice clothes we were in line for that day.

'No. No,' Auntie answered. 'Pattie cannot come. Your mother an' father want you back. It's their right,' and she walked away.

I couldn't imagine life without Auntie Agnes or Pattie. Apart from seeing my parents in the flesh, I couldn't see a reason for going to England. I was happy where I was. 'I will come back, as soon as I can,' I told Pattie.

On a school day, before it was light, Auntie Agnes sent Pattie off with our playmate Antoine's mum, whilst me and her went to town. It felt strange because I'd never been to town without Pattie. I was wearing a pretty red dress with a can-can skirt and ribbon at the waist that had come in one of the parcels from England. I had special pictures taken, which I saw later in a little book Auntie Agnes said was my passport. I would need it to travel, she told me. The only thing I recognised about me in the book was my picture.

'Where's my name?' I asked Auntie.

'Here,' she said, closing the book to show me the words: Yvette Angelina Francis printed in a white space at the bottom of the hard navy cover.

'But I'm Ruthie,' I said.

'From today, you will use your real name. Yvette.'

'It's not as nice as Ruthie,' I said, and she told me that from now on, Pattie was going to be called by her real name too: Dionne.

'What's a ci-ti-zen?' I asked Auntie, when I came across the word in my passport.

'It tells people which country you belong to. Dis,' she said, taking the book from my hand, 'means you belong to Englan'. You are English. It's the place you was born. An' when you come back to see us, you will be speaking English, just like the queen.'

The queen? I had no idea who that was or why I'd be speaking like her. Anyway, me and Pattie decided we didn't care what Auntie Agnes said: we'd never stop calling each other by our home-names: her Pattie and me Ruthie. I didn't see myself as an Yvette, nor Pattie as a Dionne, and that was that.

Then before I could ask any more questions, or accept what was coming, I was off – on my way to England, lost on a ship with others similar to me. I missed Pattie more than anything. And after what felt like months – instead of the fourteen days I later found out it was – I was there, dressed in layers of clothes, thick socks and shiny new shoes, which didn't take the cold away. And they – the parents who'd sent for me – were waiting by the big boat.

Mum looked everything like the picture Auntie Agnes had shown me: slim, light skin, small nose and painted lips.

'Well, look at my little girl,' she said, grabbing my arm. 'She skinny.' She was talking to the man standing behind her, wearing a dark coat and a trilby hat. My papa. Her eyes fell back on me. 'Who is your mother?'

'What kind of question is dat to ask de chile, Doli?' Papa said.

But she carried on staring at me, waiting for an answer.

'Dor – Dolina,' I said.

'Dolina?' she repeated, leaning over me, her thick lashes flicking in my face. 'Mummy. You must call me Mummy. Mummy or Mum.'

'Mummy,' I repeated, looking at her.

'You don't see you confusing de poor chile?' Papa told her. 'Come on, *ich mwen,* my child. She must be cole, Doli.' He put the red coat he was holding over his arm on me and picked me up, relieving the pinch I was feeling from the new shoes the woman taking care of us on the boat had made me put on.

England was a big country, crowded with buildings. There was too much to get used to. My new home was strange. We had to share everywhere, except our bedrooms, with other people Mum told me were tenants, like us. Not family or friends.

There were no goats, sheep, lizards or frogs. Only dogs and cats who lived inside people's houses. I wasn't even allowed to play outside. It wasn't safe, Mum and Papa said. There was no one to play with out there anyway. Days came and went when the idea of making my way back to St Lucia – to Pattie and Auntie Agnes – wouldn't leave my head.

I had no one to share my deepest thoughts with, thoughts only Pattie would understand. Her first letter came with one from Auntie Agnes. She wanted to know when I was coming back. All I could say was 'soon'. Though I had no idea when soon would be.

Her letters lifted any mood I was in. I couldn't wait to reply. I looked forward to them, but they couldn't replace having her with me. I missed us making mud pies under the house for our dollies; stealing off to eat guavas in the bushes Auntie Agnes said we weren't allowed to go to. I'd climb up and throw them down to Pattie. After filling our bellies, we'd wipe our mouths, pat our clothes clean and head back home before Auntie Agnes wondered where we were.

In one of my letters, I told Pattie about me watching snow fall from the sky like tiny feathers, how quickly each one melted once it touched your skin, tongue, even your eyelash. But if it fell on something else that wasn't warm, it stayed for a while, one icy feather on top of another, painting the trees, cars, pavements, everything a glittering white. We agreed that, one day, she would visit me and we'd persuade Papa and Mama to let us play outside like I'd seen the white children doing: bringing a lot of the snow together and making a fat, round man, putting a scarf around its neck, a hat on its head, a pipe in its mouth. We'd make our very own snowman.

She told me she'd learnt to stand on her hands. I told her I'd tried, but kept falling sideways.

I never imagined life without Pattie's letters, the precious link to the life I'd left behind; the connection that felt like my right to breathe, that kept me afloat, especially when things between Papa and Mum started falling apart. Then Mum never had anything nice to say about Papa anymore, though he was nothing but nice to me. His caring and thoughtful nature led him to pick up where Mum left off with me.

Often, he'd lie across the foot of my bed listening to me read. If he drifted off, I'd poke him.

'Papa, you're not listening,' I'd say.

He'd raise his head to look at me. 'Your voice so sof'',' he'd say.

I'd giggle, but let him close his eyes again.

Other times, he'd drive me into fits of laughter, folding his eyelids so that only the soft, pink skin underneath it showed. Then he'd suck his cheeks in and make silly faces at me. And his tickles sent me into such hysterics, Mum would leave whatever she was doing to come and see what all the noise was about. That was when things were good.

But after I hit my teens Pattie's letters stopped, and so did the constant arguments between Mum and Papa, because he left. I was alone with Mum, and Papa grew further and further away from me.

Chapter Three

Yvette

I was standing in front of the bathroom mirror, face contorted, plucking a hair from my chin, when the phone rang. I went to my bedroom to answer it.

'Angel?'

I sat on the bed. 'Oh, Papa. It's so good to hear from you. How you doing?'

'I… I'm in de hospital.'

'What? What for?' I stood up. 'What's happened?'

'It's de Royal London.' There was a ripple in his voice. 'Whitechapel.'

'Why, Papa? What's wrong?'

'You can come?'

'Of course. But—'

'Just come.'

I rushed around, squashing – one by one – the ideas popping up in my head about why Papa might be in hospital.

I had to cancel Mum.

'An emergency?' she asked, when I told her. 'What kind of emergency?'

'It's… work. I'm sorry. I'll call you later, Mum,' I said, and hung up.

On the bus ride to the hospital, my mind drifted to the nights me and Mum used to stay awake in our beds, listening for the sound of the front door opening, Papa's feet brushing over the door mat, his muffled footsteps climbing the stairs.

As soon as any of those sounds floated up the stairs, I'd exhale. Low tones from their bedroom would give me permission to sleep.

I walked into the hospital and checked my bag for the lavender-scented hanky I kept with me in case I came across unfriendly smells.

The only person at the nurses' station was on the phone, the side of her face to me. I unzipped my coat. She shot me a glance.

'Okay. Right… Right,' she said, then put the phone down. 'How can I help?'

'I've come to see Mr Francis. Joseph Francis?' I said.

'Francis? Ah, yes. Second door on the right, before the main ward,' she said, pointing.

Why was Papa in a side room instead of on the main ward?

I knocked lightly on the door. No response, so I opened it. Papa seemed to be asleep. I stepped closer to the bed. He was wearing a hospital gown, lying on his back, clean shaven, as usual. He coughed. I stepped back, almost falling into the armchair behind me.

'Mmm,' he said, opening his eyes, then blinking. 'Angel?'

'I didn't want to wake you,' I said, coming forward again.

He pulled himself into a sitting position and pain deepened the two lines shaped like brackets around his nose and mouth. He cleared his throat and reached for his brown trilby on the bedside table.

'Aaah,' he said, his long, bony fingers adjusting the hat on his head. 'Getting ole, *ich mwen*, my child. Your papa getting ole.'

'So what's going on, Papa? Why are you here?'

'I get stab.'

'What? What d'you mean? By whom?'

'I didn't want to tell you dat over de phone,' he said. 'Papa caa take a fight no more.' He shook his head. 'Eh-eh.'

My bum found the edge of the chair I'd almost fallen into, my eyes stayed focused on him. 'How? How did it happen?'

'It was just a newspaper I went to de shop to get,' he began. 'When, bam! – I don't know where de fella come from. He grab me, pull me in de dirty alley. Next thing I know is pure blood. De fella stab me.'

'Papa.' The thought of someone shoving a knife into Papa sent a shiver through me. This wasn't one of the scenarios that had run through my mind after his call.

'After dat' – Papa shrugged – 'I find myself in here.'

'Where did he stab you?'

'Dere. Dere, in my side.' He pointed to the ribbed area under his right arm. 'Take my wallet – lucky he didn't get my keys.'

'How bad? Is… is there any internal damage?'

'No. Dey say I was lucky.' He put his hands to rest on his lap.

'Thank God, Papa.' I sighed. 'That's a blessing.'

We were both silent, listening to the sound of approaching footsteps.

'So why have they put you in here, on your own?' I asked, after they faded.

'De post office. Insurance. Dey paying,' Papa said, like it was trivial information.

'Oh, and how long have you been here?'

He raised his thin eyebrows and looked towards the ceiling. 'Two days now, I believe.'

'And you've only just contacted me?'

'I have your number at home amongst my papers an' I caa keep too much numbers in my head dese days, Angel.'

'If you used it more often, Papa, you'd—'

'Ahh… I was going to call your mother, but you know how she is already.'

'It was an emergency, Papa. Mum wouldn't be funny about that,' I said. But who was I trying to fool? We both knew how awkward Mum could be, especially if it was something to do with Papa.

'Anyway, Bobotte manage to find your number for me.'

'I can't believe it, Papa. Stabbed?'

'An' in big, broad daylight – just going to get a paper.' He sounded like he was still trying to accept it.

'It could have been so much worse, though.'

'Is true,' he nodded. A dazed look crept over his face. 'Even de police say dat.'

'Yes, the police – what're they saying? They caught anyone?'

Papa turned his head towards the wall and made a long hissing sound as he kissed his teeth. 'Police? Police?' he said, then turned to me again.

'But they—'

'Dey come here a while ago with some pictures for me to look at.' His voice drifted.

'You recognise anyone?'

He kissed his teeth again. This time short and sharp, like a bird's tweet. 'Uh-uh.' He shook his head. 'No police ever going to find dat man.'

'Somebody must have seen something.'

'Uh-uh.' He shook his head again. 'Nobody see nothing – nothing for de police to go on, dey say. Dat fella,' he added, after a pause, 'must be long gone. Bobotte tell me sometimes dese fellas target certain areas – certain people too.'

'Who's going to target you, Papa?'

'Anyway, I tell de police everything I had to tell dem.' He waved a hand in front of him. 'Everything I know. But you looking well, Angel,' he said.

I wished I could say the same about him. His face had aged since the last time I saw him, ten months ago. He'd get the rest he needed in here.

'You got everything you need? Where're your pyjamas?'

'Dey say it's better if I wear dis. Easier for dem.'

'What about toiletries and stuff?' I said. The surfaces in his bedside cupboards were empty. I hadn't brought anything, in my rush to get here.

'I have what I need.'

'I'll pop out and get you some fruit,' I said, slipping into dietician mode. It was my job, after all. 'No mangoes, though.' We both smiled. It was our favourite fruit, but only the Caribbean ones. 'I won't be long.'

'Angel?' he said, as I pulled the door open.

'Yes, Papa?' I turned to him.

'I'm glad you come.'

'Me too, Papa.'

'Don't mind how bird vex—'

'—it caa vex with tree.' I finished the proverb he'd repeated to me since my childhood. 'I know Papa.' I smiled.

No matter how upset you get with someone you need in your life, you must keep returning to them.

Today, I sensed the 'vexed' bird was me. Papa, the tree.

Outside it was raining. Mid-morning. The lack of sun suggested a murky dusk was on its way. That would normally dampen my mood, but a good feeling was brewing inside me. It was horrible to see Papa in so much pain and scary to think how much worse it could have been, but it was comforting knowing exactly where he was.

This misfortune could turn out to be a turning point for us. We could spend lots more time together, doing stuff, like in the old days when we'd sit at the kitchen table tucking into our fish and chips, Papa splashing hot sauce over his, Mum's accusations of us turning English. Or maybe we'd start meeting again at the club, for a catch-up and a drink.

An hour later, I was rushing up the hospital steps again, a carrier bag in each hand. The first had my dripping umbrella, some tangerines, pears and bananas; the second, water, juice, deodorant, some of Papa's favourite Imperial Leather soap and a couple of wash rags.

I was turning the handle on the door to Papa's room when a different nurse, with 'Sister Lisa Thompson' written on her badge, stopped me.

'He's left,' she said, remorse and indignation stamped on her face.

'But I—'

'He's discharged himself. Against our advice, I might add,' she said, frowning.

I felt a complete idiot.

'He asked me to give you this.'

I took the piece of paper she handed me and thanked her.

At least he'd had the decency to leave me his address.

The driver of the cab I picked up said he knew where Fairchilds Estate was. Once seated, I tried to calm myself. I'd never been to Papa's new home. The last time I visited him, I hadn't seen him for six months. That time, I expected to find him in his flat-share in Stamford Hill, but the person who opened the door told me he'd moved. So, I'd found myself in Tottenham, at his domino club, targeting Mr Bobotte, his closest friend.

'It'll be Father's Day in a couple of weeks,' I'd told Mr Bobotte, after the usual 'nice to see' you, stuff. 'I've got to at least send Papa a card.'

Mr Bobotte's querying expression had softened. 'Of course. Of course,' he'd said, in his baritone voice that brought melted dark chocolate to mind. And he'd given me a new address for Papa.

A light-skinned woman with a nose like a cabbage had opened the door to me.

'Does Joseph Francis live here?' I'd asked, as she looked me over.

'Joseph?' she repeated, greasy remnants of red lipstick around her mouth. 'Come.' She widened the gap in the door. 'Joe?' she started shouting, her bare feet going at a gallop up the staircase filled with the suffocating smell of burning fat. 'A young lady here to see you.'

Papa had met us on the landing, wearing a green and white chequered lumberjack shirt with the sleeves rolled halfway up his slim, hairy arms.

'Angel? Dat's my angel! My daughter, Yvette,' he told the woman, handing her the spatula he was holding. 'Dis is my frien',' he'd said, referring to the woman as he hugged me. She'd eyed me some more.

Papa's display of joy had made me feel special, but I knew I wouldn't see or hear from him again until the next time I found him. Past discussions with him about this always turned out to be a waste of time. He'd make light of it, saying he knew I could take care of myself and if anything happened to me, he was sure someone would let him know. I couldn't get him to see what his making an effort to stay in touch would mean to me.

That day, tears had been in my eyes even before I could get through the front door. After that visit, I told myself I'd had enough of spending days or weeks getting over the sadness and disappointment each visit left me with: burying the pain it caused, pretending it was okay. So, I'd stopped tracking him.

'Fairchilds Estate.' The cab driver's voice interrupted my thoughts. I paid and got out.

According to the signage, number twenty-nine was on the third floor, which was where the lift appeared to be stuck. My experiences of home visits to clients living in places like this made me brace myself for the stench of stale pee. And only God knew what else I might stumble upon on my way up.

I took a deep breath, juggled the carrier bags around, exhaled and took a firmer grip of my hanky.

Chapter Four

Doli

I hear the crying before I could even knock on the door. Then Bel standing in front of me holding a baby – face wet an' stain with tears, even though it stop crying. The chile big, sad eyes take one look at me an' it start crying again.

'I didn't know I was so ugly,' I say, stepping inside.

'Oh, hush, hush, baby,' Bel say, in a sof' voice I never hear her use before, an' she start stroking the fine hair on the baby head. 'That's Granny's good-good friend, Miss Doli. A nice lady. Say, "Hello, Miss Doli",' she say, looking at the chile. Then she speak for him: 'My name is Justin.'

'Hello, little Justin,' I say, although I know the chile not interested in me nor my hello.

'Doli, I'm so sorry,' Bel start to say, 'but Michelle bring Justin over this morning. He has the chickenpox and she don't want to catch it. I tell her I'm sure she already had the thing when she was little, but she say she's not taking any chances. I'm so sorry, Doli. I called your house, but you must have already left.'

Ever since Bel retire, two years back, in 1998, the most I see she have time for is housework an' taking care of the grandchildren her Michelle an' Darren, give her. Not even the soca aerobics class she can make nowadays.

I really get to know Bel after my fall at the beer factory. She was one of the few people who come to see me in hospital an' secretly advise me to make a claim against the company. She was doing the same machine operator job like me dere, until dey ask her to help out as a switchboard operator.

Rosemary, one of the girls working with us, did tell me she feel Bel get the job by lying on her back, but if you know Bel you would see Rosemary was just being malicious. Bel love her dead husban' too much. Besides, Bel is a *dougla* with fair skin an' sof', pretty hair. She can speak like the English well too. Those things bring plenty opportunities to her.

I find myself stepping over toys an' moving all sorts of baby things to find space to sit down in the room.

'What can I do?' Bel say. 'You want a cup of tea or anything?'

I tell her no. Is like everybody plotting for me not to get a new outfit for Margaret an' Winston wedding anniversary party. First Yvette cancel on me, now Bel. Maybe I should go to Petticoat Lane alone.

Watching Bel stroking her grandson while he lie across her legs sucking his thumb, eyes struggling to stay open, take me right back.

I don't remember having dat kind of closeness with Yvette as a baby. Maybe it's because she wasn't with me for so long. When I told my sister, Agnes, how hard it was for me to work an' do the English, typing an' shorthand course I wanted to do, I was more than grateful when she suggest I send the baby back for her. Mama had passed an' Agnes lose all interest in coming to Englan'. She was happy with her dressmaking, but was alone an' it look like, as far as she was concerned, no man was good enough for her.

'My little niece would be good company for me,' she said. 'An' you can send back for her when you are ready.'

Plenty women used to send their children back to their mother, sister or other family who was able to take care of dem so dey could work. After all, we didn't come to Englan' for no holiday. We come to work, make money to send home or save for us to go back.

'We will send for her before she ready to start school,' I did tell Joe.

Dat help to make him see sense. The next thing I had to do was find somebody I trust who was going back home on holiday. An' a blessing come when Velma, a good frien' of mine, at the time, agree to take the baby home for us.

'But Doli, you must be able to find something nice in your wardrobe, girl,' I hear Bel saying. 'Is not every party or dance you need a new outfit for.'

'What?' I look at her.

Justin start to moan an' Bel voice sof'en up again. 'All right. All right, darling,' she tell him, an' start bouncing her legs up an' down while she stroke his head. 'I myself wearing that purple dress with the sequins. You remember it?'

'Mm? Yes. Yes,' I tell her, though my mind is not fully with her.

'Just pick a outfit you know nobody eh see you in for a while. And you know you look good in everything – with that young, sexy body you have.'

She lean across to tap my leg an' Justin start to fuss again.

'Pass me the calamine lotion over there,' she say, pointing at the pink bottle beside me on the floor. I hand it to her an' glance at my watch. Petticoat Lane will be chock-a-block with people, pushchairs, an' everything at dis time. It didn't make sense for me to go dere now.

Is up an' down, up an' down, I always have to walk on Auntie Lucille doorstep, before either she or Uncle can let me in. An' today the wind so bold, it want to drag me to where I don't necessarily want to go.

Auntie an Uncle house is at the end of a row of houses in what dey call a cul-de-sac. Running the Partner – where six of us put a little money in a pot each week an' take turns to cash in – allow dem to save up enough to buy it. Three big bedrooms an' another spare one downstairs on the way to the kitchen. Dat give dem more than enough rooms to rent out, but Auntie say, she finish with sharing a house with strangers.

After a sufficient amount of clicking an' clacking, Uncle open the door an' the smell of Sunday lunch rush to me. The stewed chicken would be a boiler, like the yard fowl we used to have back home. Dey would never buy the sof' white chicken, quick to fall off the bone in less than a hour on the fire. 'Dey growing dem chickens in a factory somewhere,' Uncle always say. An' Auntie agree with him.

'Good afternoon, Uncle,' I say.

'*Mwen la. Mwen la.* I'm dere, by the grace of God,' he reply, after I ask how he is. 'Look like you doing fine too.'

'It's only me,' I shout out to Auntie as I coming down the stairs. 'You all right, Auntie?'

'God is love,' she say, moving across the kitchen like her body is a heavy load.

I sit down an' listen to her complaining about the pain in her hips. Looking at her face, I start wishing again dat Mama was still alive. Mama was Auntie's big sister an' so much about Auntie, even the way she talk, remind me of her.

'I cannot take dis cole anymore,' Auntie say. Then, 'What a terrible shame it is about Joe, eh?'

'Joe?' Every part of me stand to attention.

Auntie lift the heavy cover from the Dutch pot. 'You mean Yvette don't tell you he in hospital?' She stir the pot, put a little gravy in her hand an' make a noise with her mouth as she taste it. 'An' it is very bad too, from what I hear.'

'But what? What happen to him, Auntie?' I say.

She put the cover back on the pot. 'Some kind of stabbing.'

'Mugging an' stabbing.' Uncle voice make me stand to attention again.

'Yes, his frien' Bobotte call here to say he was trying to get in touch with Yvette.'

'When?'

'Yesterday. First thing,' Uncle say an' sit down beside me.

'Bobotte?' I say. Why Yvette didn't tell me any of dat? An' why Bobotte didn't call me instead of Auntie? It couldn't be dat Joe forget my number, but remember Auntie's. 'So is here he have to phone to get his own chile number?'

'We try to phone Yvette ourself too, after he call,' Uncle say.

'But we didn't get her,' Auntie jump in. 'Dese young people always so busy.'

I start to pull off my cardigan.

'Lunch almost ready, but you want a cup of tea?'

'No – no, thank you, Auntie,' I say.

'I tell Anthony, we will have to go an' see him. You never know with dese things. One minute you hear somebody sick, next thing – you never know.'

'Which hospital he in?'

'Royal London, I believe,' Auntie say, an' turn the fire off under the rice.

I help to make the salad an' put everything on the table, all the while listening to everything Auntie an' Uncle have to say about what happen to Joe.

Chapter Five

Joe

He'd been over his attack too many times in his head; then the visit from that Sergeant Peters, with all of those pictures for him to look at, had Joe all uncomfortable again. One look at picture number four and a heat ran through his body. His fingers shook when his eyes fell on the crew cut around that slim face, those vicious, light brown eyes, laughing at him, making him feel like he was less of a man.

'Recognise someone?' the sergeant asked him. Joe must have been looking at the picture for too long.

'Mmm… No. No,' he told the sergeant and shook his head. 'I don't think so. I… I'm sure de person was lighter an'… an' his nose… Uh-uh. No, he's not dere.' Joe put the picture back among the rest, on the blanket covering his legs.

The sergeant took a long breath in and let it out. 'Okay,' he said, as he stood up to take the pictures from Joe.

'I… I don't want to make a mistake. You understan'?' Joe said, trying to clear his thoughts.

'Well, you've got our details. Give us a call if you remember anything,' the sergeant said, shuffling the pictures and pushing them back into a large envelope. He wished Joe well and left.

Joe didn't feel at ease with police and others like them. Even before he had come to England, in 1961, black people had been catching hell from white people with this nasty racism – and especially from the police. It had taken a while for Joe to understand how a set of people could hate another group so much, just because they had a different skin colour. And, for that, they would even kill. 'If dey don't like our colour, den why dey come an' call us?' he had asked Jacob, the friend he was sharing his first room with on Portobello Road.

Joe sighed, looking up at the hospital room's ceiling. He knew about 'police brutality', 'wrongful arrests' and 'deaths in police custody'. He'd almost joined in with one or two of the marches against Hackney police for beating that young boy, Trevor Monerville.

When Mr Monerville had come to talk to the domino club members about what the police had done to his son, Joe could see, from the tightness in his jaw and the redness in his eyes, what that father was going through. While the police had the man's child in custody, they gave the young boy such a beating, it damaged his brain. And which one of those police people was going to point a finger to identify those responsible?

Any one of those young fellas in the mugshots – even the one who'd stabbed him – could end up dead in a police cell. No. Joe wasn't going to push any young black boy into the hands of the police.

Joe lay cushioned in his favourite position on his long settee, his hat resting comfortably on his forehead to keep out the light. Yes. His home. This was the best place for him.

Sleep was crawling over his body when the bang on the door shook him.

'Uh?' Joe's sudden movement tipped the trilby onto his chest. 'What de—?'

He couldn't get up straight away, even if he wanted to. The tightness in his joints and pain in his side forced him to linger before dragging his body out of the sweet hole in the settee that hugged him like a hammock.

Maybe he should have left his telephone number and not his address. But what the hell. His daughter was only showing how much she cared. It bothered him that she was always the one taking the trouble to find him. He should have done better. He *should* do better. He'd told himself that over the years. But he couldn't put his pride aside. Couldn't stop himself from feeling judged. By Doli. By Yvette. Yvette's little comments, subtle criticisms, only added to his sense of guilt. Inadequacy. Mixed in with the joy of seeing Yvette was always the reminder of how much he'd let her down. But what is done is done.

For so long he'd wanted a home that didn't bring that look he had learnt to recognise as disappointment or embarrassment to his daughter's face when she visited. But as Mama always used to say, 'You have one plan and God have another.'

'Hello, *doudou*. Darling,' he said, as he opened the door.

'Papa.' He could see she was upset. 'You discharged yourself? Why did you do that, Papa? Why?'

'I couldn't stay dere, Angel,' Joe said, taking easy baby steps back towards the settee. 'Dese kinds of places not for me.'

His head was feeling like when he had his liquors in. But it was weeks since he'd touched a drink. It had to be due to those drugs they had given him in the hospital.

'Why didn't you wait for me?' Yvette said. 'I wasn't gone that long, Papa.'

'I tell you, I didn't feel comfortable dere.'

'What? Was the bed too lumpy?'

'So dey give you my note.'

'They wouldn't want to keep you in hospital if they didn't need to, Papa. Bed spaces are precious, you know, even private ones.'

'Huh,' Joe said. Best to let her have her say. 'Switch de heating on over dere for me please, Angel,' he said, pointing at the dial on the wall by the sitting room door. 'It feel like winter moving in with me.'

'D'you want a hot drink?'

'No. No. Just turn up de heating an' pass one of dem blankets on top of de wardrobe for me.'

Sometime later, Joe heard his daughter saying something about *bouyon*, compelling him to open his eyes.

'I can manage,' he said, when she tried to help him up. She had moved the blanket, and the cold and pain was coming back. He used all his strength to pull himself up, then let Yvette hold his arm until he reached the table.

'*Bouyon*, eh?' he said, sucking up the smell of the St Lucian soup. He imagined the dumplings and yam soaking in the thick, tasty liquid.

Yvette waited for him to pick up his spoon, then she sat opposite him, her bowl in front of her.

'Eddoes?' he said, dipping his spoon in to check the solid pieces in the bowl.

'Of course. And pumpkin – the way you like it.'

Joe tasted the liquid. 'Mmm. Nice,' he said, and cleared some phlegm from his throat. He put a piece of eddoe in his mouth and started to chew, but as soon as he swallowed, that troublesome cough started again.

'You all right?' Yvette said.

'I...' He pointed at his throat with the spoon. 'I have a... cough.'

'Here.' She put a glass of water in front of him.

In no time she was standing next to him, tapping, rubbing and slapping his back as he coughed and tried to take in some air.

'Uh-uh,' he said, pushing her away.

'Papa, you're bleeding,' she said.

'Uh? What…?' Joe was praying for something to happen so he could breathe.

The little strength he had started to leave. Angel was shouting… *hospital.* He had to lie down.

Chapter Six

Yvette

The air in Papa's little flat had been stale when he opened the door to me. He said he was cold, but I had to crack a couple of windows open. The bathroom and kitchen needed a deep clean. I couldn't even satisfy my caffeine craving with the solid crust I'd found in his 'instant' jar in the kitchen. The only things in the fridge were dregs of a tub of Stork margarine, half a pint of sour milk and a couple of spongy, sprouting potatoes. The freezer compartment was bursting – ice over a pack of mixed vegetables next to a Tupperware container with remnants of tinned tomatoes. Papa's bin was an old carrier bag on the floor with an empty bottle and two Guinness cans.

After cleaning up in there, I'd checked on him. He looked so peaceful and content sleeping on his old sofa. I sneaked out to the shops to get the ingredients for the soup. It was supposed to have helped with his recovery – not send him into a coughing fit.

His body had turned to jelly on the floor. He'd always been slim, but as I shifted him so that he wasn't lying on his wound, I realised how bony he'd become.

When I called the ambulance, the woman on the phone told me: 'We need to make sure nothing's blocking his air passage.'

'I've already done that.' I told her I was CPR-trained.

I kept a close eye on the bleeding, whilst praying for the ambulance to arrive.

There were three attendants: two men and a woman.

'Is he on any medication?' the woman asked. She took notes while the men attended to Papa.

'No… I'm not sure,' I said.

Papa was responding with odd moans to questions from the paramedic.

They stabilised Papa, then slid him onto the stretcher and carried him to the lift with me scuttling along behind. Downstairs, passers-by stood watching the stretcher being raised into the back of the ambulance.

'Discharged too early, eh?' one of the paramedics said, once we were on our way.

'No. He left,' I said, quietly annoyed at having to admit to my father's negligence. 'Discharged himself.'

The woman tutted. 'Never a good idea,' she said, and added something to her notes.

As the ambulance moved in and out of the bus lanes, I glanced at Papa, lying on the stretcher with a transparent mask over his nose. Where had that cough come from? It wouldn't even let him speak. He needed air, but his clothing was already loose at the neck. Papa needed more caring for than he realised.

Another moan came from him. The woman's walkie-talkie was muttering.

'Is he in pain?' I said.

'Possibly.' The paramedic gave me a weak smile. 'Shouldn't be too long. He'll probably be taken straight back to surgery.'

As soon as they wheeled Papa off to theatre, I called Perpetua. Pe, the friend who'd become like a sister since we'd met at uni. I waited at the hospital entrance for her.

'Why you out here in the cold?' she said, when she arrived, diverting my thoughts from what was going on with Papa. We hugged. 'I brought you a mochaccino.'

She followed me back inside to a waiting area not far from where they'd taken Papa. We joined other people sitting on the metal chairs close to the reception area, which was busier than a chip shop on a Friday night, though the staff seemed to be taking it in their stride. They were used to the belly-aches and sports injuries Saturday afternoon brought through the A&E doors. A young doctor wearing a brown sari with yellow flowers walked by, conversing with a man with a folder in his hand.

'Good job you were there,' Pe said.

'Huh?' I held my cup near my nose so I could take in the cocoa and caffeine mix. 'I felt so useless,' I said. 'Shit scared.'

Pe took a sip from her drink and smacked her lips. 'You were there, girl. Imagine what could have happened if he was on his own.'

Pe was thirteen when she came home to find her mum in a diabetic coma that she never came out of, leaving Pe at the mercy of Social Services. Her dad had been somewhere in Canada with a new family, so she'd ended up in long-term foster care.

I rubbed the top of my arm where Papa had gripped me earlier. My mind fell into the shivering thought of Papa bleeding to death, alone in his flat. Why, after all these years, hadn't he met that person I hoped he would?

A nurse called for a Jonathan somebody. A young man in shorts, supported by another carrying his football boots, hopped gingerly towards her.

'Did they say how long he might be?'

'What's that?' I asked, turning to Pe.

'Did they say how long he might be in there?'

'No. No, they didn't. But, listen, you go, if you have to.'

She'd left her four-year-old son, Temi, at home with her partner, Addae.

'I'll be all right. Honestly,' I said. 'I'll call you when he's out.'

'Don't be silly,' she said, nudging me with her thigh.

Someone behind me coughed. I leaned forward. Hospitals are where you're close to the most germs.

Minutes later, they were calling my name. A tired-looking surgeon, still wearing his blue gown and rubber shoes, stood in a corner with me. He said the procedure had gone well.

'Thank goodness.' I sighed.

'There was a small blood clot which we removed successfully. He should be fine now.'

'What about the coughing?' I said.

'Umm. That, you'll need to discuss with his consultant.'

Chapter Seven

Yvette

I'd just got back from my morning run around Hackney Marshes when Aaron called from Dominica, where he'd been for two weeks at a family reunion. He'd asked me to come with him and his mother, but after months of deliberation I decided going would be torturing myself – not when I didn't see us having a future together. I loved him, but after three and a half years it was obvious that he wasn't going to sign up to the future I wanted: him and me living as a family with one or two children. As hard as that might be, I'd have to move on – try to find someone else before my ovaries shut down.

'Hi, babes,' he said, when I answered the phone.

'You're up late, or should I say early?' I said.

'I meant to call last night, but things got slightly crazy down here.'

'Same here.' I gave him a quick summary of what had happened with Papa.

'He's gonna be all right, though?'

'I think so. How's it all going with you?'

'Oh, good. But miss you though, girl. Wish you'd come.'

'You'll be back next week.' I smiled, watching the coffee brew, the aroma comforting me.

'Mmm. Want me to bring anything special back for you?'

'Sunshine would be good.'

He chuckled. I could see the slight gap he had between his top two middle teeth, and the squint of his brown eyes.

'I'll give it a go,' he said. 'See you soon. Greet your paps for me, eh?'

'Okay.'

'Love you.'

'Yeah.' I hesitated, then added: 'Love you, too.'

Before Aaron, I'd come out of my longest relationship, of eighteen months, with Richard, who'd ended up doing a sly one with some girl he met at the gym.

For almost a year after that I gave up on meeting anyone I could take seriously. I said yes to the odd date, but if it got heavier than a good-night peck on the doorstep, I said my goodbyes.

Most men seem promising at the start, but after the usual six months 'best behaviour' period, their nasty bits started to show. Then Pe, on a mission for us both to meet some decent 'white collar' men, announced she'd bought us tickets to the black solicitors' ball.

We needed a change from what she referred to as 'those losers, with five children from five different women scattered all around London.'

I was on board.

She went home empty-handed that night, whilst I ended up exchanging numbers with Aaron, who'd simply tapped my arm as Pe and I were about to climb the stairs leading to the exit, and asked me to dance.

Pe had given me her quietly excited look: lips pursed, brows raised over glaring eyes, followed by a gentle nudge, then quickly took my coat from me.

I turned back to Aaron who, in the semi-darkness, took my arm.

He called me the next day.

Pe couldn't stop laughing when I told her he was an electrician and not the white-collar calibre we had been expecting to meet.

'But he's running his own business,' I said.

I warmed to him quickly. He's mature and reliable, and never comes before I do. And if he does, give him half an hour, at the most, and he'll be ready to go again.

But it's not all about sex and being reliable, is it?

I'd thought it was a big plus when he said he didn't have any children. At least he wouldn't be bringing that kind of baggage.

'Hey,' I'd said to Pe, after giving it more thought. 'You think there might be something wrong with him? How many black men do you know deep into their thirties without any children?'

'Think he might be firing blanks?' she said.

'Oh, God.'

We laughed it off at the time then, around a year into our relationship, Aaron admitted to me that he didn't have children because he didn't want any.

'It's just not something I've wanted in my life,' he said.

'He's probably not met the right woman,' Pe said, when I told her.

She had to be right. So, I put that worry in a box and convinced myself that time would make him see how different I was from the rest.

But three years on hadn't done it so far. I mean, all I want is what your average woman around my age wants, if they don't already have it. Was that really asking for too much?

'I've waited long enough,' I told Pe, a few weeks ago. She reminded me how hard it is to find a man like Aaron. 'Has he ever cheated on you?' she said.

'Not as far as I know, but it's been three and a half years, Pe – 2001 will be here in a few months, and it's not gonna catch me still dithering.'

*

I'd almost finished cooking lunch. The chicken was browning nicely in the oven and the pot of rice and peas was drying out on a low flame. This was probably the best time to make my regular weekend call to Auntie Agnes. It might be too late by the time I got back from seeing Papa.

Living apart from Auntie Agnes for over thirty years hasn't turned us into strangers, like me and Pattie – I mean Dionne. Auntie Agnes has never stopped calling or writing to me and still feels more like a mother than an aunt. But since Dionne stopped writing, all news about her has been through Auntie Agnes. Like she's married, has a daughter, who must be around nine or ten years old now, and she's a lawyer – something Auntie Agnes is so proud about. It was Mum and Auntie Lucille who told me that Dionne and I weren't really related, because she was adopted by Auntie Agnes. But that didn't change anything for me. I still see Dionne as a once-close relative. A cousin. The deep connection from our childhood is still there for me. That's why her cutting me off hurt so much. Plus, Auntie Agnes was Mum's sister and treated Dionne like she was her only child and me a loving niece.

'Oh, it's you, Yvie?' Auntie Agnes said, hearing my voice. 'I thought it might be Dionne, but I was planning to call you anyhow. Auntie Lucille just told me about your father. I am so sorry.'

I answered her questions and told her I was about to go to the hospital.

'You think dey will find the person who did dat?'

'Don't know, Auntie.'

'Englan' is such a big place. Criminals have more places to hide. I'll pray he makes a quick recovery. What a blessing dere was no serious damage. But, dat must be putting a little pressure on you.'

'Yeah,' I said, 'but I'm okay.'

'Well, I don't want to keep you back,' she said.

'Yeah. Give my love to Dionne, when you speak to her.'

'Oh, yes, of course I will do dat,' Auntie Agnes said. 'Do what you can for your father, as I am sure you will. You already know you can call me any time, eh?'

I could hear her husband in the background. At sixty-eight, Auntie Agnes was newlywed to Leonce, a returnee and widower, from Canada. They'd met through the catechism lessons she taught in church, had a brief courtship that I knew nothing about, and their marriage was a quiet affair.

'I'm not getting any younger, Yvie,' she'd said, when I asked why she got married so suddenly. 'An', besides, you know I don't like all of dat big fuss.'

I told her I understood, to avoid getting into it, but really I felt excluded, pushed aside.

There was no one at the nurses' station when I came in. And again, Papa was asleep.

I sat down, studying his face. His ears were larger than I remembered. Ears grow as we get older, I'd read somewhere. Seemed Papa had reached that stage.

I was getting up to go back to the nurses' station for an update on Papa's condition, when I heard him saying, '*Ladjé mwen.* Let me go. *Mwen di ladjé…* I say…'

'Papa?' I said.

His eyes were still closed, but his voice was getting louder. 'Uh?' He looked up at me.

'You okay?'

'Uh? Angel?'

'Yes, it's me, Papa,' I said. 'Having a bad dream, eh?'

'What?'

'You're sweating,' I said, and pulled out a tissue to wipe his forehead. 'Who were you telling to let you go?'

'Let me go?'

'Yes, you were saying it in your sleep. *Ladjé mwen.*'

'Dat's what I said?' He kissed his teeth. 'Just some stupid dream.'

'You're supposed to be relaxing in here, Paps, not stressing.'

'Who can relax in here?' he mumbled.

Apart from the traffic noise outside and the occasional voices and footsteps passing his door, I found Papa's room to be quiet enough.

'I brought you some lunch,' I said. 'Hope you haven't already eaten.'

'Uh?'

'Lunch. I've brought you some.'

'I don't have much appetite. Anyway, dey say is drinks or sof' food I must eat for now.'

'Oh,' I said. 'Have they told you how everything went?'

'Uh?' He gave me a questioning look.

'The bleeding… coughing. You know. Is it all sorted?'

'I believe so.'

I asked the nurse at the desk if I could speak to someone about my father. 'Mr Francis – room three.'

'Sister's got her hands full at the moment,' the nurse said. 'But perhaps I could help. Mr Francis, you said?'

I nodded and waited while she skimmed through the first couple of pages of what I assumed were Papa's notes.

'From what I can see,' she said, looking at me, 'his condition is stable.'

'When will the sister be available?' I asked. 'It's just that I need more information than that.'

She hesitated and looked towards the main ward. 'I'm really not sure. The doctor's due to see him again tomorrow morning, during his rounds.'

'Oh. What time would that be?'

She said it would be between seven and ten. I thanked her and headed back to Papa's room.

Making it to the hospital for that time would mean rearranging the performance review meeting I'd scheduled for a newish member of the team, and the assessment of a GP referral. But I needed to be clear about Papa's condition. I'd have to juggle my work schedule around.

'*Mi'y ka vini*. Look, she coming,' Papa said, as I pushed the door to his room open. It felt suddenly crowded.

'Angel, you know Mr Bobotte, of course,' he said, a glisten in his eyes.

Mr Bobotte's greying beard stood out against his dark skin. 'Hello,' he said in that mellow voice of his. His puffy eyes almost closed as he smiled. His stomach was protruding from obvious over-indulgence and non-calorie-burning activities. Being a staunch domino player could do that to you. 'It's nice to see you again.'

'An' dis is Elsa,' Papa said. 'You remember her?'

I looked across at the woman sitting close to Papa's bed, wearing a lime-green, knitted hat with a peak.

'I remember you,' she said, her eyes on me.

Chapter Eight

Doli

I was twenty years of age when I first set eyes on dat man, an' I still get a sof' feeling inside me when I think about it.

I was especially happy because as soon as the Christmas season celebrations was over, Mama was going to pay my passage to Englan'. Agnes was to follow behind me, as soon as Mama could put another passage together. I was happy to wait so me an' Agnes could make the voyage together, but Mama said it was best for me to go first.

Dis was going to be my last New Year here with Mama an' Agnes for a while, so Mama didn't give no trouble for us to go to the New Year's dance.

'You all children make sure you behave yourself, eh?' she told us dat night. Me an' Agnes was drunk already, but only with excitement.

Mama knew dat dere would be plenty eyes on us from the older people who come to sit an' tap to the music. I remember Agnes jooking me in my side with her sharp finger every time she catch Joe looking at me. An' each time I was taking a dance with one of the other fellas, Joe would cut in an' ask me for the next one. I knew full well he was trying to chat me or lyrics me, as the young people say nowadays, when he ask me who I come with.

Later, as the celebrations finish, a heavy rain begin to fall. We girls start screaming, covering our head as we run for shelter to stop the rain from wetting the hair we had spend so much time pressing earlier.

Joe showed up under the shelter we all rushed to an' took a chance to whisper in my ear how he longed to see me again. Before I could turn to look at him an' take in the nice smell he had on him, Agnes was pulling me away. Dat shower was finished, but we had to rush to get home before the next one.

I didn't see Joe again until I was about to get on the boat to Englan'.

'Mum? You scared the life out of me,' Yvette say, when she see me leaning by her front door, hands deep in my pocket, even though I have on gloves.

'You know how long I here waiting for you?' I tell her.

'Sorry.'

'I knocked a few times, but since I see your car, I say maybe you not far. I was walking up an' down the road like is something I selling.'

Yvette giggle. 'Selling? Mum!' She shake her head an' push her key in the door. 'Come in.'

'Dat's how you rush off on me yesterday?'

The door open an' dat funny smell of flowers she call a 'relaxing scent' enter my nose.

'I told you it was an' emergency.'

'An' you was going to call me later.'

'I was too busy, Mum,' she say.

I rush up to use her bathroom.

'You shouldn't be out on the street this late,' she say, when I come back.

'Eight o'clock is not late for a big woman. I'm not working tomorrow.'

'The streets can be dangerous, you know.'

I follow her to the kitchen. 'So you finish with your emergency?'

'Sort of.'

'An' it take you all day?'

'Yeah,' she say, an' put two cups by the kettle. 'Sit down, Mum. And what's with all these questions? Peppermint, isn't it? No sugar?'

I bursting to mention Joe, but waiting to see how mistrusting my daughter can be. Instead, I ask if she all right.

'Just tired,' she say.

'No date with the boyfriend tonight?'

She tell me her Aaron is away in Dominica. Why she would let dat good-looking boy go all the way to Dominica without her, I do not know. Every young girl will be after him, especially since he is from Englan'.

'You didn't want to go with him?'

'Oh, you know how work is,' she say, as though she not entitled to any vacation.

'Looks like your work is taking up a lot of your time – even your Saturdays,' I tell her.

She look down at her cup. 'It can get like that sometimes, you know. You manage to get anything for the party?'

'I will find something in my wardrobe.'

'Good idea,' she say, an' offer to give me a lift home, after my tea.

'No. You do enough already for one day. An' you yourself say how you tired.'

I could not even look at her face, neither finish my tea. I call my regular cab office an' leave.

Of course, dis was not the first time Yvette show me dat side of her, not the second or third time either. Fifteen, she was, when I find out she was meeting up with Joe without telling me. If I didn't find the black leather jacket I know full well I did not buy for her, in her room, I would never know.

'Papa gave me the money,' she say, big tears in her eyes.

'It's not dat I don't want you to see your father,' I tell her. 'I just don't want you to do it in secret.'

'All right,' she say, an' we agree she will not meet with Joe again unless she let me know.

Then, not long after dat, I agree for her to go to the three o'clock matinee with a nice little half-caste frien' she used to have. But around four o'clock, as I was coming home on the bus from Ridley Road market, I see the same little half-caste girl coming out of the library.

I sacrifice so much for dat chile: go without to send money home for Agnes to feed her, send her dolls, pretty clothes, shoes; then I bring her back here so she can get a good, English education. It wasn't easy for me, when Joe leave an' decide he not coming back. He send the maintenance for her, but nothing dat would help me make ends meet – for electricity, gas an' such. An' as soon as Yvette finish college, is Birmingham she decide to go an' study an' leave me alone in the house.

Imagine, I feeling so proud my chile going to university, an' is quite Birmingham she want to go.

'You have fam'ly in Birmingham?' I ask her.

'I'll make friends,' she say, as though frien's can ever replace fam'ly.

'You just eighteen, Yvette. I never leave my mother house until I—'

'I know. I know,' she tell me, raising her voice. 'When you were my age you didn't have a choice.'

She was right. I left school with good enough grades for my teacher to ask me to come back an' teach, but Mama was against it. A seamstress was what she had planned for me.

'Your Auntie Lucille say dere is plenty of seamstress work in Englan',' she did tell me.

I could not argue with my mother, no matter how vex I was. When Mama say is so, it was so. But, my own daughter, Yvette, always did want to challenge me an' talk back to me as though me an' her was equal. At the time, I went to find Joe an' ask him to talk to her. But, when all was said an' done, she still pack up an' head for Birmingham.

Four years later, I preparing for her to come back home, thinking both of us will work. It will make things easier when it come to paying the bills an' I could turn a extra hand in the Partner to push up my savings. But she inform me she going to live with dat African girl, Perpetua.

Ungrateful. Dat's my daughter, Yvette.

Life never give me such choices nor opportunities. I get pregnant, before I know myself or the man I married. I send the chile back home to my sister so I could try to improve myself, but Teddy Boys – dis country's racism – force me to give up my ambition. The factory was where I end up. The money was regular an' I learn to get used to the shifts. But up to now, I caa even find a good man to settle down with.

Chapter Nine

Yvette

Papa raised his eyebrows to the knock on the door. 'Yes?'

A short young nurse with brown, shoulder-length hair came in. 'How're you feeling today, Mr Francis?' she asked, smiling.

'Not too bad,' Papa replied.

She looked at me. 'Your daughter? Angel?'

'It's Yvette,' I said. 'Only he calls me Angel.'

Papa nodded and fidgeted with his bedclothes.

'Nice to meet you. I'm Emily,' the nurse said, putting her hand out to me.

I smiled. 'Good to meet you too.'

She turned to Papa. 'Would you still like us to speak to her alone?'

He nodded. Emily asked me to come with her. I told her I didn't want to miss the doctor. 'He'll know where to find us,' she said.

'I'll be back soon,' I told Papa.

A crease appeared in his forehead. I rubbed his foot lightly and left with Emily, who led me past reception to a small room with four comfy chairs around a table with magazines scattered over it.

It was when she asked whether I wanted any tea or coffee that the Macmillan badge, pinned on the top pocket of her uniform, stood out to me.

'No, thank you,' I said. My morning caffeine shot was still doing its job. 'Are—?'

The door opened. A serious-looking man in a suit walked in, carrying a blue folder.

He said he was Papa's consultant, Mr Sutton. I shook his hand and he sat down opposite us.

'I was going to ask,' I said, slowing down my words, as I looked at Emily. 'Are… you a cancer nurse?'

'Yes, I am,' she said, with a faint smile.

'Does… does my father have cancer?' I leaned towards her.

'I'm afraid he does,' Mr Sutton said. His blue eyes flattened with sadness.

For a minute I couldn't think, couldn't find any words. Then, 'Cancer?' I said. 'What type?'

'The lungs,' Mr Sutton said, softly.

'I'm so sorry.' Emily touched my arm.

'But… but he's never smoked,' I said.

'It can happen.'

'Does your mum smoke?' Emily asked.

'No. And they're not together.' I exhaled. 'Can anything be done? How far – is there any spread?'

'That's very possible,' Mr Sutton said. 'We can't be sure, since he is refusing further tests or treatment.'

Mr Sutton's words were coming at me like runaway traffic on a narrow stretch. Who was he talking about? Papa? My father?

'It's quite aggressive. Stage three, which on his last scan showed some indications of spread.'

I dragged up the courage to respond and braced myself for the answer. 'D'you… d'you know how long he might have?'

'We can't be precise,' he said, looking at me.

'But… my God.' I slumped back in my seat. No way was I prepared for this.

'Maybe you can persuade him to let us help,' Emily said.

'Especially in relation to the trouble he's having swallowing,' Mr Sutton said.

'You think there's a connection?'

'It's possible,' Mr Sutton said.

We sat in a crushing silence, then he leaned towards me and said: 'If there's nothing else…'

I couldn't find any words again. Loss. Death. Disaster blocked all thoughts.

'Nurse Dawson will give you my contact details.' He looked at Emily. 'In case you—'

'Of course,' Emily said.

The door closed behind Mr Sutton.

'I can't believe it,' I said, wiping my nose. 'I had no idea.'

'People handle their diagnosis differently,' Emily said. 'You'll need some time to come to terms with it yourself.'

'But—'

'Persuading him to comply with treatment might be the key right now.'

I stood up, trying to reel in a scrap of stability.

'I'm here if you need to talk,' Emily said.

Papa looked straight at me as I walked in. 'You all right?' he said.

'Oh, Papa.' I burst into tears. 'Why didn't you tell me?'

'You see? You see? Dis is what I didn't want,' he said. The frown came back on his face. 'Stop dis. Stop dis crying.'

I sat next to him on the little bed, slumped over, looking at my hands.

'How… how long have you known?'

'A while,' he said, quietly.

'A while, Papa?' I looked at him. 'What's a while?'

'Easter,' he mumbled.

'Six months?' I sniffed. 'What are we going to do, Papa?'

'Shhh…' He patted my shoulder. 'I… I didn't know how to tell you, *doudou.*'

'Oh, Papa…' I was unravelling again. Panic and fear resurfacing.

'I couldn't tell you. Sorry. Sorry, *ich mwen.*'

Torn, ruffled, confused, I stumbled back to my car and sat at the steering wheel like a rag doll, a mishmash of thoughts colliding in my head. *Cancer. Papa? Spread?* There had to be a way for them to help him. How long did he have? A week? A month? My insides knotted at the thought. My chest tightened. Tears flooded my eyes. I couldn't bear it.

'Yvie?' Pe said, half smiling as she opened her front door to me.

'Bad time, isn't it?' I sniffed. 'I did text.'

'Sorry.' She gave me one of her quirky apologetic faces. 'I haven't seen it.'

She was wearing tights and ankle boots which meant she'd either just got in or was about to go out.

'Auntie Yvie!' Temi ran towards me, shouting.

Pe put a hand out to steady him. 'Yvie, you look – what's happened?'

I pick Temi up. 'How's my little sweetie?' I said, hugging him. 'Auntie's missed you.'

Addae appeared in the corridor. 'Hi, Yvie,' he said. 'Sorry to hear about your dad. How's he doing?'

'Not great. Thanks for asking,' I replied. 'Listen, call me later,' I told Pe, kissing Temi and lowering him back to the floor.

'No, you don't,' she said, taking my arm. 'Come in.'

I followed, Temi bobbing along beside us to the living room, where he bounced onto the sofa.

'You coming with us?' he said. The shrill of excitement in his little voice made me wish I could abandon the troubles I'd come to share and sink into his cushioned four-year-old world.

'Where to?' I said.

He was on my lap now.

'We're going to meet Nana Onu.'

'Airport,' Pe said, lowering her voice.

'Oh, God. Sorry,' I said. 'You did tell me.'

'Auntie Yvie can come too, can't she, Mummy?' Temi asked, looking up at Pe.

'No.' Pe hesitated. 'Auntie won't be able to. Not this time. Just a minute, Yvie,' she said and left the room, leaving me quizzing Temi about his nursery friends.

Pe came back with Addae trailing behind her.

'Come on, Temi,' Addae said, waving Temi's coat at him.

'Give Auntie another kiss first,' I said, and sunk my lips into one of his cheeks again.

'They don't need me there,' Pe said. 'His sister's going as well. They'll drive up together.'

'But you'd planned to go with them,' I said, getting up.

'And? Plans change. Don't you dare go,' she said, glaring.

'See you girls later,' Addae said, a rucksack on his shoulder and little Temi on his arm.

Temi shouted more goodbyes and Pe left me alone to see him and Addae off at the door.

'Wine or coffee?' she asked, as soon as she came back.

'Listen,' I started to say, 'I don't want to stop—'

'Stop what?' Pe said. 'I don't think Addae's mother's desperate to see me at the airport. Now, wine or coffee? Talk.'

*

'My God,' Pe said, her eyes bulging as I told her what had happened at the hospital. 'I'm so sorry, Yvie. He's been carrying all of that by himself?'

'I feel so bad, Pe,' I said. 'I've… I've practically abandoned him in the last few months and now… now he's got *cancer*. I wasn't even there to help. If I'd known… my God. If he hadn't got stabbed, I might have just got a call saying he'd died. God.'

'That would have been awful. Much worse than this, Yvie,' she said. 'But there are treatments, even trial drugs.'

I'd been sitting with my chin on my hand and lifted my head to ease the pressure on my elbow. 'But he's refusing all of that, they said.' I sniffed. 'How could he refuse treatment, Pe? He wants to die.' I leaned back in the chair. 'Die.' I leaned over again, my head in my hands.

'He'll probably change his mind about the treatment, especially now that you know.'

'You think?' I said.

'You'll have to make him see sense.'

I turned my head and looked at her. 'I wish I could. Oh, Pe. What if it's too late?'

'Course you can. You know your dad better than the medical people. It's worth a try. It has to be.'

Pe was right. I had to get Papa to see reason.

'He needs you right now, Yvie.'

'But he's had this cancer for all those months, Pe, and he… he never felt he needed to tell me, to get my help—'

'That's your dad. You know what he's like,' she said. 'He called you though, didn't he?'

'He did. But…' I sighed. 'Listen.' I looked at Pe. 'Thanks for staying behind for me. I wasn't expecting you to. I just needed—'

'You don't need to say that, Yvette. Haven't we always been there for each other?'

'Yeah,' I sighed again and took a sip of my wine.

Chapter Ten

Joe

Joe studied the room. Gazed at the two chairs – one pushed inside the other, by the toilet and shower. The soft green chair Yvette preferred to sit in was close to his bed.

He squeezed his eyes shut and wiped them on his sleeve, but the material didn't soak up the moisture. He hated how things had turned out, but he couldn't see a way out. What he wanted was to stop disappointing his child.

From what he could see, keeping himself away hurt her the same as when he was close to her. He had been sure the cancer nurse would be better at explaining things to her than he ever could, but maybe he was wrong.

'Mr Francis?' the young woman wearing a purple tunic said, when she came through the door. 'Is it okay to do some bloods?' She smiled.

He was tempted to ask how much more of his blood they were planning to take, but 'Of course,' was what he said, and started to push his sleeve up.

He kept his eyes on the needle and flinched for less than a second when he felt the prick. Nursing. That was one of Doli's ambitions after she gave up on the evening classes in English, typing and shorthand. It was the reason she had given him for sending baby Yvette to her sister in St Lucia.

'But you still feeding her,' Joe had reminded her. She informed him that Cow & Gate would serve the baby just as well as breast milk. Joe could see that sending the baby back home would make it easier for both him and Doli to work, and she could do her night classes, too. They would send for her in time for her to start school.

'Agnes so looking forward to her arriving,' Doli said.

Finally, he agreed. And in no time Doli had made arrangements for the baby to travel with her friend.

The baby hadn't even finished the fourteen-day journey to St Lucia when Doli decided she was finished with night school.

'Auntie tell me, it's not safe,' she had said. 'Too much Teddy Boys on the street, especially at night.'

When he offered to come and meet her after her class was finished, she said there was no use in both of them getting killed. After that, she came up with the nursing idea.

'You know nurses have to do night work?' he told her.

They agreed this time, that he would pick her up. But in less than six weeks on the training, she started to complain. The work was too dirty, this woman didn't like her.

'Is not everybody you work with must like you, Doli,' he had told her. Eventually, she had ended up at the brewery. To this day Joe could not bring himself to understand how a smart woman like Doli could get satisfaction out of factory work.

He never took the factory route himself, but he'd had his share of hard work. And he wasn't afraid of it.

While most people had had their minds set on going to England to make money, Joe had taken cane cutting work in America. He hadn't wanted to be too far away from Mama.

And in America, from when the sun rose until it dropped down again, he and the other boys had stood in deep dirt, chopping, cleaning and piling cane in preparation for transport. He was getting used to it when he had to rush back home: Mama was sick, bleeding from somewhere inside her.

Before she died, she made him promise he would go to England. Try to make something of himself.

The savings from the money he used to send her and from the little she used to make selling fishcakes and bakes, helped to bury her. The remainder wasn't sufficient for a passage to England, so he had to put that on hold while he saved some more from the driving job he managed to get with Geest.

Finally, he had made it to England and after a few general labouring jobs, Bobotte, whom he'd met while working on the building site, helped him to get more reliable work at the Post Office. Shuffling letters day in and day out, walking the streets in the freezing cold, busting his arse on the snow and making sure vicious dogs didn't take a piece out of him, was not easy. But in the long run, Joe's way of making sure no one could question his work gave him over twenty years at the Post Office.

'A sociable fella, polite, intelligent and hardworking' was what his manager had to say about him in his speech at Joe's retirement. It had made Joe feel proud that this white man could see these things in him and see it enough to tell everybody present.

'You enjoy nursing?' he asked the young woman now, watching her pulling the needle from his vein.

'Oh, I'm a phlebotomist. Not a nurse,' she said, chuckling.

'Phlebotomist?' Joe repeated.

'We just take blood from patients. All done.' She put a cover over the needle she pulled from his arm.

Joe pulled his sleeve down.

'I'll leave you in peace now,' she said.

Joe thanked her, although he wasn't sure why, then he let his head fall back on the pillows behind him.

Chapter Eleven

Yvette

As a team leader, I had to set a good example, so never put my personal life before work. But this was unavoidable. And, to my surprise, when I told my manager, Brenda, I'd need to take time off to care for my father, she didn't make too much of an issue of it.

'We'll arrange the appropriate cover. Just keep me in the loop,' she said, in her plummy English accent.

You'd never know Brenda was black, if you didn't see her. She was Nigerian, had married 'white', and lived in lily-white Chelmsford. That was one thing, but she'd also decided to take on as much upper-class Englishness as she could. I found her constant cups of tea, bone-straight weaves and wigs, and references to 'we' and 'us' when talking about England or the English, disturbing. I resented her for that: putting tofty-white above her – no, *our* –blackness. Telling herself and the world that being black was something to run away from, to hide under a cloak, instead of embracing and loving her Nigerian heritage. I felt sorry for her in some ways: struggling to be someone she would never be. Still, I was grateful for her understanding around Papa.

After ten days in hospital, Papa's bandages were off and his stitches were healing nicely so they let him go home with the proviso that I'd be around to keep a close eye on him.

It had kept me awake practically every night, but I hadn't yet worked out how best to address the issue of treatment or tests with him. 'Aggressive' was the word Mr Sutton used about Papa's cancer. That meant fast-spreading. Only the tests could tell us what was happening with it now.

'Don't you want it?' I asked him, opening and closing his bedside cupboards to make sure they were empty. 'Your carrot juice – you're not drinking it.'

'I empty out all of dem cupboards already,' he said. 'Since last night, after your auntie an' uncle leave.'

'Auntie Lucille? They came? That's nice.' I smiled inwardly.

'Dey surprise me.'

'Why?'

'You are a blessing to me you know, chile,' Papa said.

'Did they tell you that?' I teased, sitting next to him on the unmade bed.

'I don't need nobody to tell me dat. You are a good chile,' he said, avoiding my eyes, the way he'd been doing lately.

'Drink the carrot juice, Papa,' I said. 'The longer you leave it the less nutritional value—'

'Dat man who stab me,' Papa said, staring at the empty space in front of him, 'is best he did kill me one time.'

'Papa.' I glared at him.

'It's true. You are a very intelligent young lady. You know. I am no good as a father an' your mother will tell you de same for me as a husban'.'

'You're not a perfect father, Papa, and you and Mum… well, you just couldn't get on. But that doesn't mean you should have died. What a thing to say, Papa.'

Papa pointed at the drink on the bedside table. I passed it to him. 'An' cut dis for me,' he said, putting his arm out. I sawed through his plastic name band with the jagged side of my key. 'Now let's go.' He swallowed the rest of the juice.

'Great.' I kissed his forehead. 'Let's go.'

I tried to take his bag but he wouldn't let me, even after I reminded him about his stitches. I rushed off to get the car, leaving him waiting for me at the hospital entrance.

A lump came to my throat when I came back to find him outside looking cold and shivery, even though he was wearing his coat and scarf. *Poor old Papa.* I hurried towards him.

'Dat's a fancy car you driving,' he said, finally letting me take his bag.

'Being a convertible doesn't make it fancy, Papa.'

'But dis must be expensive,' he said, settling into the front seat beside me.

'I don't have any children. It's my treat to myself. Anyway, it's reliable and economical on petrol.'

'A car cannot replace a chile, you know,' he said, 'but it's nice.'

I knew more than anyone that a car couldn't replace the child I wanted. Nothing could.

I turned on the engine and drum beats pounded out from the CD I was playing earlier.

'You can leave it on,' he said, as I was about to stop it.

'Oh. You like my "Sounds of Blackness", then?' I edged the car slowly forward.

'Dat's what you young people like?' he said.

'Young, Papa? I find it inspirational. Lifts my spirits.' I turned the volume down.

'Ins-per-ray-tion-al,' Papa repeated, as we joined the main road. He said it again, but faster. 'American?'

'Uh-huh,' I nodded.

I couldn't remember ever driving Papa anywhere before. And memories of him dropping me off or picking me and Mum up from Auntie Lucille's, church or shopping, flooded my mind;

that childish sense that people, buildings, trees – everything out there – were moving past us as he drove, instead of it being the car and not the outside world that was moving.

We mastered the Saturday shopping traffic and arrived outside Papa's flats. He hobbled out. I moved ahead of him and pressed the lift button with my gloved hand. It arrived, and we stepped aside for an Asian lady to manoeuvre a double buggy with two well-wrapped babies out. The unsanitary smell inside thickened as the heavy doors closed behind us. I tried to breathe as shallowly as possible until they opened again – but the air directly outside the door wasn't much better either.

'You got your keys?' I asked Papa.

He did, but not handy. I waited for him to find them.

'Aah,' he said, when he stepped into the living room. 'I know is you fix in here up like dat.'

'Yep. Glad you approve, Papa.'

Chapter Twelve

Doli

Bel already tell me she not going to make it to the soca aerobics class today, so I decide to just come for my regular gym session.

At first, I didn't feel comfortable with all of dis gym business – taking exercise, an' all by myself. But it's over six years since my accident at the brewery, when I did find myself rolling down those hard stairs an' losing all dat amount of blood. I didn't plan to be going through the remainder of my years walking funny like I see some people doing after dey get a stroke an' looking ole before their time. The nasty scar dat fall leave on my leg was enough. So, I follow Dr Wilson advice.

'Just two or three times a week. You won't regret it,' he did tell me.

Now, Yvette say I am 'addicted'. She, of all people, should know dis is good for me. My exercises put me in better shape than some of those young women I see by the showers, their thighs an' backside full of dimples.

Outside feel cole after the warm shower I take in the gym. A mind tell me to rush straight home, but I need to go to Dalston to pick up a few things.

I say thank you to the woman behind the counter in the bakery an' put my rolls in my bag.

'Well, hello,' I hear a man voice say. 'Number seventy-eight, isn't it?'

I look to see who's saying my house number.

'Your gas man,' a dark-skin man, not much taller than me, say as I move from the counter for the next person to get served.

'What?' Why dis black, black man, who look not too far from my age, talking like he is English?

'Don't s'pose you recognise me.' He leave his place in the queue to come an' talk to me. 'I read your meter earlier,' he say, bringing his voice down.

Dis morning, after I finish take two painkillers for my head, I opened the door for a gas man. I showed him where the meter he come to read was, an' in no time he was gone.

'Oh,' I say.

His smile broad like he want me to see the good teeth in his mouth. 'Name's Cedric. Cedric James,' he say, an' he put out his hand.

I didn't want to touch it but being it would look as if I was rude, I put out my left hand for him an' hope he notice the ring.

I leave the shop quick, but as I was at the traffic lights waiting to cross, I hear: 'Off to the market then, eh?' The bloody man beside me again. 'I'm going that way myself,' he say, looking at me in a way dat force me to move my eyes from his. 'Friend of mine's got a stall there. You like ground provisions – your yams and stuff?'

'Of course,' I tell him, looking straight ahead of me. 'I'm a West Indian.'

'Come with me and I'll introduce you. You'll get a better price. His stuff comes straight from Jamaica.'

What the hell he mean? He think St Lucia an' other smaller islands don't have yam an' dasheen too?

'I do not need any today,' I tell him, although it's a lie.

'You must think I'm pushy, but I'd love to see you again.'

'For what?'

Men have been approaching me ever since I was young – even too young to want man. Agnes used to tell me not to complain, when I tell her. 'A lot of us wish we was pretty like you,' she used to say.

'I'd love to take you out... maybe for a meal, or anything else you might prefer,' Cedric say.

'I don't think so,' I tell him, although I couldn't tell you a man ever give me dat line before. A meal? When a man is after me, is a dance or his home he usually want to take me. I was tired of dat.

'Please. There'll be no funny business. Promise,' he say, smiling.

By then I reach my regular butcher's. 'No. Sorry,' I say, an' push open the door.

Later, the headache start troubling me so much, I call Bel an' tell her I cannot make the party.

'What, because you didn't buy a new outfit?' she say.

I tell her is not dat. 'Dis headache just not going away.'

'But is a nice party you need to raise your spirits, girl.'

'I know. I know,' I tell her, 'but I caa go to a party in dis kind of pain.'

'So is me and Gracie alone going out tonight?'

Gracie used to work with us at the brewery an' she don't live too far from Bel. I was sure dey would have a good time, even without me, but agree to let Bel know if things change with me.

The headache did ease off, but I didn't go out, believing a good sleep was bound to make me feel fresh in the morning. But if

I tell you how I struggle to sleep, last night, you would say I'm a liar. All three o'clock I lying in bed with my eyes wide open, imagining my neighbours Lucy an' Simon snuggle up close, close, in their double bed an' Suzanne an' Patrick on the other side doing the same.

After spending so long doing shift work, if four o'clock come an' my eyes still wide open, I know is best I get up.

Eight o'clock, I still in my dressing gown with a piece of toast in my mouth, when my doorbell ring. I open the door an' find a sweet-smelling bunch of flowers wrap up nice in the corner of the little shelter dey call the alcove. I look around but couldn't see nobody dat could have put it dere. The little card in it say, *The scent brought you to my mind, Cedric*, an' he write his telephone number on it. *Bondyé*. My God. I smile. Is a long while since I get flowers from a man.

I rinse out a vase to put dem in an' as I was deciding which room would be best for dem, the telephone start to ring.

'You going to live long, girl,' I tell Bel. 'I was about to phone you. The party was good?'

'Oh, yes. You miss out, girl.'

'You know what, Bel? Dat Cedric man just ring my doorbell an' leave flowers for me.'

'Cedric? You mean the English black man, you tell me about? Just like that?'

'Dat's what I telling you.'

'He must really like you, Doli,' she say, then bring down her voice: 'You think you'll end up giving him a piece?'

'Me? A Jamaican?'

'Doli, you need to change this attitude you have about Jamaicans. And you're not even sure if he is one.'

'He look like one. An' dat's where he say his friend getting the hard food from.'

Bel laugh. 'Doli, you too funny, girl.'

'I tell you already how much trouble those people give me when I was working in the clothes factory. Dey will step on your toe just to get the opportunity to call you a smallie – as if Jamaica so big. Not me with dem, you hear.'

Bel laugh again. 'I find the majority of them to be okay.'

'You come from big island.'

'But, Doli, you must know not all Jamaicans are the same. Margaret and Winston not nice?'

'Dey… dey not so ignorant an'—'

'So you going to let a nice, romantic man like that get away because you suspect he's Jamaican?'

Now I wish I didn't tell her about the man. 'He talk too funny for me.'

'Look like you want that sweetness between your legs to dry up?'

'Dat can never dry up. What about you? When last you let a man even touch dem big bouncy breasts you have?'

'Don't worry about that,' she say. 'Mr Cedric sounds like he is an absolute gentleman,' she say, putting on the English voice she use when she answering the telephone or talking with white people.

'Huh.'

'Anyway, that was not why I call you,' she say. 'You see the paper?'

'What paper?'

I hope she didn't want to send me to read something about dat poor young boy, Stephen Lawrence, an' his mother. All the suffering an' fighting dat woman an' her husban' have to do since dem National Front people kill her son. It's too terrible – just too terrible for me to read. I always say, the only thing any government ever do good for me is give me the opportunity to buy my council place I pay so much rent for already.

'There's a story in there,' Bel say. 'I believe it's about your husband, Joe. From what you tell me, I'm sure is him.'

'He's not my husban',' I tell her. 'Not in dat sense.'

'But you still married. And wearing the ring.'

I look at the ole wedding ring on my finger. 'You know dis ring is jus—'

'I know,' she say, 'but you didn't tell me how you show Cedric your married hand and yet still he bring flowers for you? You think he feel you have a husband inside that house?'

'Which paper you talking about?'

'The free East End paper, girl. I cut the section out to show you.'

'I will call you back.'

'Page four. You hear? Page four,' she say, before I put down the phone.

I go back to the kitchen to search through the pile of newspapers I keep to line the dustbin an' wrap ole food in before I throw it. It was the second in the pile. I open it an' read:

> *A 67-year-old man was stabbed and robbed of his mobile phone and wallet in Bow, on Thursday morning. The victim, who has not yet been named, was found outside his home on the Fairchilds Estate and taken to hospital. Detective Sergeant Peters from the Violent Crime Taskforce, who is leading the investigation, appealed for witnesses to contact the police. He said, 'This is a cowardly attack on an elderly man in broad daylight. I appeal to anyone who has information on it to please come forward.' Anyone with information is asked to contact Tower Hamlets Violent Crime Taskforce on…*

Sweat burst on my body as if I slide back into menopause. I caa believe Joe is really in the papers.

'My God,' I say, when I call Bel back, 'you right. Look like it's him. Imagine dat. Bel, I have to go.'

'Oh, hi, Mum,' Yvette say, when she hear is me.

'I phone to tell you, your father in the paper.'

'What you talking about? What paper? Why would he be in the paper?' she say, because she think she smart.

'The free East End paper. You will not be getting it in your area. So you think I didn't know somebody attack him the other day? Why you would want to hide dat from me, Yvette? You had arranged to come out with me. You cancel it, last minute, to go an' see to Joe. The next day, I even come to your house to give you the opportunity to tell me, but – how long you did plan to continue dis lie, Yvette?'

'I… I wasn't lying or… or planning anything,' she say. 'I didn't think you'd be that interested. What's the big deal? You're not exactly going to go and see him or send him a get-well card, are you?'

'Me? I'm sure your father already have enough people coming to see him.'

'So why are you calling, Mum? To gloat, or to prove that you're in the know?'

'What you mean by dat?'

'You don't really care, Mum. That's what I mean.'

'An' Joe? He care?'

'I'm sure he'd care if he heard you were laid up in hospital. When you had your accident, didn't he call… try to come and see you? It was you who didn't want to see him.'

Yvette making me vex like hell. 'You spending your whole life making excuses for Joe. But one thing. You know where I live, an' my telephone number. Look how trouble hit him an' he don't even have your number to call.'

'That's because—'

'No. Your number in my head,' I tell her. 'Whether my phone cut off or what. Your number in my head, Yvette. But I know nothing I do is sufficient for you.'

'That's not true, Mum.'

'You know damn well it's true. Whenever it come to Joe, you find a way to excuse an' forgive him. You think because he calling you 'doudou', 'darling', 'Angel' an' all of dat, it mean something? When Joe ready, he always have a sweet mouth. Man always have a sweet mouth. Your father is no different. He know how to sof'en you up.'

'That's rubbish. I... I... He doesn't. I don't care what you say.'

'I know. Is only Joe dat matter to you.'

'You know what, Mum? Both you and Papa have your faults – we all do. And you're the one who chose him to be my father. Not me.'

'An' what a big mistake dat was, eh?' I chups my teeth. Dat chile too blasted rude for me. 'Let me go, you hear? I have a million things to do. Ba-bye.'

A part of me was glad when me an' Yvette come home from church dat Sunday morning. I'll never forget. It was 1975 – two days before I turned thirty-five. We come in an' I see his keys on the kitchen table.

'Joe gone,' I remember I tell her, before I pick dem up.

'To the club?' she ask me.

'Club? He leave us.'

Dat crampy feeling did take hold of my insides. I was the one who was supposed to leave him; make him give me my share of the house so I could buy myself another place, meet a nice man to settle down with. Not one dat prefer to be at a domino club than at home with me. Yvette would want to stay with him, of course, an' I would be free to do whatever I want with my life while age was on my side.

I did like Joe a lot, before I marry him, but I wasn't ready for no chile or no marriage, when I did find myself pregnant with Yvette. Mama had always warn me an' Agnes against letting a boy make us pregnant without marriage. An' everybody – Mama, Auntie Lucille, Agnes – was happy when I tell dem Joe say he want to marry me. Eventually, I was happy too, so I became Mrs Dolina Francis.

The next person I tell about Joe leaving was Auntie. 'I'm sure is another woman he have,' I did tell her.

'You cannot let another woman take your husban' an' make your marriage finish like dat,' she tell me. 'Go and find him, you hear? The two of you have to talk. You have a chile, Doli.'

What Auntie was saying did make sense. Yvette never stop asking me question after question about when Joe coming home. And trying to make ends meet without him might not be as easy as all dat. I take Auntie advice, start reading Acts of Contrition three times in the morning an' before I go to sleep. I find Joe, ask him to come for us to talk.

Then on a Friday, soon after Yvette leave for school, he show up at the house.

'So you finally decide to come?' I tell him, although I was well glad to see him.

'I had a lot of things to take care of,' he say, glancing upstairs. 'Angel gone?'

'Yes,' I tell him. He give me a bag with a few things for her an' follow me to the kitchen.

'You afraid to take off your coat?' I ask him.

He open the buttons, take off his hat an' hook it on a chair.

When I offer him, he say he don't want no drink. He not long finish have breakfast.

I sit down beside him. 'So, where you living now, Joe?'

He clear his throat an' shuffle his bottom on the chair. 'A frien' helping me out.'

I did already hear from Frederick wife, Sylvianne, dat is a woman name Elsa he living at. But she an' Joe telling everybody dey don't have nothing.

'Since when Elsa is your frien'?'

He jump when I say dat. 'Doli, you don't want me.'

I ask him how he could leave me an' Yvette like dat, if he is happy. Really, happy.

He say: 'How many times you have to tell me to leave before you can expect me to go?'

'Regardless of our disagreements, I didn't take care of you, Joe?' I say.

His eyes not moving from the window in front of him.

'What I didn't do right, Joe? Follow you to your domino club every week? Listen to your frien's tell their stupid jokes… drink until… until—'

'You see dat?' He get up an' pick up his hat. 'Dat is the reason I didn't want to come here.'

'All right. All right,' I say. Dis is how he does get vex when I talk about his frien's. 'Dat's not the reason I ask you to come.'

'So why?'

'I want you to come back home, Joe,' I say.

Chapter Thirteen

Yvette

After Mum's call, I sat quietly, mulling over our conversation. Why did I let her draw me into that argument? I could have just apologised and explained why I hadn't told her about Papa's attack; that I found not sharing information about them to each other was easier for me to manage.

It was true – Papa did go months without contacting me, but things between me and him are so different to what me and Mum have. It's been that way since the first day we met. An invisible bond. Whereas Mum's always been kind of distant.

She seemed pleased when I did well at school, but Papa was the one who never stopped encouraging me to strive for my goals. 'Take every opportunity dis country give you, *ich mwen*,' he'd always said. 'If you make ten pounds, make sure you save two…'

Who made a special effort to take me to see the bonfire display on Guy Fawkes Night, because he knew I loved it? Who, after Mum made it clear she wasn't interested, would rescue me from boredom and take me to the domino club with him?

'Come an' go to the club with Papa, Angel,' he'd say, getting up from his nap or lifting his head from the newspaper he was reading.

Mum would object, of course. 'Dat's the kind of place you see to take a chile?' she'd say and try to find a million reasons why I couldn't go right now: I had homework, dishes to wash, he'd be back too late and I wouldn't be able to get up in the morning.

Anything she could dream up. But I'd be ready to rush through the front door with him.

The fact that Mum had an unhappy marriage with Papa wasn't any of my doing. It wasn't my fault, either, that she couldn't stand the one thing he loved doing most – playing dominoes. She'd never stopped being jealous of my closeness with him and resentful of the times he and I spent together. Yes, I might sympathise with him more than I did with her, but life hadn't been that good to him. When she had a nice roof over her head, he was struggling to get decent housing.

If Mum was different, less hostile and a bit more forgiving towards Papa, I would've been more honest with her about loads of things, including why I couldn't go shopping with her last Saturday. *It's a two-way street, Mum.*

Still agitated, I picked myself up, sighed and went downstairs to finish cooking and give Pe a call to see how things were going with her and Addae's mum's visit, before heading off to the hospital.

The double lock on my front door was opened. I smelt stewed fish.

'At last.' Aaron's voice shot up from the kitchen as soon as I closed the front door behind me. I hadn't expected him to come over until tomorrow. Thought he'd be too jet-lagged.

'Come here, you,' he said, rushing up to me in the hallway.

I was beaming inside as I tugged my arm out of my coat sleeve. His hug brought a mingling of spices and Hugo Boss to my nostrils. Our lips touched and my urge for him bubbled.

'Been soaking in the sun, eh?' I said, as we slowly separated.

The deep brown skin he'd left with was now a healthy near-black. 'Fish?' I said, screwing my face up at the faint taste in my mouth.

'Yeah, and breadfruit,' he said, putting his arms around me again and squeezing my bottom. 'I... mmm' – he started kissing my neck – 'sneaked it in. Hungry?'

'Not for breadfruit,' I said. I wanted him now and, judging from the lump pressing against me, he wanted me too.

I left Aaron dozing and went downstairs to put the food away. On my way back up, the light was on in the bathroom, but I went on to the bedroom.

'Where've you been?' he said, ambling back in.

'Tidying up the kitchen.'

He crawled back into bed squeezed up close to me, then pulled the duvet over us.

'I forgot to ask how your pap's doing?' he said.

'Didn't give you a chance, did I?' My mood shifted as I told him about the cancer.

'No treatment?'

'No.' Fear of the extent of Papa's condition crept back into me. 'All he's agreed to is wound care and physio.'

'Boy. That's hard.' He sighed and snuggled closer. 'Missed you so much.'

'Missed you too,' I said.

'It's got to be worrying, though – your pap's condition.'

'Mm.'

'I wish you'd come with us to Dominica, Yvie. You would have loved it. Met so much family I didn't know. You and Mum have to make time to teach me that *kwéyòl*. People were talking to me in the lingo and I had to either pretend I understood or just tell them I didn't.'

'I've offered too many times.'

St Lucia and Dominica, like some other countries colonised by the French, share the same language, and since Mum and Papa spoke it to each other and to me when I was a child, I understand it well. Though I have to rehearse most of what I want to say in my head before saying it.

'And, hey, everybody was trying to get me a girlfriend. I showed them your picture. Told them no one could match you.' He chuckled.

There was that word again: girlfriend. I was tired of being just that. He didn't exactly have to propose marriage – not right now, but I was more than ready for us to move in together.

'You okay?' he said.

'Yeah.'

'You sure?' He pulled me towards him, his dick resurrecting against me.

'Thought you'd be jet-lagged,' I said.

'This is nice.'

'Mmm.'

His fingers started making curly patterns over my bottom, then he turned me gently onto my back. As he kissed me, I felt the tenderness in my mouth from the earlier session. 'I've missed you so much,' he whispered, licking my nipples.

I pushed my chest up for a deeper suck. He ran his hand lightly over my thighs then slid his fingers between my legs. I let him feel the sharpness from my nails over his back then eased him in.

When I woke up, he was gone. I rushed off to Papa's, arriving later than planned, and found he'd already had breakfast and was out of his pyjamas. On my way to get myself some coffee, my mobile rang.

'Why d'you sneak out like that?' I said quietly into the phone.

'I told you last night, I'd have to shoot off early,' Aaron said. 'I've got such a backlog of jobs to sort out. Text me your pap's address.'

'Oh. Okay,' I said, surprised.

I walked ahead of Aaron, towards the front room. 'It's Aaron, Papa,' I said, loudly.

'Who?' Papa said, repositioning himself on the sofa to get a better look at his visitor.

'Aaron. My friend.'

'Good morning, Mr Francis,' Aaron said, his solid frame moving steadily towards Papa. 'Nice to meet you again.' He leaned over to shake Papa's hand.

'Dis is your… your young man?'

'Yes. You've met him before, Papa.'

'I did?'

'Don't tell me you've forgotten. He played dominoes with you all at the club—'

'Eh-eh. Is dat so?' Papa said, smiling and straightening up.

'Yes,' Aaron said. 'And you wiped the floor with us, I remember. You and your partner—'

'Bobotte?'

'Not sure,' Aaron said, taking a couple of steps back after Papa released his hand, 'it was a woman – gave us two six loves in a row. That was painful.' Aaron chuckled.

'Yeah?' Papa laughed.

Aaron pulled up one of the dining chairs and sat close to him.

'Well, it's very nice of you to come an' see me,' Papa said. 'Angel, you getting a drink for the young man?' He turned to Aaron again. 'So I give you a beating to remember?'

'You certainly did,' Aaron said, as I left the room to get him some juice.

'Yes, is good when you can work for yourself,' I caught Papa saying, on my way back in. 'Uh-huh. All your money coming straight to you. No middle man.'

'Yeap.' Aaron nodded, politely.

'You have a very smart man, Angel,' Papa said, looking at me.

Seeing them together like this brought back memories of the time I had first introduced Aaron to Papa, at his domino club, when he'd started giving him the third degree about his 'intentions' towards me.

'Papa? You don't need to ask him that,' I'd said, trying to rescue Aaron.

'Well, I want to know,' Papa had replied, looking at Aaron.

'Well… well, we're serious, if that's what you mean, Mr Francis,' Aaron had said.

'You sure? He serious, Angel?' Papa had turned to me. 'He treat you good?'

'Yes, Papa,' I said, and proposed joining him in a game.

The cosiness of having him and Aaron together for the second time didn't last. Aaron was already looking at his phone. He edged off his chair, raised his eyebrows and looked up at me.

'Gonna have to shoot off,' he said, edging further forward.

'Back to work?' Papa asked, like he wished he had somewhere important he had to be too, instead of parked on his sofa.

'Yeah,' Aaron said, checking his phone again. He hadn't even managed to finish his drink.

We sneaked in a quick kiss at the front door. 'Call you later,' he said.

The flat was quiet after that. Then things turned topsy-turvy.

Mr Bobotte and his wife, Miss Merle, arrived. Miss Merle was a good-looking lady. Plump, especially round the midriff. If she'd come to me at work, I might have advised her to lay off the cakes, pastries and other sugary intakes and move around more.

'How's tricks?' Mr Bobotte asked Papa.

'*Sa ka fèt*, Joe? How you doing, Joe?' Merle asked.

'*Mwen la.* I'm there. *Mwen la*,' Papa said.

Mr Bobotte put the blue carrier bag he was holding on the table and they started joking about Papa being missed at the game last night.

The talk was about Papa's life away from me – about the people he'd always found time for.

I started to ask if they'd like a hot drink and before the words could get out of my mouth, Papa was directing me to where I'd find the tumblers. Then Mr Bobotte pulled a bottle of Mount Gay rum out of the bag.

I threw a disapproving look at Papa. Pouring more toxins in his body couldn't be good.

'De fellas missing you, man,' Mr Bobotte said, and gave a list of people who were due to pay Papa a visit.

'Um… bring… bring some chaser, Angel,' Papa said, waving a finger in my direction. 'An' some ice.'

I was about to tell him he didn't have any 'chasers', and certainly no ice, when he pointed to the bottom of the cabinet. 'Look in dere.'

'In dere' housed another two bottles of Mount Gay rum and half a bottle of brandy. There were also cans of lemonade and coke. I put a tin of each on the table and brought them water in place of ice.

By now the smell of the fish I had in the oven had taken over the flat. I asked if anyone wanted to eat. They all declined.

I was beginning to feel out of place so made myself busy in the kitchen, tidying things that didn't need tidying. Miss Merle gave me a sympathetic smile when I came back.

Mr Bobotte poured himself what I suspected was a top-up, then passed the bottle to Papa.

'Papa? I don't think—'

'Just a little one,' Mr Bobotte said. He gave me a playful wink.

'Just a taste,' Papa said, and took the bottle from his friend.

I couldn't stomach witnessing Papa's frivolousness, his disregard for his health, so said I had to pop out for a while and left.

The wind blew my coat wide open, putting a stop to the walk I had in mind. I folded my arms around me, got in my car and sat with the engine on. Why would Papa do this? It was enough that all those years of domino playing in stuffy back rooms and bars had given him lung cancer; that he wasn't undergoing any treatment or on any medication – he wanted to add another bunch of poisons to the mix? A toxin-free body was what he should be aiming for. The life he used to lead had to change. I couldn't condone it. No. Wouldn't sit around watching him pour more toxins into his body.

I felt a sudden urge to drive away. Now. Forget about Papa and his self-destructive behaviour. Keep away, like I was doing before. But it wasn't that straightforward anymore. He needed me, and I needed for him to stay alive.

I watched people – young mums, young men and the elderly – going in and out of the depressing-looking council blocks, then pushed a Randy Crawford tape into the cassette player. Shit. Mr Bobotte was standing in front of the flats, a cigarette in his mouth. He wasn't likely to see me since I was parked yards away from the entrance, but I ducked down anyway.

He finished his cigarette, Miss Merle appeared, hooked her arm into his and they walked off together.

'Angel,' Papa called out, as soon as I stepped inside. 'How you can make me ashame' like dat in front of de people?'

'Do you seriously think you should be drinking, Papa?'

'Dese – dese people are my frien's.'

'Your friends? Do they know you have cancer?'

Papa made a huffing sound.

'Why do you do it, Papa?' I said. 'Why would you be drinking rum when you… you know it's… it's not good, Papa.' The tears I'd been suppressing started choking me. 'It's like you… you don't *care*. And it hurts me to watch you throw it – throw your life away.'

'Come. Come an' sit here.' Papa patted a space on the sofa next to him and shuffled backwards.

I sat down on the space he'd created. He put his arm around me and triggered more tears.

'All right. All right,' he said, tapping my hand. 'It's not dat I don't care. By all means, I care. If I didn't care, you think I would send Bobotte out to smoke his cigarette?'

'You shouldn't be drinking alcohol, especially that strong stuff, Papa.'

He kissed his teeth. 'With dat thing I have inside me, you think a little drink going to make matters any worse?'

I didn't answer. He was probably right.

'I didn't even taste de rum, anyhow.'

I pulled out a tissue I had stuffed up my sleeve and wiped my nose.

'Stop it. Stop. Dat's enough crying.'

His hold started to loosen around me. 'Mr Bobotte drank all of that?' I said, sniffing. A quarter of the rum in the bottle on the table was gone.

'An' Merle.'

'Sure you didn't help?'

Papa picked his glass off the floor by the sofa and held it up to me. 'Look,' he said. 'Smell my mouth if you don't believe me,' and he opened his mouth like he was preparing for a dental inspection. 'Come an' smell it, onh?'

'Huh.' I tutted.

'What you see in dat glass is de same shot you see me put in it before you leave. I don't even have de taste for dese things again,' he said.

'Good.'

We both laughed and I squashed up closer to him, my head on his chest.

'Angel?' he said. His voice sounded hollow and distant above my head.

'Yes, Papa?'

'Dere's something I have to tell you.'

I sniffed again, sat up and looked at him. 'What?'

'About de man dat stab me.' He paused.

I hoped he wasn't going to be saying anything about dying again.

'Something about him,' Papa said. 'Or maybe it was just de way things happen, make me remember dis fella.' Papa paused.

I sat up straight and looked at him. 'A fellow, Papa. Who? Did you tell the police?'

He shook his head. 'It's not like dat.'

'What d'you mean?' I looked intently at him.

'Listen,' he said. 'When we... me an' your mother, was coming to Englan' on de boat, dere was a man. Ian.' He paused, seemed disconnected from me and everything else in the room for a moment, then continued. 'Ian was one of dose... one of dose men I see did like your mother.'

'Yeah?' No surprises there: even the bus drivers tried to chat Mum up when I got on the bus with her.

'One night – de last night on de boat, I was walking about on de top deck. De boat was sending me from right to left, when

I meet up with him. Maybe he was even following me, I don't know, but he start asking me questions like… like where I think dat pretty brown-skin girl he see me chatting to is right now.'

'Mum?'

'Yes. He say some disrespectful things about her. You understan'?'

'Like what?'

Papa paused. 'Well… like if I get to touch dem full round breasts she have an' telling me I best forget about her because he have his own plans for her.'

'Okay, Papa. I understand,' I said. I felt uneasy hearing him talk about Mum in a sexual way.

'I'm sorry, Angel, I just want to tell you everything.'

I nodded. 'Okay.' And let him continue.

'When I try to tell him don't talk about de woman – your mother – like dat, he start with me, telling me he sure I caa even get close enough to Doli to take her smell, let alone touch her… how I must be a buller man. Me, you know, he calling a buller.' Papa shuffled in his seat. 'Huh. If he did know how much I love woman, especially dem days.'

I made a grunting sound. 'I get it, Papa,' I said.

'He come up close, close up in my face,' Papa continued. 'I push him away… caa understan' why dis fella behaving like dat. I mean, I only meet him on de boat.' Papa frowned.

'Anyways. I tell him something like, "Man, know your place," an' push him from in front of me. He take a swing for me. I grab him. He hold my arm tight. "Let me go," I tell him, an' push him hard against de railings.

'Dat was when I see his body start to shake. I see he losing his balance, so I try to hold him. Next thing I know, de man face start to change, twitching, eyeballs getting big, spit dripping from his mouth. I figure he real vex or drunk. I didn't know what to do.

Nobody was around. I let him go. De fella fall back on de railings, den brucks on de floor. I look around again. Don't see nobody.'

'He had a fit, Papa,' I said, quietly. 'An' epileptic fit.'

'I didn't know nothing about fits in dose days. It was dark. De first thing I think was to run an' find somebody dat could help him. Den a mind tell me, "Joe, you want dem to deport you even before you reach Englan'? What happen if de fella dead? Dey will put it on you." I go straight to my room, fix up myself an' go back up to de dance dey was holding in de hall.'

'So what happened to him?' I asked. 'Somebody must have found him.'

'Up to now,' Papa's fixed stare pulled me further into his story, 'I am still not sure if de fella fall down dead or somebody find him alive.'

'And you never reported it to anyone?'

'I tell you I was too afraid. Afraid dey would accuse me. All I know is next day, we reach Englan' an' I or nobody else I ask don't see him.'

'Oh, Papa. I'm sure he was okay.'

'Dat's what I want you to find out for me.'

The story Papa had just told me was disturbing enough on its own. Asking me to find the man seemed weird and out of place. 'What, Papa?'

'I need to know. What happen with him? Maybe he… find out if he is alive for me. Because, I tell you, dat boy who stab me resemble Ian so much he could be his son.'

I took a deep breath. 'Oh, Papa. Lots of people look alike and have no connection with each other. You know how many people have told me I look like someone they know? Or asked if I'm such and such a person's sister?'

'I know. I know. Dat's what I keep telling myself, but – find out for me, please, *ich mwen*. Find out if… where he is.'

'Papa, I can tell you the man's most likely alive and getting on with his life somewhere.'

'Dere was a time when I did force myself to believe dat, but…' Papa's thoughts seemed to wander for a while. 'I would be so grateful if you could find out, Angel. Is not so much how de boy face make me recall Ian, but de whole thing disturb my spirit so hard, have me worrying, causing me to…' Papa's voice became childlike. His face ruffled. He was serious.

'Papa.' I stood up and faced him. I'd never seen him like this before. 'Okay. Okay. I'll try,' I said. 'But I don't think it will be easy to find him.'

'Please, *ich mwen*. Please. I must know if he die on de boat or leave alive.'

Papa had never asked the adult me to do anything for him, let alone something as serious as this.

'I'll do my best. But what was his surname?'

Papa shrugged. 'I never did know his title. Well, maybe I did, but I forget. Angel? I… I have to know what happen… before it's too—'

'Papa, okay. I'll do what I can.'

'One thing, though,' he said, holding my arm. 'What I tell you happen on de boat is between you an' me, eh?' He raised his eyebrows and looked directly at me. 'You understan'?'

'Yes, Papa, I understand,' I said.

After eating Papa fell asleep, but his story wouldn't leave my mind.

I suppose it was possible that this Ian man had died on the ship. But it was also possible that he managed to get help and left the ship the following day, like all the other passengers. More importantly, how was I going to find out whether he was dead or alive? I wished I hadn't agreed to it at all, but saying no would have been too harsh. And, I had to admit, deep down, I was pleased that Papa had asked me to do something that would keep him in my life, at least for a while.

Chapter Fourteen

Yvette

Papa said this Ian had definitely known Mum, so it was worth checking whether she remembered anything about him. I wasn't sure what mood she'd be in. We hadn't spoken since that head-butt last Sunday, but I took a chance and popped by her house on my way home to see what she could tell me.

'Eh-eh, is you?' she said, when she opened the door and found me standing in her alcove with a bunch of orange and white lilies in my hand.

'Sorry, but they're not from me. I found them here,' I confessed, sniffing the flowers. 'They're gorgeous, though. What's the occasion?' I was keen to get an insight into a part of Mum's life that she did her best to keep closed to me.

'No occasion. You making all the cole come in.' She waved me in and took the flowers. I leaned in and put a peck on her cheek.

'Eh-eh. A kiss too?'

I ignored her sarky comments. She smiled. I took my coat off, hung it on one of the hooks by the front door and followed her to the kitchen, where she put the flowers to stand in a pot of water.

'You not opening the card?'

'Later. So you not vex with me?'

'Course I'm not upset with you, Mum,' I said. 'In fact, I've been thinking, some of the things you said about me and Papa the other day had some truth.'

She gave me a smug look.

'And I was grateful that you told me about the article.'

'Mmm. If you did tell me you was coming I would have prepared something for you. Is only some stale food I have there from last night.'

'I'm okay, thanks,' I said, touching my stomach. 'Peppermint tea will be fine.' I sat down, watching her fill the kettle, the scent from the lilies lifting my mood.

'So, what's going on with him – your father?'

'Oh, he's recovering,' I said. I couldn't tell her about the cancer.

She sucked in her cheeks and frowned like there was a sour taste in her mouth.

'Mum?' I said.

'Uh-huh?'

'You know when you and Papa were coming to England on that ship?'

'You mean dat boat? *Carlotta C*?' she said, a longing in her voice.

'Is that what it was called?'

'Uh-huh.' She turned the fire off under the whistling kettle.

I dug a notepad and pen from my bag. 'Do you remember a man called Ian?'

'Ian?' Mum turned to me, the kettle in her hand. 'What? What you doing?' she asked.

'Taking notes,' I said, sitting poised, ready to write.

'Notes? For what?'

'So I don't forget stuff.' I had to handle this carefully, so she wouldn't clam up or become irritated at the mention of Papa, and I didn't want to lie either. 'D'you remember him, Mum? Papa said he travelled with you all.'

'Joe? *Sa ki wivé,* Joe? What happen to Joe?' She put the kettle down and faced me, a hand on her hip. 'What's going on?'

'Papa's asked me to find Ian for him.'

'For what?'

'He said there was a man on the ship when you were coming over. The man's name was Ian and he'd really like to get in touch with him. That's all. D'you remember him?'

She grunted. 'Yvette, I don't understand. Out of all of the men an' women on dat big boat, why is *dis* man Joe decide he want to get in touch with?'

'So you know… remember him?'

'Well… well, yes, of course.' She picked up the kettle again, poured steaming water into the cups, put one in front of me, then sat down with hers. 'But what Joe want with the man?'

'He just wants me to find out if he's still alive.'

'Alive? Why would he not be alive? An' why Joe, all of a sudden, want to know dat? It's almost forty years.'

'What d'you remember about him? Ian.'

Mum blinked a couple of times. Her gaze fell on the table.

'Please, Mum. It's important,' I said. 'He says he's been think-ing about Ian a lot.'

'Ian?' She lifted her head again. 'Why?'

'I… I need to get – you don't remember his surname at all, do you?'

'Me? If I did ever know the man title, you think I would hold dat in my head?'

'So you wouldn't know which island he was from or what part of England he planned to go to?'

'No,' she said, frowning and shaking her head. 'Not really. He could have come from Antigua, St Vincent, any one of those places. People did come from all around. How you can expect me to remember dat kind of thing after so long?'

'Didn't you all hang out together, at meal times and stuff?'

'Yes. When things wasn't rough an' the boat wasn't making people feel too sick to leave their cabin, the men would mostly be playing cards, dominoes. Us girls might watch, sit in our room chatting or, if it wasn't too cole, go for a stroll on deck.'

'So during your socialising and stuff, you must have found out something about him.'

She looked away and kissed her teeth. 'Yvette, best you go an' help the police find who stab your father than to try an' play Columbo with me. If Ian did want to make friends with Joe, he himself wouldn't make contact?'

'I know, Mum,' I said, leaning forward, 'but I promised Papa I'd try. I can only try. And to find him I'll need to at least know his surname.'

'Well, it's not me you should ask,' she said, like it was her final word on the matter.

'Papa said he knew you, said he quite liked you.'

'How Joe would know dat?' She looked away, blushing. 'I tell you already, dere was a lot of people on dat boat.'

'*Carlotta C*, eh?'

Mum leaned over to see what I was writing. 'You really have to write dat?'

'I don't want to forget anything.'

'Young girl like you?' She continued staring at the notepad.

'Can you remember the actual date you arrived?'

'I know it wasn't as cole as I was expecting it to be.'

I asked if I could take a look at her old passport. 'It would give me all of that information,' I said. 'Please, Mum.'

'Your father don't have a passport, too?' she said, fidgeting with the corner of an old newspaper on the table.

'Yeah, but you know you're much more organised than him.'

I made eye contact with her. For as long as I could remember, she had kept her important papers in an off-white, heart-shaped vanity case on top of her wardrobe. I could picture it now, filled with yellowing documents.

'It won't take long, Mum. Come on.'

'Another day, Yvette,' she said. 'Not now. Drink your tea.'

'It would really help.' I lowered my voice. 'Pleeease?'

She stood up abruptly and looked down at me. 'What's going to happen if you don't find dis Ian man? You or Joe going to die?'

'If you won't help,' I said, picking up my notebook. 'I'll have to find another—'

'You just want to know the date we arrive?'

'Please,' I said, sensing a breakthrough.

She took her handbag off one of the chairs that was pushed under the table and retrieved a set of keys.

'Come,' she said.

I expected we were going to her bedroom, but she went to my old room – which had totally changed.

The previous green, patterned wallpaper had been replaced with a beige, textured one. The busy floral carpet was now a plain brown and all of the bedroom furniture was gone. Instead, there was a desk with a computer on it. The room looked and smelt freshly done.

'When did you get this?' I asked.

'The other day,' she said, as she moved past me and opened the bottom drawer of the desk.

'So you can use the computer now?'

'I am planning to,' she mumbled.

'Oh, that's great.'

'Dis is what you want?' She stood up and handed me the old passport. I sensed something was upsetting her, and it didn't surprise me since our whole conversation was about me helping Papa.

'Can I take some notes?'

'Go ahead, as long as you leave my passport here,' she said, and left me alone in her new study.

British Passport, the little navy-blue book read. Colony of Saint Lucia. Date of issue: December 1960. A large, blue 'CANCELLED' was stamped on the second page over her full name: Miss Dolina Morella St Clair. Profession: Seamstress. Place and date of birth: Desruisseaux, St Lucia, 10 July 1940. Height: 5 feet 5 inches. Colour of eyes: Brown. Colour of hair: Brown.

The face of the young Dolina who left St Lucia in 1961 was the same as the one that had met me when I was brought back to England, six years later. In the picture, she was wearing a black shirt or dress. Her thick hair was pulled up on her head and sat in a mop of curls, a style that suited her oval-shaped face. I turned the page. In the middle of the statement: 'Valid for all parts of the Commonwealth…' was another 'CAN-CELLED' stamp. Two pages on was the date I was looking for: 10 AUGUST 1961.

'You finish?' Mum's voice startled me.

'You look so gorgeous in there,' I said, turning to her, the passport in my hand.

'Mmm,' she said, coming further in. 'You sure your father don't have another reason why he want to find Ian?'

'Like what?' I said, handing the passport to her. 'I shouldn't really tell you, but he said the man who attacked him reminded him of Ian.'

'The man who attack him? *Bondyé*. Your father head not good.' She locked the passport back in the drawer.

'That's what brought the memories of this Ian back to him,' I said, on our way back downstairs.

'Huh.'

'I told him the resemblance had to be a coincidence. Happens all the time. Thanks, though, Mum.'

'It's okay.'

'I'll finish my tea now,' I said, when we reached the bottom
of the stairs. We sat at the kitchen table again. I asked how Miss
Belvina was.

'Bel?' Mum's voice was quiet now. 'She okay. It's a while since
I see her.'

'You not gym-mates anymore?'

'She busy with her grandchildren. She ask me to give you her
regards, you know, after she hear about your father.'

'Ahh. Tell her thanks and give her my love when you next
speak to her.'

'Mmm.' Mum nodded.

'You want me to help you sort your flowers out? You've got
enough there for two vases and still haven't opened the card,' I
teased, looking past her at the bouquet. 'Looks like somebody
else apart from me thinks you're very special.'

'You?' she said.

'Yes. Me.'

'Don't worry. I will fix dem.'

'Okay.' I pushed my chair back. 'I better be off.'

'All right.'

I stood up and gave her another peck on the cheek.

'Mind yourself on the road,' she said, half smiling.

I said I would.

Chapter Fifteen

Doli

If I remember Ian? Shiny shoes, dress sharp as a sailor. The kind of boy Mama would tell me I need to keep far from. He used to come to my mind a lot after we reached Englan', especially after dat last night on the boat.

But dat Joe really know how to interfere with somebody, eh? Causing Yvette to come bringing all these questions about Ian. What the hell?

Agnes was standing with her arm over Mama's shoulder as I walked away to board the little boat dat would take us to the big, white one far out in the harbour.

'Don't forget us when you reach Englan', you hear?' Mama did shout after me.

Excitement was running through me, but I was afraid. 'Take care of Mama, Agnes,' I shout back. Although I know I could always rely on her to do dat.

Agnes wave. I wave too an' rush to join the line of people getting in the small boat.

When we reach the big one dat was going to take us to Englan', we had to climb some wooden steps with only rope on each side to hold on to. Between each step was deep sea water. Any stumble would make somebody have to pull a drowned Dolina from the sea. My heart was beating fast. Mama should not have let me go without Agnes.

Never in my life had I seen so much people in one place, at the same time, than when I set foot on dat big boat. People were crying from joy an' sorrow. Plenty were shouting, laughing too; some pushing their way to the front to give the last wave to fam'ly an' frien's we were all leaving behind.

My chest start to swell. I wanted to scream. Tell dem to stop; to take me back. I don't want to leave Mama, Agnes, the rest of the fam'ly an' all my frien's behind. I didn't know where to put myself amongst all of those people.

After a while, a loud horn dat sound like somebody passing wind start to blow. My St Lucia was getting smaller an' smaller as the boat back away. It never cross my mind, at the time, dat I would never see Mama again.

A white woman wearing a uniform with a hat come an' take me down some hard steps dat made a ping-ping noise when my shoe heel hit it.

'This is your cabin,' she say, when we reach what I was sure, by the sound of a heavy engine an' smell of hot iron, was the bottom of the boat. My inside start to tremble again.

A little while after, two women, Moira an' Carmen, come in an' find me sitting on my bed, looking around. Moira had left her little girl with her mother an' Carmen say she planning to get herself a husban' when she reach Englan'.

'You don't have to wait until you reach Englan' for dat. Look, plenty man on dis boat already,' Moira tell her. 'An' some of dem nice!' She make her voice small like a mouse.

'Dey don't have no job,' Carmen say.

We laugh.

I tell dem I want to study. Learn to read, write an' speak good English. Then get a nice job, before all of dat husban' an' children business.

After the boat stop in Antigua, Deidre join us an' occupy the last bed.

'Come. Come see dis,' Moira call out to us on our way to dinner. 'Look at all dis water, eh?'

The four of us stand there, with a few others, women holding their hair, men their hats, looking out at nothing but sea water upon sea water, making bubbles as the ship drive through it. The salty smell on the wind an' dat amount of sea water made me think about what Mama used to say – dat the sea don't have no back door. Once you fall in, is only one way out.

'Come on,' Deidre say, 'before I bring up my guts.'

An' as we turn, I notice him. Dat sweet *saga* boy with his honey eyes on me.

Chapter Sixteen

Yvette

'You just came to my mind,' Auntie Agnes said, when I answered the phone, 'so I say let me call. How things going with your father?'

I told her about Papa asking me to find Ian, making sure nothing about the altercation slipped out.

'After so many years?' she said. 'He want to find somebody from the boat?'

'And I don't even know if, or how, I'll be able to. I'm hoping to find the shipping company, see if they have records of their old passenger lists.'

'Dat sounds very involved.'

'Yeah.' The thought alone was exhausting. 'But I'll need to find his surname or anything else that could help find him,' I said. 'I've tried Mum, but she says she just about remembers him, although from what Papa says this Ian man was keen on her. But how are you, anyway, Auntie?'

'I'm fine. I'm just a little worried about your cousin.'

'Dionne? Why? There's nothing wrong with her, is there? She's not ill or anything?' The idea of Dionne being ill unsettled me.

'No. It's just dat… well, I haven't heard from her in a while.'

'I'm sure she's fine, Auntie,' I said. 'She's probably tied up with something. You know how life can get busy.'

'Yes.' Auntie was worried. I could tell, even though she was doing her best to mask it. But Dionne was a grown woman. Couldn't Auntie see that?

'Don't worry. I'm sure you'll hear from her soon,' I told her before we said goodbye.

But after the call, it occurred to me that Dionne might be distancing herself from Auntie, like she'd done with me. That would hurt Auntie terribly. Gut me, too. Severing her link with Auntie would close the only avenue I had of knowing anything about Dionne, keeping our connection alive. I didn't want to lose that any more than Auntie did.

My eyes flicked open. Someone was closing the front door. I lifted my head.

'You were in some sleep,' Aaron said, walking into the front room. 'You didn't hear me knocking?'

'Mmm.' I covered my mouth to yawn.

It irritated me sometimes that he'd only use the keys I'd given him if I wasn't in. I'd stayed on the sofa after speaking to Auntie Agnes and obviously fallen asleep. As he leaned over to kiss me, the phone started ringing on the floor next to me. 'Oh, Auntie?' I said, still half-asleep. Aaron tapped my hand. I looked up. He was miming. I squinched up my face and whispered, 'What?' back, then he left the room.

'You still dere?' Auntie said.

'Yes… yes, Auntie. I'm here,' I said, refocusing.

'I was thinking,' she said, 'after I finished speaking to you earlier, how I remember when Doli reached Englan' she wrote to tell me about some of the boys on the boat who did take a fancy to her.'

'That would most likely be Papa,' I said.

'Yes, him too, but dere were others. I just check amongst my old letters – you know how I don't throw those kinds of sentimental things away.'

'And?' I moved from reclining to a sitting position. 'Did you find anything?'

'Yes.'

'Hold on. Hold on, Auntie,' I said and stretched across to the computer table to get paper and something to write with. 'I'm ready.'

'Ian was definitely one. Some of dese letters are not too easy to read now, but from what I can see, she mention him more dan once in dem.'

'Right. Is there a surname?'

'No. She didn't give his title. No.'

'What about the island he was from? Anything about that?'

'Oh, yes. St Vincent. Ian was definitely from dere.'

'Wow. Oh, that's great, Auntie. That's something,' I said, the phone wedged between my chin and shoulder. 'Thanks, Auntie. At least we have the country. That should help. Something else to go on.'

'What's all this about St Vincent?' Aaron wanted to know after I finished the call. He'd heard more than I thought he had when he came back into the room.

'There's this man Papa wants me to find for him,' I said. 'They met on the ship when he was coming to England. Lost touch. Now he wants me to find out where he is.'

'And what's your auntie got to do with it?'

'It's a bit of a long story,' I said.

Aaron gave me that raised eyebrow and slow nod of his which meant, *Okay, I'll stay out of your business if that's what you want.*

I got up and switched on the computer.

'What you doing now?' he said.

'Writing to a shipping company.'

'Come on, you can do that tomorrow,' he said, then came over and started nibbling my ears. 'I'll help with it tomorrow,' he whispered, swivelling my chair around so I was facing him.

I let him lead me upstairs.

'You're not with me, are you?' Aaron said, leaning off me on the bed.

'Sorry,' I said.

'Your paps, uh?'

'Yeah. And I can't stop wondering whether I'll be able to find this guy or what's the best route to take.'

'I told you I'll help.'

'You? Mr "lots of jobs to catch up on"?' I turned onto my back and stared at the ceiling.

'It won't be me directly,' he said. 'I know someone.'

'What d'you mean?'

'A friend of mine. He's a private dick.'

'A what?'

'Private investigator. We go way back. I've known him since school.'

'Oh. Have I met him?' I said.

'Maybe not.'

'Private investigators are expensive, though.'

'I thought this was important to you and your paps.' He turned to lie on his back too, his hands supporting his head.

'Course it is,' I said, moving to face him.

'So, what's the problem?'

I considered it for a moment.

'You're a bloody genius,' I said.

'Rob has access to all sorts. Birth and death certificates, police records, movements in and out of the country – you'll be surprised.'

'God. That's great.'

'You'll have to give me all the information you know about this guy you wanna find, though. I mean everything. I can call Rob tomorrow.'

'What's his name? Your private dick,' I said, smirking.

'Rob. Rob Payne.'

'Let's hope he can relieve mine.'

'What?' He turned towards me. 'You in some kind of pain, little lady?' He started tickling me and kissing my neck.

'What d'you think Rob Payne's likely to charge?' I asked Aaron, in the morning. I'd taken some unpaid leave to look after Papa so any extra spending would have to come out of my savings.

We'd overslept, and Aaron was rushing through the coffee and toast I'd made him.

'Don't worry about it, for now,' he said. 'I'll sort it out.'

'Ask him for an estimate at least, yeah? I'm gonna need to budget.'

'You and your bloody budgets,' he said, taking the piece of paper with the information about Ian on it. 'I'll sort it out. 'See you later.' He kissed me and rushed off.

Chapter Seventeen

Yvette

'Hello, my dear.' I heard her voice before she opened Papa's front door to me. It took a couple of seconds for me to recognise Miss Elsa without the hat. She looked younger, prettier.

'I come to keep your father company,' she said.

I stared at her. My feet felt stuck to the mat.

'You afraid of me? Of course not.' She answered herself. 'Then come in, nuh?' She stepped aside.

'Angel?' Papa called from the living room.

'Yes. Your Angel is here,' Miss Elsa said.

'Hi, Papa,' I said. 'You okay?'

'Elsa here with me,' he said.

'I see,' I said, kissing his forehead.

'Your father and me are good friends, you know,' Miss Elsa said. 'For too long, eh, Joe? You think it's too long, Joe?' she teased. 'Look, I almost forget.' She pulled a box like a jewellery case out of the bag on the floor next to her.

'My medal?' Papa said, smiling. 'Although I didn't play?'

Miss Elsa gave an approving grin. 'East London champion,' she said. 'When you come down you'll see the trophy. This one is real special. We kicking ass, Joey-boy.'

'Put it dere on the shelf for me, please, *doudou*,' Papa said, handing me the medal with his name inscribed below the Flyers Domino Club logo – an eagle, wings opened in flight.

'We not forgetting our chairman,' Miss Elsa said, still jovial. 'Our man Joey, eh?'

'Mmm,' Papa said, and relaxed back into the sofa.

I uncovered a pot of soup in the kitchen.

'So how you holding up?' Miss Elsa's voice startled me.

'Okay,' I said, putting the lid back down.

'I know it must be hard. No matter what you say. And don't mind him there, acting all tough an' all. He's a man, and must let people believe he strong, but he's as afraid as you. I know that, even though I playing along.'

'You know about the cancer?' I said, lowering my voice.

'Yes, but not because he tell me. I come across a letter on the table before he get a chance to move it.'

'You know he's refusing treatment?'

She took a quick step back, like something was about to fall on her feet, and double blinked. 'No,' she said. Her curly lashes became more noticeable with her glare. 'He didn't tell me that. And each time I ask how he is, all he say is, he's there.'

I leaned towards her. 'D'you think you can talk to him? About having treatment?'

Miss Elsa shrugged. 'I can try. But… I will try,' she said.

Without thinking, I hugged her. Her hold was light. Gentle. 'Thank you,' I whispered, quickly letting go. 'Don't let him know I told you,' I whispered.

'Our secret,' she said quietly back. 'And, by the way, I like what he let you do to the place.'

'He wasn't around to stop me,' I said.

'We will try to maintain it.' She gave me a playful nudge and walked off.

'Remember, Joe,' she was saying as I joined them, 'when we was back home, the old people had a bush tea for every sickness you have?'

'Umm,' Papa replied, his hat tipped over his forehead.

'Saturday was molasses day, to clean you out. You remember that?'

'Mmm,' Papa replied.

'I can keep Joe company for you today, if you like,' Miss Elsa said. 'Jackie's coming over later.' She turned to Papa, then me again. 'Jackie is my friend.'

'Go, go,' Papa said, flicking loose fingers at me. 'Your young man must be missing you.'

I was hoping for space to tell Papa about the private investigator, but that would have to wait. He had good company and Sunday lunch.

'Thanks, Miss Elsa,' I said again, leaving.

When I got home, I gave Auntie Lucille a quick call. On my way to the kitchen, there was a knock on the front door.

'Mum?' I said.

'I just pass by on my way from church.'

I left her to hang her coat up. 'I'll be in the kitchen,' I said, but stopped when there was another knock on the door.

It was Aaron this time. I was expecting him. 'Hi – good afternoon, Mrs Francis,' he said, when he saw Mum. 'It's nice to see you.'

'Nice to see you too,' Mum said. 'How are you? It look like West Indian sun agree with you?'

'I loved it.' Aaron smiled.

They both followed me to the kitchen. Aaron washed his hands and started setting the table while I put the food out.

'Yeah. He's got a serious tan, hasn't he?' I said, and invited Mum to have lunch with us.

'If you have enough. But I already cook, so you don't need to trouble yourself.' She sighed and sat down. 'Any more news?'

'About what?' I said.

'Your father. He doing all right?'

I told her Papa was home now.

'An' dis stupid thing about finding Ian? He finish with dat?'

'No. I'm going to hire a private investigator to do it,' I said, as we sat down. 'Save me a lot of bother.'

'Dat's not expensive?' she said, spooning some rice onto her plate. She cleared her throat. 'You find out his title?'

'Not yet, but I found out which island he was from.'

'Who tell you?'

'I've been doing some digging of my own.'

Auntie Agnes wouldn't appreciate me letting Mum know she'd shared what her sister had told her in her letters, with me.

Mum raised her eyebrows at me. 'Oh? So you will not need any more information about Ian from me after all. How was Dominica, Aaron?'

Aaron started filling her in on his family reunion. She was looking at him, but didn't seem to be listening. Mid-way between him telling her about the food and weather, she announced she had to go and was soon out of the door, leaving most of her food on the plate.

'That was strange,' Aaron said, after she left. 'And did you notice?'

'What?' I was washing up, while he tidied the table.

'Her, checking me out.'

'No,' I said. But I had.

I too had noticed her eyes lingering on his backside, though I'd prefer to believe it was his general physique, when he got up to get the wine for me and him; the pleased look on her face at the time. My own mother eying up my man. Yuck.

Her dropping in like this, after church, which was closer to her house than mine, was strange. Was she that concerned about Papa?

'Hey, you with me?' Aaron tapped my shoulder.

'Mm?'

'I said, do you fancy going to see a film one evening this week?'

'Mmm… this week? Depends on what's happening with Papa,' I said.

'I was thinking maybe Friday night?'

Friday night. His usual stay-over night. I was tired of that, too. Needed more. Why didn't he?

'It's one of those thrillers you like. Think it's called "What Lies Beneath".'

I placed the last pan upside down on the drainer and stared at the window in front of me. Aaron came and stood next to me, his back against the work surface.

'Something wrong?' he said, looking at the side of my face.

I wanted to wait until things were more settled with Papa before tackling things with Aaron again. But the longer I left it, the more fake our relationship felt. If we were going to split up, it would be best to get it over with and start mopping everything up.

I sighed and picked up a towel to wipe my hands.

'Worrying about your paps? I know it can't be easy.'

'No. It's us. Our future together,' I said, turning to face him.

'Oh, Yvie. Not that again.' A sullen look spread across his face. 'Can't we talk about this another time?'

'When? We don't want the same things in life. And I'm tired of—'

'Hold on. Hold on,' he said, raising his hand to stop me as he pulled his phone from his pocket. 'I have to take this.'

'Where?' he said, wandering out of the kitchen. 'Good…' His voice became too muffled for me to hear anything else he was saying. Then there was the sound of his feet coming back to the kitchen. He stood there, holding his jacket and phone.

'I'm sorry about that,' he said. 'Something's come up. I've got to go.'

'What, now? You have to go *now*?' I said.

'I'm really sorry, Yvette,' he said again, half-facing me. 'I know it's the worst time, but I have to.'

'Okay,' I said, looking away.

'I'll explain later.'

I turned back to him. 'Tell me now, Aaron, or don't bother.'

'Aah. Don't be like that, Yvie. Please. It's business.'

I pulled away before he could touch me.

'Yvie, please,' he said. 'I have to rush. It's urgent.' He gave me a lingering look as he fumbled with his jacket.

'I'm not stopping you,' I said.

'I'll call. We'll sort this out.'

'Oh, don't bother!' I shouted.

He hesitated for a few seconds at the door and sighed. My frustration intensified as he walked away.

He's gone, I told myself, hearing the front door shut. *What's the point?*

I poured myself a glass of wine and, on my way upstairs, almost tripped over the duffle bag he'd left on the landing in his rush to leave. I'd wasted too much of my time waiting for this relationship to move up a notch. I wouldn't waste any more.

I had just checked in on Papa before getting ready for bed, when a text came in from Aaron.

> *Have to take a short trip to Holland. Will explain and be in touch ASAP. Love you*

I was tempted to reply: *Really?* Instead, I ran a hot bath.

Chapter Eighteen

Yvette

I was preparing to go back to work on reduced hours, and popped into the office to finalise it with Brenda.

I had also finished proofreading Pe's application for a Masters in HR Management she was applying for. Her office was only a stone's throw from mine and we'd agreed to meet in the car park so I could give it back to her.

For her, getting this Masters was a gateway to furthering her career. Addae wasn't so keen. He wanted them to have another child. As an accountant, he felt he earned enough money for Pe to carry on working part-time while they raised their children.

'It's good,' I said, handing the envelope to her.

'Thanks,' she said.

'You told Addae yet?'

'Not yet,' she whispered back, looking over her shoulder. 'Anything from Aaron?'

I told her about the text I'd got. 'I have to end this,' I said. 'Can't carry on living a lie.'

'You can sort it out when he gets back.'

'He's not gonna change his mind about wanting any children, Pe. And Holland, you know? Holland. When he's been going on about how busy he is here.

'I really thought he was gonna be different.'

'You wouldn't have been with him all this time if he wasn't.'

Yeah. Aaron *was* different and in so many ways that mattered, but what was I going to do with this longing, my need to have a child, a family of my own? There was no point in me being with him if he didn't want that too.

'Mmm.'

Pe waved to someone entering the carpark.

'Listen, you better get back to work. Tell Addae about the application. He loves you. He'll understand,' I said.

'I will.' She hesitated. 'I will.'

Rob Payne's office was in an old building above a Turkish welfare advice place, across the road from Dalston Junction.

As annoyed as I was with Aaron, there was no question that his idea of getting a private investigator to find Ian was a good one. I'd thought about using a different company, but it was best to go with someone recommended, especially on something like this. So, I'd found Rob Payne's number in the telephone directory and arranged to see him on Wednesday morning. Papa was good at getting his own breakfast now. He needed fewer painkillers as well, though his mood was still low.

I stood under my umbrella, my back to the bellow of traffic on the busy main road, and pressed the dusty buzzer with 'Payne's PI Services 3rd floor' printed under it. A female voice answered and let me into the damp, musty smell that travelled up the stairway with me. At the top, I took a deep breath, then said, 'Good morning,' to the black woman, who moved her attention from the computer screen to me.

'Good morning,' she said, looking over her glasses. Her dark lips spread into a smile. 'Mrs—?'

'Miss Francis.'

'Sorry, Miss.' She nodded. 'Mr Payne's ten o'clock appointment?'

'Yes.' I nodded back.

She asked me to take a seat. 'Mr Payne will be wit' you shortly.'

I thanked her and sat on one of the four wooden chairs in the chilly reception area. She invited me to help myself to tea or coffee from the facilities on a table nearby. I told her I was fine.

She got up, exposing her neat body that was fitted snugly into a black-and-white semi-formal dress, and knocked on the door to her right.

'Your ten o'clock is here, Mr Payne,' she said, popping her head inside.

Less than a minute later, a tall, slim, clean-shaven white man came out. 'Miss Francis?' he said, raising his eyebrows. At least he hadn't given me a non-existent husband.

I stood up abruptly and my handbag fell to the floor. I scooped it up and walked towards Mr Payne.

His office was just big enough for his large desk, three chairs and the four metal filing cabinets that were neatly fitted along the walls.

'Inez offer you a drink?' Rob Payne asked, after a quick handshake.

'Er... yes,' I said, sitting down.

The large sash windows behind him were closed, but the cold air was finding a way in from outside. I suppose it helped to clear the smell of stale cigarette smoke wedged in the room.

His desk was sparse, with only a pencil sharpener attached to one of the corners, and a cream-coloured file lying on it.

'Well it's... it's good to meet you.' His grey eyes peered at me.

'Yes. Aaron recommended you, so—'

'Lucky me, eh?' he said, his face brightening up. 'Yes, he's given me a few details. A difficult one. I suspect he's told you.' His tone was formal again. I was surprised that Aaron had already managed to get the information to him. 'Well…' he continued, 'the distance in time – it was so long ago and we don't have many facts to go on: names, addresses, age, etcetera.'

'Oh.' I felt a sudden drain of optimism.

'We've only been on it for a couple of days, but I can tell you' – Rob Payne tilted his head to the side – 'these shipping companies don't keep very good records now, let alone in the sixties.'

'Not even a passenger list? You know, to show who travelled?' I said.

'Well, yes.' He pulled his lower lip up. 'But if they do have them, they won't necessarily go back forty years.'

'Oh.' I was starting to lose faith in this Rob Payne. This was going to be a waste of time.

'But don't lose heart,' he said. 'I have some contacts. St Vincent, you say he travelled from?'

'Yes. Yes. That's what we believe.' Hope was edging closer.

'Could it be another island?'

'I don't think so.'

'If only we had his surname. It would narrow things down. Ian isn't exactly an unusual name. Then we have the question of whether that was his official name.'

I looked at him wide-eyed, my optimism beginning on another downward spiral. 'What do you mean?'

'It's just that people sometimes use pseudonyms – unofficial names, you know.'

'Yes, I do.' Practically everybody back home had one. Mine was Ruthie. This search would be bloody useless if Ian was this man's pseudo or home-name.

'Not to worry, though,' Rob Payne said. 'I have one or two leads to start with.'

'I know you said it's difficult, but in your experience how long is it all likely to take?'

'To find him?'

'Uh-huh.' I nodded.

'I'm afraid these things take as long as they have to. Sometimes leads dry up. Sometimes… I sense there's some kind of urgency?'

'Yes, there is.' Clearly Aaron hadn't told him that bit. 'You see I… I need… Everything I tell you is strictly confidential, isn't it?' I wanted to be sure he wouldn't share this information with Aaron.

'Of course. It's the nature of our work, Miss Francis.' He gave me a reassuring smile that made him look quite attractive for a white man.

'I need to find him… this Ian man, for my father. He's very sick and… this thing's haunting him. He needs to know of this man's whereabouts – even if it turns out that he's dead.'

'I see,' Rob Payne said. 'Believe me, we will do our best to locate Mr Ian. Our absolute best.'

'And can you contact me direct, please, if you find anything?'

His eyes widened slightly as he looked at me.

'I know Aaron gave you the case,' I said, 'but it was on my behalf, so—'

'I understand perfectly.' He nodded.

I hoped I hadn't opened a door that I should have kept closed – that Rob Payne was not detecting the rumblings in my relationship with Aaron. I wasn't sure how much this Rob Payne knew about Aaron's life – about me. Would Aaron be that close to a white guy? Not likely, or I would've met him before now.

I took up my bag in preparation to leave.

'Maybe you can keep asking your father – or anyone else you think might have known Ian – more questions.'

'I will,' I said. Mum came immediately to mind.

'If you find it problematic, we can speak to them ourselves – if they don't mind.'

I told him I didn't think that would be possible right now.

'But it might be our only avenue, if we draw a blank in any crucial areas. With all respect, we'd probably be better at teasing information out of people than the average—'

'I know,' I said. 'Do you charge on a daily basis?'

'No. We take an initial engagement fee – which Aaron has already taken care of.' A flicker of a smile crossed his lips. 'The additional costs will depend on the amount of time we need to spend on the case.'

'Right,' I said, and thanked him for seeing me at such short notice.

Rob Payne walked me to the top of the stairs, assuring me he'd be in touch.

The heavy door closed behind me and I stepped out into the noise and pollution. The pavement was still wet, although the rain had stopped. I walked around the corner to where I'd parked my car. Damn. There was a parking ticket on my windscreen.

Things didn't improve much throughout the rest of the day. My 1.30 didn't show and everyone was talking about an upcoming restructuring of the department. At the last team meeting, Brenda had assured everyone that our section wouldn't be touched, but now one of the other dieticians, a trade union rep, was saying different. I couldn't afford to lose my job, what with everything else that was going on in my life. Scanning for jobs, filling in application forms – that whole job-hunting thing? I wasn't in the space for that. All of this uncertainty was dragging me down.

I called Pe from the car after work. Working in Human Resources she sometimes got inside information on things like this. She confirmed that the service was going to be under review, but wasn't sure yet about job losses. We agreed to talk later.

*

Elsa was with Papa when I called before leaving work, so that evening I dropped in on Mum instead. I needed to get more information on Ian. And so far, she was the next best person to Papa for that.

'Hi, Mum,' I said, at the door.

'Eh-eh, you come an' see me again?' She stressed the 'again'.

I gave her a light hug and followed her into the zesty scent that grew stronger as we got closer to the kitchen. She was making the lemonade I'd loved as a child. If she couldn't get her preferred option: limes, then lemons would do.

'How is the boyfriend?' she asked.

I put the kettle on, while she poured brown sugar into the jug of juice and added a few drops of vanilla essence.

'Fine,' I said.

'You don't want juice instead?'

I told her no, for fear of acid erosion.

She stirred the mixture with a long wooden spoon, tasted it, added more water, then got a glass from the drainer and poured herself some. The remainder she put in the fridge.

When we were both seated at the table, I got my notebook out.

'What you writing now?' she said, pushing her chair back. 'So dat's why you come here?'

'No,' I said. 'I've come to see you, but thought while I was here, I might see if you remembered anything else about Ian.'

'Like what?' She folded her arms and looked down her nose at my notebook.

'His surname. D'you remember it at all?'

'Why you think I would know dat? Ask your father. Why would I know more about Ian than him?'

'I have and will probably ask him again,' I said, 'but I wanted to make sure you hadn't left anything out from what you've already told me. And I really need his surname.'

Her gaze strayed. 'No. I don't know. I caa remember.'

'Okay. Okay,' I said, and stopped writing. 'But... sorry, Mum, just one more thing. Do you know if he had any other names?'

'But I just tell you—'

'I mean pet names, you know – like how they used to call me Ruthie back home.'

'I never give you no name like dat, onh,' she said, glaring at me. 'But Agnes did tell me it's only a home-name, an' I couldn't do nothing about it from here.'

'Mum, we're talking about Ian's home-name. Not mine.'

'How you think I would know what dey used to call Ian where he come from?'

'I heard he quite fancied you.'

'Me?'

'Yes. You, Mum. Men fancy you, Mum. Just the other day, you got flowers from an admirer. Did you fancy him as well? Ian.'

She looked away. 'Well...' She ran a hand along the soft skin on the front of her neck and seemed disconnected from me for a few seconds. 'He was a good-looking man.'

'Really?' I said.

'Yes, really.' She picked up her glass again. 'Dat's all.'

She might have known more, but I didn't want to push it.

Chapter Nineteen

Joe

They say when you're dying you see dead people. Yesterday, it had been his sister, Ethel, that Joe had caught sitting at the foot of his bed, when he woke up from one of his dreams in a hot-cold sweat, calling Ian's name.

Ethel's clothes were white, even the *mouchwè* tied around her head. She was holding the baby in her arms. Didn't speak, just sat and looked straight at him. As soon as he moved to get a better view, she was gone.

Today, when he lifted his head from the pillow, looking around for a cloth to wipe the sweat from his face and neck, she was standing by the wardrobe door, just looking again, but without the baby.

There was a lot of quarrelling when Mama had found out Ethel was pregnant. She couldn't stop letting Ethel know how disappointed she was.

'Mama, we will manage,' Joe remembered telling her. 'Is only milk de baby will be drinking for a good while, isn't it?'

'But how she going to work, Joe?' Mama said. The hurt was there in her eyes.

Joe wished he could have done more to help. Earned more money to make life easier for all of them.

Mama couldn't even rely on getting a red cent from Davis. He was too busy in the rum shop to bother about Mama or how she was feeding the three children she had for him.

His older brother, Bradley, had left for Curaçao two years before, and the money and letters he had been sending stopped after the first six months. Every cent Joe made from loading bananas, and Ethel made from taking care of rich white people's children, was needed for the three of them to live.

And it was plain to see that Ryan, the baby's father, was not interested in Ethel anymore, let alone the child she was carrying for him. Ethel stopped coming home late from work so there was no cut-eye look from Mama, but her belly was still swelling.

One day, Joe arrived home from work to discover that Ethel was in labour. He was sitting out in the yard as daylight was leaving, waiting to get the all clear, maybe hear a baby cry, but instead Mama stumbled out and dropped to her knees, screaming.

'Bondyé, ich mwen mò. My God, my child is dead. Ich mwen mò. Bondyé!'

The whole of Mabouya Valley rushed over to see what was happening, and people started to gather in the darkening yard.

Mama was still on her knees conversing with God when they brought both Ethel and the baby's bodies out. Uncle Henry made Joe leave the women and marched him down to the rum shop to deal with his grief.

Each shot of white rum Joe took set a fire in the back of his throat. The water he was instructed to send down after it didn't help much either, but Uncle Henry and the rest of the men said this was the best cure for Joe's suffering.

*

Lying there on his bed, all those years later, Joe supposed it wouldn't be long before Mama started showing up round his little flat, too.

He heard the front door open then close again. Yvette, his Angel, had her own key now. It was easier, she'd said. 'Saves you having to get up to let me in.'

'I coming,' Joe shouted, in response to her call.

Her habit was to breeze off to the kitchen – the room she was mostly in and out of. The smell of the flowers she always came with would be everywhere, even after she'd left.

Joe went to the sitting room, picked up the newspaper she had brought for him and walked over to the window. It was a habit – his new way of keeping in touch with the outside. There wasn't a hint of blue in the sky and the draught seeping in through the gaps in the window reminded him how much colder it had to be out there.

'How you been today, Papa?' She was back, standing on her toes to kiss his cheek, then sitting down by the table. 'What did you have for breakfast? There's only a cup in the sink.'

'Couple of bananas,' he said, 'an' some coffee.' He edged closer to the sofa.

'Is that all?'

'An' one or two digestives.'

'You managed to get that down?'

He hadn't, but didn't want to worry her. He sat down, brought his legs to their usual position, thought about flicking through the paper, then said: 'You get any news from dat private detective man about Ian?'

'Not yet, Papa,' she said. Just what he expected. 'But you know that ship you and Mum came up in? That *Carlotta C*?'

'Uh-huh.' He put the paper to rest on his lap.

'It sank, just a year after bringing you lot here.'

'People drown?'

'One.'

'That *Empire Windrush* – the one that brought people here from the West Indies in the forties. That caught fire and sank as well – way back in 1954, before you and Mum came.'

'How you know all dis?'

'Mr Payne. The private investigator,' she said. 'These ships weren't built to last, were they?'

'You sure dat man know what he doing?'

'I think so.'

'I hope so.'

They knew which island Ian had boarded from, the name of the boat they had travelled to England on, the date it docked in England. *Now dey even know it sink, yet still dey cannot find de man?* Joe hadn't run into any other Ians on that boat, but that didn't mean there weren't any there. Like Joseph, Ian was a common kind of name.

Joe was losing hope.

'Glad that *Carlotta C* didn't sink when you and Mum were on it,' Yvette said.

'Mm. *Carlotta C*, eh?' Joe's voice trailed.

'Yeah, but it doesn't exist anymore.' She got up to see to his supper.

There were plenty of good-looking women on *Carlotta C* – some Joe took a fancy to himself. Doli had passed him on her way to the smaller boat waiting to ferry them to the ship. He'd seen her, trying to hold on to her hat, as she waved goodbye to her family. But with so many people on that ship, he didn't see her again until he was in the line for food. On the first evening, she was way ahead of him. His intention was to quickly get his food then find a seat as close to her as possible, but even before they finished serving him, all of those spaces were taken.

As he saw Doli get up to leave the table, he'd gone after her. 'Hey.' He had touched her lightly on her shoulder. 'You remember me?'

Both she and the girl she was walking with turned to look at him.

'Oh, of course,' Doli said.

Just seeing her made him feel good.

'You'll meet me,' the girl said to Doli, and she walked on ahead.

Doli shouted for her to wait. 'I coming,' she said, looking at Joe as if she was in two minds. Then she said, 'I… I… later. I'll see you later,' and ran off after the girl.

Even though he knew that Doli liked him, over that two-week journey, his jealousy had brimmed over each time he'd seen Ian eyeing her or conversing with her. He'd observed the shy way she looked at Ian too. It was similar to how she looked at him, but to her he was special. She'd told him so when they'd stolen time together in his cabin, when the other fellas weren't around.

Ian's taunts had made Joe's blood boil even more on that last night at sea. He'd felt compelled to put the boy in order. He'd always regretted having to leave him there, but he wasn't going to put the opportunities – chances for a good life – waiting for him in England at risk for that crazy fella.

Years later, when all he wished he had to worry about was an upcoming domino match, it was this damn Ian that was occupying his mind, slipping into his head even when he was asleep. Worrying him even more than his cancer.

*

'Papa?' Joe heard Yvette saying, reminding him she was here.

'Uh?'

'You having it there or at the table?'

He wasn't really ready to eat right now but, 'Bring it,' he said. 'I'll take it here.' Then he told her he'd be fine on his own.

'I know,' Yvette said, as she handed him the tray with the fish soup. 'But don't you want a little company?'

'It's Friday. Bobotte coming here in a while, so go. Go ahead an' do your business.'

'It's okay, Papa,' she insisted.

Joe looked at the light liquid in the bowl – the small bits of spaghetti-looking things. The whole thing tasted good, but he was afraid of activating the cough that followed after every swallow of solids. He sighed and put his spoon down. At least he had Bobotte's visit to look forward to.

Thoughts of Doli, and then Bobotte, took Joe's mind elsewhere. Some years into their marriage, when because of Doli's bad attitude, Bobotte, who was closer to him than his own brother Bradley had ever been, stopped coming to their house.

'Why she must behave so, man?' Bobotte had asked him one day, after Doli, knowing full well that a couple of the boys had dropped by, refused to come into the front room to even say a good evening.

'Dey don't come here for me,' she'd told him. Where, he wondered, were all the good manners she never stopped claiming her mother gave her?

Yes, he did stay out late at the club come a Friday and Saturday night, but he didn't sleep out – not unless a match or club dance was too far to make it back home the same night. And after all was said and done, except for the one or two dances, he had never touched another woman while he was living with Doli. Why would he? He had a warm bed and a beautiful wife waiting for him at home. As vexed as Doli might be with him, she would never say no for long. But a point came when he felt more comfortable at the domino club than in his own home.

When he'd married Doli he really did believe it would be as they say: 'Till death do you part'. Stupid. Love can do that to you.

Chapter Twenty

Doli

Why would Joe want to make it his business to find Ian? The question caa stop running through my mind, as I push open the front door. What? I step on a white envelope, open it an' find a piece of paper inside. *Can we talk? Please. Cedric.* An' he put his telephone number again.

It's four days now since dis man stop leaving flowers by my door. Now he send me dis. I chups, drop the paper an' envelope in my bag an' take my tired self upstairs to soak in the bath. Afterwards, I cream my skin, put on my gown an' go back down to the kitchen, all the while thinking about the note. As the kettle boiling, I go an' take the paper from my bag.

About what dis Cedric want to talk to me? I take the tea to the bedroom an' make myself comfortable: my back resting on the bedhead an' my legs stretch out in front of me. As I pick up the tea I hope will give me a deep sleep tonight, I look at the telephone sitting beside it. I taste the tea an' glance at the note, put the cup down an' dial his number.

'Is… is dat Cedric?'

'Gosh, you've just made my night. My day,' Cedric say. 'How are you?'

'Okay,' I reply. 'I wanted to say thank you for the flowers, but… I'm sorry for phoning you so late.'

'God, it's only – what – nine o'clock? And I'm happy to hear your voice at any time. I've been thinking about you a lot,' he say.

'Why you doing dat?' I fix my gown so it cover more of my legs.

'Lots of reasons. D'you know how beautiful you are?'

The first time dis man see me I had not long get out of bed. The second time I had just come from the gym, an' he find I look beautiful?

'You are a real sweet-talker, eh, Mr Cedric.'

'I'm not any kind of sweet-talker. I tell the truth. That's all. You... you're single, aren't you?'

'Well, I am married, but we not together now.'

'Oh, good – I mean, I'm sorry because break-ups, especially if it's like a marriage, can be quite rough. But I'm glad there's no husband. I s'pose there might be a boyfriend, though – someone you're seeing?'

But why dis man asking me all my business like dat?

'Not really.'

'You don't sound very sure.'

I slide down on the bed, lie on my back an' fix the pillow under my head. 'Of course I'm sure. You have a woman?'

'No. No,' Cedric say. The words come fast from his mouth.

'Mm.'

'So, will you accept my offer and let me take you out for a meal?'

My eyes fall on my foot. My toes bending, so I caa even see the red polish I put on dem a couple days ago.

Dis Cedric might be different.

Saturday night come an' I wear my brown trousers an' orange blouse with the baggy sleeves an' a two-inch heel, because I don't want him to feel he's too short for me.

His eyes light up when I step out to meet him. 'You look good enough to eat,' he say, then rush back to his car to open the door for me.

'Thank you very much, Mr Cedric,' I say. My backside brush his front as I slip past him to get in the car.

Guy Fawkes Night not until next week, but somebody was already shooting fireworks in the sky.

'Gosh, you smell good,' he say, when he get in.

'You sure is not the fireworks you smelling?' I feel myself blushing an' was glad his eyes was on the road.

'Definitely not,' he say, then start the car. 'So, how've you been since our last chat?'

'Dat was only last night,' I say, 'but I'm fine.'

'You should like this place,' he say, as the car pull away. 'You do like steak, don't you?'

'Yes. I told you already.'

He laugh an' say he just making sure.

Last night, after I agree for him to take me out to dinner, he ask if I fancy West Indian. I tell him I can cook dat myself. An' as for Italian, pasta don't stay long in my belly.

Finally, I agree for him to surprise me – as long as I don't end up with no belly ache. An' after all, is his money he was spending.

He say he taking me to a place name Angus Steakhouse in the West End.

'You'll love it,' he did tell me. 'The steak's beautiful there.'

I have been to the West End before, but only for shopping an' to see a film.

Another firework fly up in the sky as we drive over Old Street roundabout.

'I love fireworks,' Cedric say, taking a corner. 'Don't you? Makes me feel like a kid all over again.'

'Mmm,' I say.

'So that'll be our next date then. Guy Fawkes Night. There's a real big display in Vicky Park. Fancy that?'

Guy Fawkes was what Yvette an' Joe did like to go to when Yvette was little. Once or twice I did go with dem, but dey seem to love it more than me an' I started to feel like an' outsider again, so after dat I begin to stay home with the television an' listen to the countless shooting of rockets an' sometimes look out the window to make sure nobody not blasting any fire in my house.

'Maybe,' I say, an' he push a cassette tape on. Bob Marley singing, how he don't want to wait in vain. 'Where you come from?' I ask him. He turn down the music an' ask me why.

'You talk like… like so—'

'English?' he say, then give a quiet laugh an' say, 'I'm from Antigua.'

'But you didn't grow up dere.'

'No.' He laugh again. 'I'm joking. I was born here. My parents are from Antigua. They came here well before most West Indians started coming. What about you? I know you weren't born here.'

'What you mean by dat?'

'Well, you've got an accent – Dominican?'

'No.'

'Got to be St Lucia then,' he say.

'Uh-huh.' We both laugh.

Cedric seem to know the West End well an' he find a parking space close to the restaurant so easy.

'Table for two?' the waiter with a red-an'-black outfit come an' ask us, after I walk through the door Cedric was holding open for me.

The seat in the restaurant cover with a strong material dat feel like carpet an' the table the waiter give us could take four people.

Cedric sit facing me. 'You'll probably want your steak well done,' he say.

I was still studying the menu an' raise my head to tell him, yes. I was not expecting to have the English 'meat an' two veg', but the more I look at the menu, the more it seem like dat was what I was going to have. I never eat asparagus before, so choose to have it with some carrots an' chips, since I didn't see rice.

'T-bones. Well done, please,' he tell the waiter. What a relief to hear he didn't want to see blood in the middle of his meat, like those English people I'm sure he spend a lot of time with. 'And a bottle of red, please.'

'You plan to drink so much wine?' I ask him.

He look at me. 'Oh, you don't—?'

'No. Er... a cup of tea, please,' I tell the waiter. Cedric change his mind an' ask for a glass of wine instead.

'So, here we are then,' he say, as soon as the waiter leave.

'Mmm. It's nice,' I tell him, an' run my eyes round the place.

'I'm so pleased you agreed to come.' His face look bright an' he start moving about in his seat.

'You feeling the cole, too?' I ask him. The place was warm, but dere was a light draff blowing round my foot.

'No,' he say. 'Not really. Just so happy to be here with you.'

I don't say nothing. Just look around.

'You got children?' he ask.

I tell him a little bit about Yvette.

'You must be proud of her,' he say.

'Of course. What about you? You have... children?'

'Yes. Bobby's in Antigua – been there with my parents since secondary school. He loves it.'

'You married?'

He shake his head. 'No. Never,' he say, as if with regret.

'Oh.'

'It's a long story. She – Bobby's mum – was white. I was – am black, and pretty dark at that. Her parents didn't approve, you know.'

The waiter bring the drinks an' leave.

I start to wonder about Cedric. I have good hair an' I know enough men does approach me, but I'm not no shabine with skin so fair people might mistake me for a half-caste or somebody with white close in their fam'ly.

'So what it is you like about white women?' I ask him.

'Nothing in particular,' he say.

'So why—?'

'It just happened. You know. One of those things.'

'Mmm.'

I drink my tea. He drink some of his wine an' soon dey come with the food.

'It looks nice,' I say, because I sense he was a little nervous now.

Cedric flash his nice even teeth an' take his cutlery out from the serviette dey have it wrap in. 'Hope you enjoy it,' he say, an' put the serviette on his lap.

The meat taste okay, even though I didn't see any sign of seasoning or gravy on it.

'You think I'm too inquisitive?' I ask him, while we was eating.

'No. I'm impressed with your honesty,' he say.

'All right. No more questions,' I tell him an' smile.

His good manners last all night. He drop me back to my door, make sure I was inside an' wish me a good night. He didn't ask if he can come in for tea, coffee or a drink like a lot of men I have been out with, whose main interest was to get inside my pantie.

After my shower, I was lying in bed thinking about the good time I had with Cedric an' how he was different, when the phone ring. It was him, calling to say goodnight.

Chapter Twenty-One

Joe

Only his neck to the top of his head was visible to Joe in the bathroom mirror, but for him that was enough. A lot of things were different on his face now. The distinct hair-line shape people used to say was the mark of his father's children was not even vaguely visible now; two small sacks hung under his dull, empty eyes; deep lines, like tracks, ran down each side of his nose.

'Uh-huh,' he said, to the face in the mirror.

Today, Bobotte was taking him down to the club. Two months away from there was a long time.

Three or four tables would be running a game. He might have to wait to join one. How would it feel not being able to fire a few liquors with the gang anymore?

'Oh, what happen—?' Bobotte said.

After his friend's third attempt to start the engine on his old Ford, Joe found himself praying it wouldn't start at all. The cold was finding a way through the three layers he was wearing and he was dreading having to see pity in the eyes of anybody at the club. Yes, he was sick and had been attacked, but that didn't stop him from being his own man.

'Better you get a mechanic to take a look at dis ole Cortina, man,' Joe told Bobotte.

'You joking. I just pick dis up from de garage yesterday,' Bobotte said.

Their conversation moved on to talk about the best cars to have these days then, after a little silence, the matches the club had ahead of them. Hitchin had just come down. After Christmas, it would be Birmingham.

Joe was feeling more and more excluded. The forty-five minutes it took to drive from Bow to Tottenham felt stretched into a whole night.

When they reached Stamford Hill and he saw the Hasidic Jews with their big furry hats and drop curls, he knew he would soon be there.

'But de place quiet,' he said to Bobotte, as they walked in to the smell of liquor and old cigarette smoke.

'Hey, Joe,' Sam called to him from behind the bar, with her usual friendly smile. 'Nice to see you.'

Bobotte waited while he talked. Then Joe followed him to the back of the building, listening for the familiar sounds of dominoes hitting against hard table tops, fellas jesting and music playing. Yes, where was the music? And the lights?

'Welcome back, Joe.' Suddenly the room, full of voices, exploded around him and the light sparked on, making Joe stumble slightly and wrestle to keep his feelings in check.

For a while, he almost forgot he had been away. Everyone gathered around him, wanting a game. Gentle taps on his shoulders, shaking of hands, the smell of cooking from the kitchen. All of it made him feel at home again. He was where he wanted to be. With good friends, laughter, banter, good tunes playing in the background. Then he was the man of the match, being handed a special get-well card with his name printed under the Pitons, the famous mountains depicted on St Lucia's national flag. Everything about the evening made him feel like he would soon be back, resuming his place in the team.

'Boy, you know you sleep from Tottenham to Bow?' Joe heard Bobotte saying as he opened his eyes.

'Huh?' He noticed the street lights and started to make sense of where he was. The car engine was off. He raised his chest, drew in some air and slowly exhaled as he looked round.

'How things really going with you, man?' Bobotte said, looking at him. 'I mean to say with de doctors an' dem?'

'All right,' Joe said, clearing his throat. 'Is just the hard food not going down too good for me.'

'An' what they, de doctors, saying about dat?'

Joe felt the weight of Bobotte's eyes on him.

'Is a while now I sense is not just de stabbing affecting you. I am right, eh?' Bobotte added, filling in the silence.

Joe nodded and cleared his throat again. 'It's true.'

'So what is it?'

'Man.' Joe hesitated. 'Is cancer dey say I have.'

Bobotte's chest rose and fell again. 'Oh, boy,' he said. 'Where?'

Joe shrugged. 'It start in my lungs, dey say. Not sure where it get to now.'

'So you on a sort of treatment?'

Joe shook his head.

'No?' Bobotte turned and leaned closer to Joe. 'But why?'

'I... I don't see de sense in it.'

'Joe... Joe... Joe,' Bobotte said, 'Take my foolish advice, man, an' go talk to de doctor. If you feel you caa do it, make your daughter do it. She know?'

Joe nodded.

'I notice your size going down too, man. Is now I understan'
why she fussing about you so.'

Joe sensed vexation mixed with worry in his friend's voice.

'Dere's a lot of people round you dat care for you, Joe.
Look how you have your chile running up an' down like she's
crazy. Cancer is no joke. If they say they can help you, why
you don't let dem, man? Dat's what de National Health Service
dere for, man.'

Joe felt chastised, a young boy again; Bobotte was Uncle
Henry.

By the time Joe made the call it was late, but it would be one less
thing on his mind if he got it over with that night.

She answered the phone sooner than he expected. He hoped
he wasn't disturbing her.

'Is me,' he said.

'Papa? Everything all right?' Yvette said. 'Why aren't you fast
asleep?'

'Sleep? No.' He was in no hurry to face sleep. Sleep would
bring on the heavy sweats, nightmares of him grabbing at nothing
in the dark; his own voice waking him.

'You sure you all right, Papa?'

'I… I decide to go ahead with de tests… what… whatever dey
say dey want to check, to see how… how things are… If it will
help me to swallow…' He paused. 'You… you dere?'

'Yes. Yes! Oh, God. Papa!' Yvette shouted in his ear.

'But I don't want to know about any kinda spread dey find.
You understan'?'

'But—'

'Dey can tell you, but I don't want to know. You understan', eh?'

'Yes. Yes, Papa. I understand. I understand, Papa. If that's what you want. You've made the right decision, Papa. Oh, God. Oh, *God*. This is great. Papa, maybe—'

'No. No maybe.'

'Oh, Papa,' she said. 'I love you so much.'

He knew if she was with him now he wouldn't be able to breathe through all the hugs and kisses she would be planting on him.

'I'll call Mr Sutton on Monday, shall I? Make an appointment.'

'Uhh,' Joe said.

Chapter Twenty-Two

Yvette

Thoughts of Aaron and the likelihood of finding Ian were tossing around in my head as I sat in bed sipping a second glass of wine, when Papa called.

His habit of constantly clearing his throat and his reduced appetite were bothering me. I'd tried to ask Emily, his Macmillan nurse, about it soon after they'd discharged him from the hospital, but she couldn't tell me anything definite.

'Each case is different,' she'd said. She wouldn't want to misinform me.

His decision to have the tests led straight to me hoping he'd agree to treatment as well. Things were beginning to move. We'd soon know what was going on with this cancer and be able to do something to at least slow it down. I was seeing more than a smattering of hope.

The drowsiness from the wine, from before Papa's call, was fading. I went to the toilet, then poured myself another glass and got back into bed. The telephone rang again.

'Papa?' I said.

'No, it's me,' Auntie Agnes said, a strain in her voice. 'I wake you?'

'No. I'm up,' I said. 'You okay, Auntie?'

'Yes, but just checking... You sure you haven't heard from your cousin?'

'Dionne? Why would I, Auntie? You know she doesn't—'

'I know. I know, but I was just checking. Everything all right with you?'

'Well… yeah. Okay,' I said. 'You mean you still haven't heard from her?'

'Yes… but—'

'Auntie, as long as she's not sick, I'd say there's nothing for you to worry about. Dionne loves you as much as I do. She'll probably be in touch soon.'

'I know. I know,' she said. But she didn't sound sure at all.

'Auntie,' I said, hesitating. 'D'you think it might help if I called her?' I couldn't think of another way to help.

'No. No,' Auntie said. 'I'm sure I will hear from her. One way or the other.'

I'd considered calling Dionne before, though I'd have to get her number from Auntie. It was my fear of more rejection that had stopped me pushing the idea in the past; I'd written numerous letters to her, asking why she'd stopped writing. She had ignored all of them. How could a person change like that?

What would her response be now if she heard my voice at the end of her phone? Hang up? Tell me to piss off using words this time, and not just actions? 'Well, let me know when you hear from her, anyhow.' Auntie's fretting was starting to affect me.

Chapter Twenty-Three

Doli

I was rushing so as not to be late to meet Bel for the soca aerobics class, but as I open the door to leave, I almost fall on the person in front of my door.

'Eh—?' I step back.

The woman was wearing a big green hat dat could make her pass for a Rasta.

'Doli?' she say.

I work out who she is an' step back inside the house, but she coming in on me, as if I give her permission to enter.

'I hope you don't mind,' Elsa start to say. Quiet, like she afraid to speak. 'I... I think we need to talk.'

'Eh-eh.' I look in her face. Her brown eyes make her resemble a cat. 'We need to talk?'

'I'm sorry for coming here like this,' she say.

My right hand on my hip now.

'Because you and I' – she talking like she so English – 'have never been friends.'

'You damn right.'

'But sometimes in life, we must put bad feelings aside... Joe...' – something in her voice make me focus on her – 'is... is very sick.'

'Sick? You don't think I know he sick. He get stab the other day. Is he send you here?'

She look straight in my face as if she don't understand me.

'No – of course not.' She shake her head. 'You… Joe would not do that. I'm here as a friend—'

'Frien'?' I look at her from head to foot. 'Dat's what you calling yourself?'

'Doli,' she say, half smiling. 'Me and Joe have nothing like that.'

'Not you he was sleeping with when he did leave dis house?'

'No. Not me, Doli.'

'Don't lie in my face, Elsa. You all was always shopping together, going to parties. You think people didn't tell me?'

Elsa straighten her body an' lift her head. 'I am not responsible for what people tell you.'

'You are responsible when you cannot keep your hands off another woman husban'. Everybody know is with you he was living after he—'

'He had nowhere else to go. I was being a friend.'

'From what I hear, you was more than dat.'

'People can talk, Doli. You yourself know that. People can talk all kinds of things. It doesn't mean there's any truth in it.'

'Dere's no smoke without fire,' I say.

'It was you he love, Doli. You, and his daughter. He cannot give anybody the love he has for you and Yvette.'

I start to feel hot standing in the house with my coat on.

'It wasn't easy for me to come here,' she say.

'So leave. I already know Joe get stab.'

'If that's all you know, then you don't know anything.' She turn her face from me.

'What you mean by dat?'

'I'm sorry, Doli. I didn't come here to upset you.'

'You don't hear?' I walk past her an' open the door wide. 'It's time for you to leave.'

After I slam the door on her tail, I feel sorry I couldn't find words to lambaste her some more. I could feel my blood pumping

through my body. I go in the kitchen an' sit down. Elsa really have
a nerve, eh? An' she want me to believe she an' Joe had nothing?

After dat first time Joe did come to see me at the house, he come
back again, as he did promise. Dis time I make sure I cook some
green fig an' salt fish, the way he like it – with plenty onions an'
tomatoes. I hang up his coat an' he go straight in the sitting room
an' sit on the settee.

He was wearing new trousers. I offer him a drink. He say no.
I ask if he hungry, he say no, so I sit beside him. Everything he
say seem to be concerning Yvette.

I agree dat he should see her. He say he don't want dem to
lose touch.

'What about me, Joe?' I ask him. 'You don't mind lose touch
with me?'

'Doli—'

'Joe, I am still your wife an' I love you.' I shuffle closer to him.
He sit stiff in the corner of the settee, looking straight ahead
at the empty shelf where his domino trophies used to be. 'You
afraid of me, Joe?'

'You wait for me to leave before you realise you love me?'
he say.

'You don't have feelings for me anymore, Joe? You not missing me?'

'Of course,' he say. 'What you think?'

I look at the side of his face an' run my hand along the front
of his jumper. Dis was the man I believed love me, would never
leave me.

'What… what you doing, Doli?' he say, but he not moving.
My eyes fall on the front of his trousers. 'I miss you, Joe.'

'Behave, Doli,' he say. 'You think dat's why I come here?'

'So you saying you don't want it?'

'I will take a drink now,' he say, an' get up to fix one from the drinks he did leave in the cabinet.

When he sit back down I come close up, take the drink from his hand an' put my mouth on his.

'I still love you, you know, Joe,' I tell him again. A sweet heat rise up all inside me. I beg him to take me upstairs.

Things started to get good with us. Then, just after I tell Auntie Lucille I believe we going to work things out an' I was planning to ask him when he coming back home, he call an' say he not coming to the house again.

'I will send the money to help you… for Yvette,' he say.

Dat was when he really break my heart. An' nobody had to tell me it was because of the big-time secretary of the domino club, Elsa.

An' after all dat – so many years later – she find herself in my house, saying she want to talk to me? Elsa?

Chapter Twenty-Four

YVETTE

Even my nails were suffering, waiting for the call from the hospital to confirm Papa's appointment. My nibbling had left all of them, except for my thumbs, prickly and uneven. The whole thing was slowing down this morning's task of auditing the patients' files, too. I dropped one into the box designated for archiving and checked the time again.

An hour later, the phone rang. I answered it.

'Oh, I am so glad to catch you,' Miss Elsa said. 'I'm so sorry. So sorry.'

'For what?'

'I didn't know. Your mother – I didn't know.'

'Mum? Didn't know what, Miss Elsa?'

'I need to see you to talk. Where you say you live again?' she said.

'I'm at work. In Islington,' I said. 'But I'll be at Papa's tomorrow morning, unless it's urgent.'

'Yes. It is... it is urgent. I have to see you. What time you finishing work?'

I looked at the pile of files on my desk. A catch-up tomorrow morning at Papa's would have suited me better. 'I... how about if I meet you around six outside Angel station? That okay?'

'Yes. That will be good,' she said.

I told her I had to go. 'I'm expecting a call from the hospital about an appointment for Papa. You know, for the tests?'

'Tests? You convince him to change his mind?'

'I thought you'd spoken to him about it.'

'No. Not me,' she said. 'I was even feeling bad because up to now I haven't been able to find the right time to do it. But that's good he agree to go. I'll see you later, then.'

What could all this be about Mum not knowing? Had she met Mum somewhere? Had they spoken about Papa? Why couldn't she tell me what she had to say over the phone? I resisted the temptation to call her back.

Four-thirty came. I was about to give up on hearing from the hospital, when Mr Sutton's secretary called. She confirmed that a bed had been reserved for Papa for first thing Thursday morning.

Papa would need to be in at eight. The tests would begin the following day.

A determined wind was blowing through the madness of the rush hour. People were scurrying around, bumping into each other, and the traffic was in typical bumper-to-bumper mode. I stood at the traffic lights waiting to cross to Angel tube station. Once there, to help keep warm, I positioned myself partially inside while scanning the area outside for a glimpse of Miss Elsa.

She was on time, her green hat replaced with a brown in the same design.

It felt strange meeting her there, like that. Like me and her were friends or something.

'I hope you haven't been waiting long. It's cold, eh?' she said, rubbing her hands. 'I forgot my gloves.'

'Oh, dear,' I said. 'I know a nice little coffee shop. Come on. It's not far.'

'You work round here, you say?' she said, as we walked.

'Yes. Down the road.'

'Joe tell me your job is something in food?'

'I'm a dietician,' I said. 'Mainly with children – young people.'

There were only a few people in the coffee shop: two older women sitting close to each other studying a tube map, another woman sitting alone staring through the window, her hands round her cup, and a man sitting at another window table flicking through a book.

I led Miss Elsa to a table as far away from anyone as possible and went to get our drinks.

'So,' I said, after I'd pulled my chair in. 'What's going on?'

'I went to see your mother.'

I leaned back on my chair, my hands flopped to my lap. 'Why?' I stared at her.

'I… I wanted to tell her she should come to see Joe. She – you don't think so?' She didn't give me a chance to answer. 'It would be good for him – maybe for her too,' she said, leaning towards me, both her hands on the table. 'I didn't know she didn't know about the… you know.'

'I haven't really told anyone,' I said, 'except—'

'But she didn't give me a chance to tell her and as soon as I realised she didn't know, I stop myself from saying any more on the subject. Now I'm afraid she might suspect something. I feel so bad.'

I braced myself for the call I was sure would be coming from Mum about Miss Elsa's visit.

'I am so sorry, Yvette. It's just that… I did it for Joe. He can't be sick like that and she don't come to see him. I know he still like her.'

Miss Elsa looked like she was about to cry. I put a hand on her shoulder. 'Don't worry about it,' I said. 'I've tried to talk to her myself, to see if she'd come, but they have a strange relationship.'

'I know, but—'

'Papa's not as bad as Mum,' I said, leaning back into my seat. 'And you'd think I'd know by now, but sometimes even I am not sure what I should keep them from knowing about each other, so I try to say as little as possible. It seems Papa doesn't want people to know about the cancer, but he'll be going in on Thursday for tests.'

'That's good,' she said, then went quiet for a while. 'I don't understand what it is Joe has done to her so much.'

'It's her pride,' I said.

'Because he left?'

'And feeling like he put the club before her.'

'Poor Joe.' She sighed. 'It must be hard for you to be in the middle of all that.'

'Sometimes. But I'm kind of used to it.'

We stopped talking, like we both had to digest what we'd just shared.

Miss Elsa sighed then said, with a fresh, uplifted voice: 'We gave him a really good celebration at the club Saturday night. He tell you? You should have seen his face.' Hers was beaming.

That was the night he called me. Maybe his experience there helped to change his mind.

'And don't worry, nobody was smoking. Me and Bobotte made sure of that.'

'Thank you.'

'I really hope me going to see Doli – your mother – will not create—'

'I'll handle it,' I said. 'It's probably time she knew, anyway.'

The break in our conversation gave me a chance to finish my coffee, then I was ready to go home.

'Miss Elsa?' I said.

Her attention had drifted. She hadn't drunk much of her tea.

'Mmm? What you say?' She glanced at me.

'Is Mum right? About… are you and Papa—?'

'Oh, no,' she said, sharply. 'Me and Joe? Uh-uh.' She shook her head.

'I just thought—'

'A lot of people used to – even now your mother's still accusing me – but me and Joe… No. Your father is like a brother to me.'

'Okay,' I said, disappointed. So she wasn't that special someone I hoped Papa had found.

She looked around and took a sip of her tea, which had to be cold now. 'We better go,' she said, and stood to gather her things.

Chapter Twenty-Five

Doli

'Busy day?' Cedric ask me, after I pick up the phone.

'Not really. Just my soca aerobics class,' I tell him.

'That's what keeps you looking so good.' He give a quiet laugh, then say: 'You sure you're all right?' when I don't answer.

'I just don't feel to talk right now,' I tell him.

How he was going to understand when neither Yvette, Auntie Lucille or Bel could see all the confusion dis stabbing Joe get bringing about?

Earlier dat day, when I tell Bel about Elsa coming here, she tell me maybe I should follow her advice an' go an' see Joe. 'The Bible say we should visit the sick, Doli. Nothing wrong in that. You could make it easy and go with Yvette,' she say.

But nobody knows how Joe leaving me an' taking up with Elsa did make me feel. The shame. Him leaving me an' going to her.

I catch Cedric saying something about company.

'Excuse me?' I say.

'I said, what you need is some company.'

'I don't think so.' What I need right now is for people to stop involving me in Joe dis an' Joe dat an' for Yvette to finish with all dis tra la la about trying to find Ian.

'I'm sure it'll lift your mood,' Cedric say.

I tell him I am not sure.

'I won't stay any longer than you want me to,' he say.

I tell him I don't know.

'It's up to you.'

I know how much of a gentleman Cedric can be an' remember how he show me so much respect – never even try to kiss me the other night when he drop me home. I respect him for dat, an' when I was with him I was able to put my troubles aside.

'Well, all right,' I say, an' tell him not to ring the bell. I will look out for him.

After dat, I running around the place. Not sure if I should bring him in the kitchen or in the sitting room.

The sitting room is best, I decide. So I move the crochet doily from under the vase on the centre table an' pass a cloth over the top, then put dem back, straighten all of the chair-backs on the settee then run upstairs an' take off my wedding ring. By the time I check my face in the mirror, Cedric already outside.

In dat cold, the man only wearing a red jumper, jeans an' a short brown scarf around his neck.

'Good evening,' he say. 'You're looking wonderful, as usual. Smell lovely too.'

The only wine I have is ginger, but I offer him some anyway, after I lead him to the sitting room.

'Not on a weekday, thanks,' he say. 'Leaves me foggy in the morning.'

He sit down on the single settee under the window, remove his scarf, an' his eyes take in the room.

'You get here quick,' I tell him. 'I didn't have time to change.'

'Oh, don't worry about that,' he say. 'You're at home. Your daughter, is it?'

I look up at the big frame picture of Yvette holding her first degree certificate tight in her hand. 'Yes,' I tell him, then sit in the middle of the long settee.

'I sensed something was bothering you, on the phone.'

I cross my legs an' fix the robe over dem. 'It's just somebody I don't want anything to do with come an' visit me today.'

'Ah, I see. Awkward, right?'

I don't answer.

'Old boyfriend?' he ask.

'Oh, no.'

'Someone you'd had a falling out with?'

'Something like dat.'

'You shouldn't let that kinda stuff bother you. Wants to be friends again, is it?'

'Something like dat.'

'It can be hard when people rake up the past.'

'Mm,' I say. 'You sure you don't want a drink? I have tea.'

'Actually, a cold drink would be nice.'

I go to the kitchen an' bring him some fresh lemonade.

He taste it an' say: 'Lovely. Homemade?'

'Uh-huh.'

He smile, drink some more then put the glass down on the side table next to his chair. 'What you need is some relaxation,' he say, then he rest back on the settee again.

I look at him.

'A massage.'

Dey have massage at the health centre. Me an' Bel did have one a long while ago. 'Maybe I'll arrange dat,' I say.

'I could give you a nice foot rub.'

'Foot rub?' I look at him, curious.

'Wouldn't take long. Mmm.' He twist up his bottom lip. 'Five, maybe ten minutes. It's really relaxing. I'm told I'm very good.'

'So you does give foot rub to all your women?'

He give a little laugh dat show his nice teeth. 'Only the special and lucky ones. Come on.' He lean forward an' look straight in my face. 'I want to do something nice for you.'

'Okay,' I say. 'I… I have to lie down?'

'It's totally up to you. You can put your legs across there' – he point to the space next to me – 'or stay exactly where you are.'

I tell him I will stay where I am an' while he getting up an' rubbing his hands, I put a foot out for him. He come an' kneel down in front of me an' take my foot in his hands. I hold the robe close so I don't expose my panties. His hands feel soft, an' a little – but not too – cole.

'You have magic fingers?'

'Just relax,' Cedric say, as if my talking interrupting him.

I don't want him to see my scar – the one I get after the fall at the beer factory. But the way he touching, rubbing an' pressing under my foot make me feel to rest my head.

'Mmmm. Dat's nice,' I say, an' my body start to sink.

The next thing I feel is my toe in somewhere sof' an' warm.

'Mmm.' Cedric start to moan an' I realise the sof'ness is inside his mouth. He start kissing my legs; his mouth moving up to my *kòkòt*. I let my body slide down, my crotch reach his face.

'Uhhh… smells good,' he say, rubbing something dat feel like it could be his nose on my *kòkòt*. Oh, God, the blood start pumping hard through me. My *kòkòt* feel like it have a heart beating inside it. It start to swell. I touch my breasts, my hard nipples. I don't want dis feeling to stop.

I raise my *kòkòt* closer up to Cedric mouth. 'Ah… aaah… ah… aah!' My body shaking. My *kòkòt* feel to explode. 'Ahhh-hhhh… *bondyé*.'

I lift my head, see Cedric look up from between my legs – an' all of a sudden, his teeth move in his mouth.

I straighten up. Pull my robe around me. He move quick an' sit beside me. 'Dat was not suppose to happen,' I say, pulling my robe tighter.

'Ah, come on, we both enjoyed it, didn't we?' He touch my leg an' I jump up.

'Is best you go now,' I tell him.

Cedric look up at me. 'I… I thought… well, okay, if that's your wish. But I had a nice time… Maybe…'

I couldn't even look at his face without seeing his false teeth moving in his mouth again.

'I'm tired,' I tell him, an' run my hand over my head to fix my hair. All I want is to put what happened behind me. Forget it did ever happen.

He pick up his scarf. 'I'll give you a call, then,' he say.

'It's okay.' I follow him to the door. Close it, lock it behind him an' put my head in my hand. 'Oh, God. Oh, God. Oh, God. What is wrong with you, Doli?' I say, an' rush upstairs, with my shame.

Chapter Twenty-Six

Yvette

Thirteen-year-old Tessa was sitting in my office with me when my phone pinged in my drawer. I'd have to check it after seeing her.

'Where's Mum today?' I asked Tessa.

It was okay seeing her on her own, but important to have a parent or guardian present. Apart from keeping them on board, they were the ones putting the food in the cupboard and fridge. Tessa was at risk of developing diabetes, like her older sister.

'She's s'pose to meet me here,' Tessa said, 'but…' She shrugged, then frowned. 'Most likely stuck at work.'

'You okay with us carrying on until she gets here?'

Tessa nodded.

We sat down and I went through my usual review questions to see how she'd been getting on. According to her, apart from adding what she described as a 'little bit' of cheese on her burger, things were okay.

'That's great, isn't it?' I said, as she stepped off the scales. She'd lost another half-kilo.

'I've been too scared to check,' she said.

'You're doing well,' I said.

When I had first seen Tessa a couple of months before, she wasn't only obese, but it had been hard to get a smile out of her. Today her smile put colour in her cheeks. There was some way to go to reach our agreed target, but we'd managed to get her BMI from thirty-five to thirty-three.

'Still managing to walk to school?' I asked her.

'Most days,' she said. 'If it's not gonna make me late.'

'D'you think you're getting enough help at home to stick with our programme?'

'Think so.'

Twenty minutes later, her mother hadn't arrived. Tessa decided to make her way home on her own.

After seeing her out, I checked my phone. The text was from Aaron.

b home by 5 today. Shall I come over?

I forwarded it to Pe, with an added message: *Got this from him.*

I hadn't heard from him since he left last Sunday, and had been accepting the fact that we're finished. If I was going to meet up with him it would only be to let him know that. And that's what I said to Pe when she called.

'But don't you wanna hear what he's got to say?'

'What for?' I pushed my office door shut to keep my conversation private.

'Why he hasn't been able to call you for the last whatever days? And at least let him have the chance to finally make his mind up about the kind of future he wants with you.'

'I don't even want to go over that with him any more, Pe. I'm sick of it. Had enough.'

'You sure?'

'What would be the point?'

'So you gonna let him come over then, tell him you're done?'

'For one, I'm not having him come to my house.'

'So where?'

I told her I'd go to his. It would be easier to tell him we're over at his house than at mine.

'But give him a chance to explain the Holland thing,' Pe advised me. 'Ending it without talking things out won't let you get proper closure. You wanna be sure you really made the right decision. At least think about it.'

I did, throughout the rest of the day, and all the way to his house.

I'm at his front door, the duffle bag he left at mine, that I've had in my car for the last few days in my hand, and the door opens.

I looked into his face and fought back anger, disappointment, longing and the urge to cry. I was reduced to a confused mess, but couldn't let him know that.

'Don't stand there like you're a stranger,' he said.

I stepped inside and he came towards me awkwardly. 'Give me your coat.'

I put his duffle bag down and pulled my coat off.

'Let's go in here,' he said, leading me to his front room.

I sat on the armchair opposite the door. Not much had changed in the room since I was last there. The walls were the same eggshell white and the black, three-seat leather sofa was in the same position, facing the unused fireplace. The wicker rocking chair might have been moved, but the large framed poster of Malcolm X holding a gun with the caption, 'By any means necessary', was still standing on the floor, next to the wooden carving of a stern-looking Maasai warrior gripping a spear.

'How's your paps doing?' Aaron said, hovering in front of me like an over-keen waiter.

'Okay, you know,' I said, my eyes locked on the carving.

'A drink? Wine or—?'

'Water, please,' I said, though some wine might have helped to loosen me up. He disappeared. I glanced around some more and was checking out the ceiling when he returned with my water.

There was a smug keenness in the way he was looking at me from where he sat, on the armchair facing me.

'Makes a change, doesn't it?' he said.

I raised my eyebrows at him.

'You visiting me,' he continued, after a pause. 'I'm so sorry about how things have worked out. And, like I said on the phone, I really didn't mean to rush off, especially like that. I know you might think it's because of what you wanted to discuss, but—'

'It doesn't matter anymore,' I said.

'There's... there's a lot I have to tell you.'

'Like what?' I sat rigid, my knees together, the glass in my hand.

'You know a while before I met you, I was seeing Vanessa.'

'Uh-huh.' Vanessa was the one before me. I'd heard the story. He'd taken two years to get over her.

'One day everything was fine, and the next, she was gone. Didn't even leave a note.'

I put the glass of water on the floor next to my chair.

'Nobody we knew, except her best friend, Felicia, could tell me any more than Vanessa had gone back home, to Curaçao,' Aaron continued. 'According to Felicia, Vanessa was pregnant.'

The word hit me with a thud. He'd left all of this out when he'd originally told me the Vanessa story.

'What're you saying, you... you have a—?'

'Hold on.' He raised his hand to silence me.

I tightened my jaw and clenched my teeth to stop myself from speaking. I didn't come here to listen to Aaron's old love story. More importantly, I didn't want to hear he had a child. A child. A five or six-year-old daughter or son.

The family *I* wanted with him.

I sat still and silent. Afraid to breathe for fear of increasing the tightness in my chest. I looked across at him, listening.

'I didn't know whether she had the child or not,' he said.

I let out a breath.

'And even if she hadn't,' he said, 'I genuinely wanted to know that she was all right. That nothing bad had happened to her because, according to sources, she hadn't turned up in Curaçao.'

'You've been tracking her?' I said, glaring at him.

'Not me directly. Rob was working on that for me.'

'Rob Payne?' I raised my eyebrows.

'Yeah. I needed to know.'

'So you've found her.' I felt redundant. There was no room for me in this scenario. No place for me here. I stood up.

'No. No.' He jumped to his feet, shuffled around me, opening his arms to block my exit. 'Come. Please, Yvette. Please hear me out. Please.'

I sat down again slowly, eyes fixed on him. 'Tell me straight, Aaron. What's going on?'

'The last time,' he said, 'that Sunday, when I was at your place – Rob called. He'd found Vanessa. That's why I went to Holland. She was dead.'

'And the child?' I held my breath, waiting for his answer.

'There wasn't one.'

Partially relieved, I sighed.

'Probably got rid of it,' he said quietly. 'Turns out she became an escort girl out there – high-end prostitution.'

'Bloody hell.' The words slipped out of my mouth. 'Well,' I sighed again. 'You've done your duty by her. Everything's all right for you now.'

'It wasn't that, Yvie.'

'What is it then, Aaron? You've gone clear across to Holland to look for your ex. Doesn't that prove how much you're really... how you must feel about her?'

'I needed to know if she had my child. The last thing I want is a child of mine running around without me knowing anything about her or him and them not knowing me. It's been bothering me. I had to know.' His gaze was on a space on the floor close to my chair.

'Listen, I'm going,' I said, getting up again.

He raised his head. 'I thought we were gonna talk.'

'We have. It's over, Aaron.'

'I'm sorry,' he said, standing. 'But – Yvie?'

I rushed out of the room and grabbed my coat off the banister. 'Drop my keys through my letterbox,' I said. 'Here are yours.' I took them out of my bag and threw them at him. 'And I understand I owe you some money.'

'For what?' Aaron looked at the keys I'd thrown lying by his feet and looked back up at me flummoxed.

'Your friend, the PI,' I said. 'Let me know how much and I'll reimburse you.' I charged out, tears pooling in my eyes.

'Yvie, hold on!' he said.

I slammed the door behind me.

Rage sent me speeding off, crossing the give-way line too soon and almost ramming into a black Volkswagen.

The driver swerved to avoid me. 'Stupid bitch. Where's your eyes?' he shouted.

I drove on, anger and frustration half blinding me.

Aaron didn't want me. He was still hung up on his old girlfriend. He'd taken time off his work and spent God knows how much money trying to find her and his possible child. But he didn't want to have a child with me.

I pushed the front door open and picked up the white envelope on the inside doormat, put it to sit on the step with my handbag while I took my coat off, then picked it up again and looked at the front. The airmail sticker across the top left-hand corner alerted me first, then the name the letter was addressed to.

'Ruthie Francis? *What?*'

It hit me like a bolt from nowhere, slipped me back into childhood, when envelopes like this, addressed to me quickened my heartbeat, thrilled and excited me. I turned it over. From Pattie? Dionne? Gosh! I rushed up to my bedroom tearing it open on my way.

My dearest Ruthie.

I sat on the bed. Ruthie. How long had it been since anyone had called me that? I continued reading.

I hope you are well. I wouldn't blame you if you have given up on me, but things have not been easy. Right now, there are important things we need to discuss, but I think it is best we do it in person. I will be in England at the end of this month and will get in touch with you again then. Please, do not tell Auntie Agnes about this letter. Let it be one of our secrets. You can email or call me if you like – I will explain everything when I see you.

Still love you. Pattie/Dionne

Why was she coming to England, and why keep it from Auntie Agnes?

She was sixteen in the last picture Auntie Agnes sent me of her. I imagined her looking the same as she did then. Slender. High cheek bones, small eyes, glossy lips. Her hair parted in the middle of her two cornrows. My longing for the sister I'd had and lost started to reawaken.

After what felt like a lifetime of blanking me, Pattie – Dionne – had written to me. She wanted to talk? And in person? 'One of our secrets', she said.

What did she mean by things not being easy? In spite of what she'd asked, surely I had to speak to Auntie Agnes? Give her the good news that Dionne was okay. But why didn't she want Auntie to know she'd written to me? And if she was okay, why couldn't Auntie Agnes get in touch with her? But when I tried to call Auntie Agnes, the phone rang and rang. No one picked up.

Chapter Twenty-Seven

Joe

Joe wasn't sure what time it was, but it was early, and he was propped up in bed thinking of Elsa. She had been good company over the last few weeks. Like brother and sister, they had become over the years. It wasn't what he'd wanted, but it was the hand God had dealt him.

The first couple of nights after Joe had left Doli, he had nowhere to sleep but in his old Vauxhall. Soon, he realised that if he was the last to leave the club, no one would know that he didn't leave until morning. It wasn't comfortable, but once he'd cleaned himself a spot, he managed to get a few hours' sleep. Nobody had to know. It would work until he found somewhere else to stay.

But one Sunday morning, he opened his eyes and Elsa was sitting on a chair beside him. She wanted to know what he was doing there, sleeping on the domino club floor.

'Me an' Doli finish,' he said.

'And it's here you think you should sleep? Joe, you have friends here. Me, Bobotte—' and she started to give him a list of people he could have gone to. 'I cannot be a replacement for Doli,' she told him, 'but I can give you a roof over your head for a while.'

That 'while' stretched into eight months, but his hope that sleeping on Elsa's sofa, their chatting, eating and going down to the club together, would amount to the two of them having something more never materialised.

*

A knock on the door was Yvette.

'Morning, Papa.'

'Morning, *ich mwen*,' Joe replied.

The smell and sound of breakfast being served in the main ward made Joe remember the 'NIL BY MOUTH' sign written above his bed.

Yvette gave him a light kiss on his forehead and sat by his feet, looking at him. 'You okay?' she said.

'Yes.'

'It'll be over soon.'

He didn't answer.

'Nervous?'

He shrugged. 'Uh-uh,' and shook his head. Telling her he was would only stir her up. He'd thought hard about what the results of the tests might say. How long they'd tell him he had left to live.

'I'll be right here when you get back,' Yvette said, looking at him. She was trying to read his face. 'It'll be fine, Papa.'

'You think so?'

'Whatever the results, we'll manage it together.'

'Mmm.'

Doubts had been creeping closer to Joe since he'd seen his brother Bradley standing in his living room, two days ago, looking not much older than when he'd left him, Ethel and Mama in St Lucia. *No need to wonder why he stopped writing now.* He had been giving Joe that half-smile of his. *Where is Mama? Why didn't she come?*

'If I come back from dat... dat, pro–procedure, all right,' Joe said.

'If? What d'you mean if?' Yvette interrupted.

Joe swallowed the lump forming in his throat. His daughter was hanging on to hope, not the reality he understood.

'It will all be fine. You'll just need some TLC.' She laughed. 'Tender loving care. And I'll be there to give it to you. Miss Elsa too.'

He forced a smile. She rubbed his hand. He said nothing.

'I hope you're not worrying about us not finding Ian,' she said, 'because we will. It's taking a while, but we'll find him.'

'I hope so.'

'I love you. You know that, Papa?'

'Papa love you, too, *ich mwen*,' he said, trying to dismiss other feelings he couldn't let go.

Yvette stood up, came closer, hugged and kissed him hard on his cheek, then rubbed the spot gently with her finger. As she leaned away, he looked up at her. Her hair was tied back in a bun, with the hair line he'd passed on to her from Davis in full display.

'What?' she said. 'Something wrong?'

'No. Nothing.'

She shifted her eyes, but he'd already seen the water building up in them, heard the change in her voice.

'Papa—?'

They both turned towards the knock on the door.

'Come in,' Joe said.

A woman wearing rubber shoes and a set of blue clothes that looked like they were made from paper, walked in with a nurse.

'Joseph Francis?' the nurse asked.

'Yes,' Joe answered.

The woman in blue asked how he was feeling and pulled out the papers Joe had signed a couple of days before. Joe confirmed that it was his signature, and they checked the plastic bracelet on his wrist.

Yvette sniffed. 'How long is he likely to be away for?' she asked the nurse.

'Two, maybe three hours,' the woman with the blue clothes said.

'You don't bound to come with us,' Joe said to Yvette, when he realised she was getting in the lift with them.

'He's in good hands,' the woman said.

'I know,' Yvette replied, hesitating.

'Don't worry about me, eh?' Joe told her.

They came out of the lift and stopped in front of two wide doors. He took in her flowery scent and felt moisture when she bent down to kiss his forehead.

'See you soon then, Papa,' she said. 'I'll be waiting.' There was an unsteadiness in her voice.

God had blessed him with a good, faithful child. He'd tried in vain, not to let her down. A tear trickled down the side of his face.

The big doors swung shut behind him.

Joe was lifted from his bed onto another one that was flat and hard. The smell and lights were different. There was nobody he could put a face or a name to. Doctors, nurses. Everyone was wearing white or blue, looking busy, busy, busy. Talking, using language he could hardly understand. They asked him his name; explained what they planned to do again; if that was his signature on the yellow paper; then asked how he was feeling. Somebody ran a little joke that made him smile and warned him about the sharp prick he was about to get in his hand.

He shut his eyes.

Chapter Twenty-Eight

Yvette

After Papa disappeared through the doors, I wiped my eyes, hung around reception for a bit, then wandered out to one of the cafes for a latte, which I brought back to his room with me. Without the bed and Papa, the room felt empty. Without meaning or significance. I sat down. The forty-five minutes that had passed felt like hours.

The months after my decision to stop tracking Papa weren't without concerns of how he was, where he might be living; hopes that he'd get in touch, then feeling rejected when he didn't. Why were those feelings creeping up on me again? Everything would turn out okay, despite the doubts I suspected he had. And was there something he wanted to say to me before that knock came on the door?

My latte was getting cold. I didn't fancy it anymore. Too much was unsettled in my mind.

Dionne's letter. What was all of that about?

I sighed and turned my attention to work. My personal development plan was due in in a couple of days. I took it out of my bag and skimmed through it, deleting and adding bits of information here and there. Almost an hour later, I was deleting temporary numbers from my work then personal phone. After that, I flicked through a dietician's journal I'd been carrying around in my bag all week, read an article about jockeys with eating disorders, then put the magazine back in my bag. I couldn't stay focused. Over two hours had passed. Probably one more to go. I needed some fresh air again. A walk would help make the time go faster.

I was getting my things together when I heard shuffling behind the door. It was Emily again. She'd popped in earlier to say hello and ask if I wanted a cup of tea. Her face looked flushed. Directly behind her was Mr Sutton, the surgeon.

I stood up.

'Would you take a seat for me, please?' Mr Sutton said, closing the door behind him. His voice had a worrying tone.

'Is everything okay?' I asked, lowering myself into the chair behind me, my eyes on Mr Sutton.

Emily pulled up the two chairs stacked by the wall. Mr Sutton took one. She positioned hers closer to me.

'I'm very sorry, Miss Francis,' Mr Sutton said.

'What's happened?' I leaned forward.

'I'm afraid we ran into complications.'

'What?' I straightened up. 'What d'you mean?'

'I'm very sorry,' Mr Sutton repeated. 'We lost him.'

Something shrivels inside me. The blood drains from my face, leaving me numb, motionless in my seat.

Mr Sutton was staring at me, shaking his head. His mouth was moving, there was anticipation in his eyes.

'Where… where is he?' I stood up.

Emily and the doctor looked up at me.

'You should sit down,' Emily said.

I ignored her. 'Wh-what happened?'

'I'm afraid his lungs collapsed,' Mr Sutton said.

For a few seconds his words stayed frozen, outside my head. They'd made a mistake. My hands clenched into fists as tight as my insides. My breath was piled at the back of my throat.

Emily stood up and touched my hand.

'His condition was worse than we thought,' Mr Sutton said, standing too.

'How… what… what happened?' I said. 'Papa. I have to see him.' I tried to get past them.

'Perhaps there is someone you'd like to call?' Emily said, her hand gentle but firm on my arm.

'No,' I said, shaking her off. 'I want to see my father. I have to… Oh, my God! Take me. Take me to see him,' I shouted, stepping towards the door again.

Mr Sutton whispered something to Emily, then edged out of the door.

'Are you sure there isn't someone I can call for you?' Emily said.

I sniffed, told her no and took a tissue from a pack she offered me.

'Come with me,' she said. 'He's still in the unit.'

Outside Papa's room, hospital activities were going on as normal. It was tea time: trolleys were rolling, cups were clinking and hot drinks were being served. Who out there knew or cared that my papa hadn't come back from theatre?

I walked, half-dazed. I couldn't – wouldn't – let my mind enter that space that said I'd never see Papa alive again. Touch him. Hear his voice. My stomach was tight, but I was floating, following Emily to the lift in silence. We got out of the lift where I'd last seen him. Emily pushed the double doors, held it back for me and continued leading the way. My heart was pounding, bang, bang, banging in my chest. But I needed to do this.

'Let me see,' Emily said, her voice low, like the words were meant for herself and she opened another door into a room like an upmarket dental surgery with stuff on wheels, movable flood lights and what looked like a TV screen on the wall. 'Here—'

I gasped as my eyes fell on Papa's body lying with a white sheet covering him up to his neck.

I went further in. 'Papa?' The word barely got past the space in my throat. His eyes were closed. 'Papa!' I repeated, willing him to hear me. Move. Show some sign of life. I looked down at his face. Seeming calm. Relaxed. Contented. 'Oh, Papa,' I said, touching his arm, his face, still warm. 'Papa?' Part of me expected a response. Demanded one. A movement of the eye lids. Something.

I stared at his chest. 'Papa?' Nothing.

I glanced at Emily, standing a few feet away, closer to the door. Papa was really gone.

'It wasn't supposed to happen like this,' I said. 'Not like this. Why?' I glanced at Emily again. 'Why did it have to happen like this?'

I was trembling, looking at Papa's face again. Tears streaming down my face.

'I should have been with him when he died. Be there to make sure he was all right.'

Emily touched my arm. 'He wouldn't have suffered. He was still under the anaesthesia,' she said.

'How could this have happened?' My knees began to buckle.

'Here.' There was something behind me. Emily took my arm, encouraged me to sit.

'No. No.' I stumbled past her towards the door, shaking, leaned up against the wall, my own arms around me, my eyes on Papa's body.

Emily touched me again. 'Shall we?' she said, trying to lead me out.

It couldn't be. This wasn't right.

'How could he die, just like that?' I spluttered. A ball of cobweb felt lodged at the back of my throat, making it hard to breathe.

'I'm really sorry,' Emily said, leading me towards the lift.

All hopes of getting Papa on meds that would slow down the cancer, making the most of remission time, recapturing some of the time we'd lost, had been brought to a halt. There was nothing left.

It didn't help that the room she took me to was the one we'd sat in when they'd first given me the news about Papa's cancer. We were about to sit down when there was a gentle knock on the door.

Mr Sutton came slowly in, looking around as though he wasn't sure whether or not it was safe.

'Would you prefer it if I left?' Emily asked me, as he sat down.

'No. It's okay,' I said.

'I can't tell you how sorry I am,' Mr Sutton said. The sombre tone hadn't left his voice.

I felt drained, but I was facing one of the last people to see my father alive. Was he responsible for my father's death? Had he slipped up?

I sniffed. 'What happened?' I asked.

'As you know, we were trying to identify the reasons for the difficulties he was having with swallowing,' Mr Sutton said.

My gaze was on him.

'It would appear that the cancer had spread much further than we'd anticipated. Unfortunately, his lungs collapsed during the procedure.'

I gasped, covering my mouth.

'All risks had been explained to Mr Francis before going ahead with the procedure. And all protocols were strictly adhered to.'

Papa's pre-admission session ran through my mind. The admission nurse, then Mr Sutton, explaining exactly what the procedure entailed; me skimming over the forms with Papa. They had all seemed pretty standard. He'd signed next to the crosses.

My strong desire for Papa to have the tests had pushed thoughts
of any serious risks or concerns about anything going wrong to
the bottom of the list.

'But this wasn't supposed to happen,' I said.

'I'm afraid a lot *can* happen,' Mr Sutton said. 'Of course, every
effort was made to resuscitate but,' he paused and looked down
at his hands, 'unfortunately it wasn't successful.'

Tears built up in my eyes again. 'At… at what point did it
happen?' I asked, 'Was… was it at the beginning or—?'

Mr Sutton sighed. 'Nine forty-five,' he said, 'but he wouldn't
have suffered any pain, due to the anaesthetic.'

Nine forty-five. What was I doing then, when Papa took his
last breath?

My brain froze.

'Are there any more questions you'd like to ask Mr Sutton?'
Emily said, jolting me back into a semblance of reality.

'I don't think so.' I shook my head. 'It's… no.'

Mr Sutton told me to contact his office if I needed to. Said
he was sorry again and left.

'Now, would you like to make any calls?' Emily asked. Her
voice was so quiet and subtle, I almost mistook it for one in my
head.

'Mmm,' I exhaled. Emily left and I called Mum, but there
was no answer from her mobile or landline.

I called Auntie Lucille. 'Auntie?'

'Yes, is me, *ich mwen*,' she said.

'Mum's not with you, is she?'

'No. It's a few days now I don't see her. Everything all right?'

'Papa's died,' I spluttered, a crack in my voice.

'*Bondyé.*' There were a few seconds of silence. I'd had more
time than her to absorb it, and still it wasn't making complete
sense to me. 'When dis happen?' she said.

'Today – just now. I mean, not long.'

'Just so?'

'He had cancer, Auntie,' I said.

'*Bondyé*. Cancer? An'—'

'He didn't want everyone to know, so I couldn't tell—'

'Where you now?'

'In the hospital, Auntie, but—'

'I sending your uncle for you.'

'No. It's all right. I've got my car,' I said.

'Anthony?' Her voice faded then returned. 'We coming.' I imagined her not knowing which way to turn, what to do next. Uncle would orientate her.

'No, Auntie,' I said. 'I've got my car here. I'll call you back.'

She made me promise that I would. After that, I called Pe.

'What?' she said, after I blurted the terrible news out to her.

'His lungs collapsed. He…' My voice left and tears took over.

The door opened. I looked up as Miss Elsa walked cautiously towards me. I told Pe I'd call her back.

'The lady… nurse sent me here,' Miss Elsa said. The pleats gathered in the middle of her forehead brought her eyebrows closer together. 'I don't see Joe in his room. They still have him down there?'

Tears trickled down my face.

'Something happen?' she said.

I nodded and swallowed the phlegm in the back of my throat. 'It didn't go well,' I said. 'He didn't come back, Miss Elsa.'

'What you mean, he didn't come back?'

I held my hand over my mouth as if that would reduce the impact of the words. 'He… he died.'

'What?'

I opened the tissue balled up in my hand and wiped my nose. 'I've seen his body. It's true… I…' The image of Papa's body on the bed in that room appeared and silenced me.

Miss Elsa lowered herself in the chair closest to her. 'My God,' she said. 'But why you didn't call me?'

'I… I didn't think – I called Mum. But she didn't answer her phone.'

For a few minutes, apart from my snuffling, it was quiet in the room. Then Miss Elsa said: 'Now we must do what we think Joe would want.'

'What?' I looked at her.

'Plan for a wake and a funeral. Oh, God, Yvette,' she said. Her voice started to quiver. 'I'm going to miss him.' I hurried over and put my arms around her. 'He was my friend.' Her body shook from her sobbing. 'My very good friend.'

There was a light knock at the door.

'Oh, I'm sorry,' Emily said, looking in. 'Didn't mean to inter-rupt. Just checking that you'd found her. I'll be at the front, if you need me.' And she left, closing the door as quietly as she'd opened it.

Miss Elsa loosened her hold on me. 'Let's come out of this place,' she said, sniffing.

We didn't speak on the way to Papa's room. Everything else going on along the corridors of the hospital felt far removed, nothing to do with us; not the nurses we passed, the patient being guided in a wheelchair, nor the cleaner pushing a mop around. They were of no significance. Near invisible.

I opened the door. Miss Elsa walked in, trance-like. I took out the few bits of clothes Papa had in the cupboard. How could this be? Papa? I got his bag and dropped the clothes inside it.

Dead? No. He couldn't be dead. Not just like that. I was getting breathless. Miss Elsa touched my arm. I picked Papa's hat up and followed her out.

We sat in the car. Miss Elsa had questions that made me go over what Mr Sutton had told me about how Papa died, including some of the risks mentioned in the documents he'd signed consenting to the procedure, and everything else that had happened before she arrived.

'You are very strong,' she said, tapping my hand, after I told her about seeing his body. It had felt so necessary to me at the time. 'But,' her voice deepened, 'you have a right to make them investigate how this come to happen.'

'I shouldn't have pressured him,' I said.

'You? How you pressure him?' she said. Her reprimanding tone reminded me of Mum.

'I don't know.' I shrugged.

My plan was to drop Miss Elsa off then head off home or to Auntie Lucille's, but Miss Elsa said: 'We must make preparations for later.'

'Later?' I gave her a quizzical look. Then it dawned on me. The Nine-Nights wake would have to start tonight. At Papa's flat.

'We must let people know,' she said. 'Get drinks, food and – oh, no,' she said, dismissing my suggestion for ordering in the food. 'I know plenty of people who will be happy to come and help. They will do it for Joe.' She turned to face me. 'How you feeling now?'

'I'm okay,' I said, staring at nothing through the windscreen.

She asked if I could drop her 'by a friend' who lived a couple of roads away. Before she got out of the car, I gave her all the notes in my purse, forty pounds, and said I'd give her more later.

'This will be sufficient,' she said. 'We will order drinks from the same people the club use. Ranjit know us. He will understand.

And what we don't use, we can return. You sure you want to go home? Your boyfriend – somebody meeting you there?'

'I'll be fine,' I said. 'You'd better take these,' and I handed her my keys to Papa's flat. His were in my boot with the rest of his things.

'You sure you going to be all right?' Miss Elsa said, her eyes fixed on my face.

'Yes. Yes.' I hoped I was doing a good job convincing her.

Events felt blurry on the journey home. Numbness was setting in.

When I pulled up, I checked the two calls I hadn't been able to answer while I was driving.

One was from Auntie Lucille, the other from Pe. I mentally prepared to deliver an apology before calling Auntie Lucille back, but after I'd assured her that I wouldn't be alone and had help with managing things, she settled on just having Papa's address.

'I will see you later,' she said.

Then I texted Pe to let her know where I was.

The lavender scent warmed me as I walked into the house. I dropped my bag at the foot of the bed, crawled under the duvet and bawled.

Chapter Twenty-Nine

Yvette

My body twitched. Someone was at the front door. I slowly uncurled myself, got out of bed and went downstairs.

'Can I come in?' Aaron said. The cold oozing through the gap in the door was as unwelcome as he was right now.

'This isn't a good time, Aaron,' I said, avoiding his eyes. My voice was throaty, like it belonged to someone else. I felt weak, worn. A drooping mess.

'Please,' he said.

I hesitated, sighed, walked slowly back towards the stairs and sat down.

'Who told you?' I said, as he came closer.

'What? I noticed your car outside and thought you might be in,' he said, looking at me.

'My… Papa died today,' I said, my face to the wall.

'Uh? No. And you're here on your own? Yvette.' His voice softened when he said my name.

'Pe's on her way. I thought it was her when you knocked.'

'God, I'm so sorry, Yvette.' He leaned towards me and put a hand on my knee. 'What happened?'

'He was having tests – a procedure. And he died,' I said.

'That's horrible. Come on. You can't be here on your own.'

I didn't budge. 'It's the best place for me.'

'But not on your own, Yvette.'

'I'm fine, Aaron.' The conversation was beginning to irritate me. Mixing me up. 'You better go,' I said.

'Yvette, why you being like this? This is not the way to solve problems.'

'Talking to you isn't gonna solve the problems I have right now,' I said.

'Yvie—'

'Aaron, please. I don't want you here.'

He huffed and shifted his weight from one side to the next. 'If you're sure that's what you want.'

I looked up when I heard him open the front door and Pe's voice rise above the traffic noise outside.

She stumbled in, her coat wide open, her long plaits partially covering her face. 'I'm so sorry I couldn't get here quicker,' she said, dropping her bag. 'I see Aaron came. Oh, Yvie.' Her eyes were locked on me. I dragged myself towards her. 'You must feel – oh God, Yvie.' She opened her arms to me. 'It's gutting. I know.'

I buried my face in the oily scent in her hair.

We went into the front room and sat close together on the sofa, her arm over my shoulder.

'Didn't see this coming, did we?' she said.

I shook my head, then stared blindly at the hibiscus batik hanging on the wall facing us.

'I'll bet he didn't, either,' Pe added.

'Maybe he did,' I said. 'Maybe he'd just had enough. I shouldn't have pressured him.'

'But you didn't,' Pe said. 'You specifically avoided doing that. Listen, if the professionals… experts… didn't know how bad the thing had spread, how was anyone else supposed to? How's your mum taking it?'

'I can't get hold of her.'

'How come?'

I shrugged. 'Not answering her phone.'

'I'll make us a hot drink.'

The sudden absence of her warmth when she took her arm off my shoulder made me wish for a blanket.

'You eaten?' she said.

'No. Tea'll be fine.'

I shut my eyes, as if to block out the horrible reality, and followed her to the kitchen, where we sipped tea in silence for a while.

'You called Aaron, then?' she said.

'Uh-uh.' I shook my head. 'He said he was just passing.'

'So you told him?'

'Mm.'

'He looked upset.'

I put my cup down, took a deep breath and stood up. 'What time is it?' I said.

Pe shuffled round. 'Twenty to four.'

'I'd better get changed.'

'For what?'

I told her about the wake.

'Nine-Nights?' she said.

'Uh-huh. It's custom.'

'Oh, of course,' she said. 'You called work?'

'I'll do it in the morning. You don't have to come tonight, you know, Pe. There'll be eight more after this one.'

'No. I'll come. I want to.'

'It can go on for a while.'

'A while?'

'Till all visitors are gone,' I said.

'Okay.'

I'd been to wakes and Nine-Nights before. This would be the first where I would be the bereaved. I was dreading it.

I left Pe washing our cups and went to get changed. Alone upstairs, Aaron's visit slipped into my mind. Under normal circumstances, his support would have brought great relief, but 'we' were no more. I had to come to terms with that.

I tried calling Mum again. Again, no one answered. This time, I tried Miss Belvina.

Just after I'd said hello, I heard a child in the background: 'Nana?'

'Yes… yes… shhhh. Hold on, Justin, baby,' she said. 'Nana is on the phone.'

'It's only me, Miss Belvina,' I said, after she finished talking to the child.

'I'm sorry about that, sweetie. How you doing?'

'Is Mum with you?' I said.

'Doli? Oh, no, darling. I haven't heard from her for a couple of days. And I've been so busy with one thing and another. Now young Justin's mother and father gone off on a dirty weekend,' she said, lowering her voice, then chuckling. 'Although, they tell me not to call it that.' She chuckled again. 'How is your father doing, I heard about the—'

'He… he passed away today. This morning.' I sniffed.

'Oh, baby, I'm so sorry to hear that. From that stabbing?'

'He had cancer.' I was trying hard not to start crying again.

'But – oh, no. That is so sad… too sad. I could hear something wasn't too right in your voice.'

'That's why I'm trying to get hold of Mum.'

'You mean she don't know?'

'I can't get hold of her,' I said.

'Right now, I have my baby grandson, Justin, you see… otherwise I would—'

'It's okay,' I said. 'I'm not on my own. I just wanted to let Mum know.'

'Good. You need the right kind of company at… at times like this. Nana coming, darling,' Miss Belvina said, her voice suddenly muffled and distant. I imagined she must have moved her mouth away from the phone. 'I'll try to get hold of your mother for you, but I'm sure you'll hear from her soon. Darling, if you need any help with, you know – organising things, I will be more than happy to. Give me your number, sweetheart.'

While she was finding pen and paper, I heard her making odd comments to her grandchild.

'I will definitely call you, but you have my number too, so don't be shy to call if you need anything,' she said. 'God bless you, darling. I'll see you soon.'

I thanked her and said goodbye.

As I made my way downstairs, Pe came out of the sitting room. 'Got hold of your mum?' she asked.

I shook my head. 'Her friend.'

'Am I gonna look out of place?' Pe said, seeing the black clothes I'd changed into. 'These are hardly mourning colours.' She looked down at the cheery, multicoloured, knee-length dress she was wearing.

'You'll be fine as you are,' I said.

A short, wide-bodied woman with smooth, plump up skin and a cute button nose opened Papa's front door to us.

'I am Jacqueline – Jackie,' she said, after I told her who I was. 'I am so very sorry 'bout your loss.'

'Thank you,' I said, determined not to cry, and introduced Pe.

She took my hand, pulling me inside.

'De kitchen full ah people,' she said, her warm hand holding mine. 'I'll tell Elsa you here.'

Pe followed me into the sitting room, where a handful of people had already gathered. They didn't seem to notice us come in. A man was stooped in front of Papa's drinks cabinet. For a moment, I thought it was Papa: his slimness, balding head and striped brown-and-beige shirt had a familiarity.

He turned, as if sensing our presence, and stood up.

'I'm Nathan,' he said, greeting us. 'You are Joe's—'

'Daughter,' I said, trying to smile. 'This is my friend, Pe.'

We shook his hand.

'Please accept my sympathy,' he said. 'Joe was a good man.'

Nothing was good about being in Papa's flat right now. Mr Bobotte came across and took my hand and, for the first time in all the years I'd known him, pulled me close and gave me a long bear hug, either trying not to cry or to disguise the fact that he was.

'Dis is a very sad time,' he said, his voice even deeper than usual. 'Very sad time.'

When he finally freed me, I realised his wife, Miss Merle, was near us.

'We never knew,' she said, rubbing my arm, 'about the other thing.'

'The cancer?' I said, quietly.

'It's only de other night he tell Bobotte.'

Mr Bobotte nodded. 'An' I advise him to let de people help him. I wish I was able to tell him dat sooner – before it was too late.' The last few words stumbled out. Miss Merle stroked her husband's shoulder.

'I wish I'd known sooner too,' I said.

The rest of the people in the room, including Mr Fredrick's wife Miss Sylvianne, and another man I didn't know, started moving towards me.

Everyone gave their sympathy and asked how I was doing.

In the middle of it all I felt a tap on my arm.

'Excuse her, eh?' Miss Elsa said, rescuing me.

'Won't be a minute, Pe,' I said, and let Miss Elsa usher me and Jackie into Papa's bedroom. It was close in there; a window needed to be opened.

'This is Jackie,' Miss Elsa said, closing the door behind us. 'My *special* friend.'

'We… we met earlier,' I said.

'Yes, but I wanted you to know – you know.'

Me and Miss Elsa sat on the bed while Jackie stood by the door.

'Like I told you,' Miss Elsa said. 'Your father was special to me, but in a different kinda way. We could have never—'

'I see,' I said, glancing at Jackie, who didn't show any signs of the awkwardness I was feeling with Miss Elsa coming clean about her sexuality in front of her lover, who I hardly knew.

'Thanks for telling me,' I said.

Her disclosure made me feel closer to her – to Jackie too.

'Now you can go back out and meet everyone,' Miss Elsa said.

'Okay. Nice to meet you again, Miss—'

'No, no. None ah dat "Miss" business fi me,' Jackie interrupted, as Miss Elsa got up to leave. 'Ah don't want no "Miss nothing". Just Jackie or Jacqueline, if you prefer. You all right with dat?' Her smile changed her eyes into two dark lines above her doll-like cheeks.

'Yes. I am.'

Miss Elsa looked at Jackie, affection in her eyes. 'I forget,' she said, turning back to me. 'Before you leave tonight, look round in here and collect all of your father's important papers. You know? You cannot leave such things lying round.'

The smell of fishcakes had filled the front room. I offered to help out in the kitchen, but Miss Elsa shooed me away. 'Too many cooks. You know what that can do,' she said. 'We have enough hands in here.'

The gathering in the front room had grown. Auntie Lucille and Uncle Anthony were sitting on the chairs close to the table with Pe, and I went straight to them.

'They remember me,' Pe said, looking pleased.

'Of course,' Auntie said, hugging me.

Auntie sat down, but Uncle stayed standing. 'Dis is a terrible thing. Dis cancer,' he said, shaking his head.

'Sit… sit down,' Auntie said to me, pulling a chair closer. 'Where Doli? She coming?'

Before I could answer her, my phone rang. I was hoping it would be Mum, but it was Rob Payne. He asked if I was able to speak.

'Er…' I hesitated and got up. 'My father passed away today. I… I'm kind of in the middle of one of his wakes.'

'Oh, goodness, I'm so sorry. Sorry about your loss and sorry for calling at such a bad time,' he said. 'Perhaps it's best we simply continue with our work then – put it all in writing to you. Assuming you want us to continue,' he said, 'given your father's passing.'

'Yes. Yes. Continue, please,' I said. I swallowed hard and closed the call. On my way back to join Pe and the others, I briefly considered his question. *Did* finding Ian matter now?

'Everything okay?' Pe asked.

'Yeah.' I nodded and put the phone away.

More visitors were trickling in, all making their way to me, embracing me, shaking my hand. It was a repetitive cycle of introductions, sympathy-giving and pitiful looks as silent acknowledgements of my pain. Almost everyone brought some kind of contribution: drinks, snacks, even bottled water.

'Oh, what a lovely girl you grow up into,' announced an old lady wearing a neat little wig. She approached me with open arms. 'I am Miss Velma,' she said. 'You will not remember me, you was just a baby – so cute. So beautiful…'

'Oh,' I said, curious, as I returned her hug.

'You travelled with us, me and my sister, Maria, back to St Lucia so long ago. Sixty-two. Maria was the only one who could stop you from crying. She alone had that special touch.'

I felt a connection with her. 'She… your sister Maria's not with you?' I asked, looking around.

'Oh, no. Maria passed a long while back. Seems like she took that trip home to die. I had to return from our eight weeks' holiday on my own,' she said.

'Oh, I'm so sorry,' I said.

There were times, way back, when thoughts of me, the baby Yvette, being sent to St Lucia with people I'd never known, would make me feel so sad, so rejected. Miss Velma must have stayed in contact over all these years, or heard about Papa's death through the grapevine and turned up to show her respects. 'I hope I was well behaved,' I said.

'But how is Doli, your mother? She here?' Miss Velma asked, looking past me.

'No,' I said. 'Not at the moment.'

'I'm so sorry for your loss,' Miss Velma said.

As I watched her wander off to greet others in the room, I felt a trickle of guilt for not having been in touch with her years ago; this kind lady and her sister, who'd changed my soiled nappies, fed me and lulled me to sleep, for two whole weeks, as a favour to my parents.

Another sad parting but, unlike this one, it was temporary and I didn't have a clue it had been happening.

As a distraction, I got Miss Elsa to agree to let me pass some of the finger-food round. Pe walked beside me with the paper plates and serviettes.

There'd been no new arrivals for a while. I put my mouth close to Pe's ear and told her she should go. I'd seen her check her phone a couple of times.

She said it was all right. Addae's mother was there to help with Temi, but I knew it bothered her that Temi's granny had a habit of ignoring bedtimes. 'I'll just check how things are going,' she said.

'Go on.' I nudged her with my elbow. 'Everyone's gonna be leaving soon.'

She glanced round the room, looking perturbed. 'You sure?'

'Yeah. It's fine.'

She moved unhurriedly, saying goodbye to Auntie and Uncle, then I followed her to do the same with Miss Elsa and Jackie.

After Pe left, I tried to encourage Auntie Lucille and Uncle to go.

'You better think again,' Auntie said, 'if you think we leaving you here by yourself.'

'I'm not by myself, Auntie,' I said.

'Unless I see de person dat's going home with you, is by me you sleeping tonight.'

Jackie came out of the kitchen and slumped herself in the chair Pe had been sitting in.

'Ah tink dat's it fi de night,' she said, and stretched her stocky legs out in front of her.

Miss Elsa too, joined us, her apron off.

'You all shoulda let us give you all a hand,' Auntie Lucille said.

As more of the other women reappeared from the kitchen, the men put the remainder of the drinks away.

When we closed the door to Papa's flat, part of me pretended we'd left him in there to get a good night's rest.

I'll see you tomorrow, Papa.

Chapter Thirty

Yvette

There was an odd sense of comfort, waking up in my old room at Auntie Lucille's. I'd slept here regularly when I was a child: Mum and Papa used to be off partying. After Papa left, it was Mum off out with friends.

I lifted the duvet, pushing back the smell of clean laundry trapped in it, and tiptoed to the bathroom in the old-lady nightie Auntie had lent me. Getting an early morning run would have been good for me today, but Auntie and Uncle didn't want anyone tampering with their front door once they'd locked up for the night.

They were already in the kitchen. 'Morning, *ich mwen*,' they both said when they saw me. Auntie was chopping onions and pumpkin for Saturday's soup.

'You sleep well last night?' Uncle asked, spreading butter on toast.

'Okay,' I said. I was so drained last night. My brain had shut down soon after my head hit the pillow. Now, I couldn't wait to get home.

Auntie put the knife down and scooped the vegetables up to drop in the pot. 'Look,' she said, 'I make some eggs an' toast. Come an' eat before everything get cole.'

I told her I wasn't hungry, but I'd have some coffee.

She turned the fire on under the kettle. 'What is going on with your Auntie Agnes?' she said. I stretched past her to get a cup from the drainer. 'Yesterday, I call her an' dat man she marry de other day – what is his name again?'

'Leonce,' I said.

'He say she gone to Trinidad to look for dat chile she did take care of.'

'Patti? Sorry, Dionne,' I said. 'She's gone to Trinidad?' Strange that she hadn't told me. Why did she feel the need to go all that way? If I'd got hold of her when I called, I could have told her that Dionne was okay.

'Some people so ungrateful, eh? Agnes take care of dat chile for so long with nothing at all from her own fam'ly. Now she turn big lawyer she not even giving poor Agnes a call.'

'Really?' I said. Dionne's letter came to mind again. Was that what she wanted to talk to me about? That maybe she'd found her real family – her mother, father maybe.

'Good luck to Agnes. Is money she have to throw away like dat?'

'When you think you will have a date for de funeral?' Uncle asked me, sending my mind hurtling back to my own problems. I hadn't given a lot of thought to organising Papa's funeral. 'Not sure,' I said.

'Dat's a lot of work you have on your hands dere, you know,' he said.

'We are all one fam'ly,' Auntie said. 'Just tell us what you want us to do to help, you hear?'

I was the only family Papa had here and any offers of help from people close to me were welcome. Miss Belvina's name was already on the list.

The lack of contact from Mum was starting to bother me. Last night Auntie Lucille said she'd left messages asking her to call, but she hadn't. And I was sure Miss Belvina would have done the same too, after speaking to me.

Chapter Thirty-One

Doli

I don't even finish brush my teeth an' somebody already knocking my door. I hope it's not dat Cedric. Since dat night he come here, I cannot bring myself to even talk to the man, let alone see him. Is not only the shock of seeing the teeth I did believe was his own, moving in his mouth dat make me caa face him, but what he must think of me after I let him do what he do to me.

'Mum.'

'Good morning, Yvette,' I say, turn an' leave the door open for her to come in.

'Where've you been?'

'I said, good morning, Yvette. Where's your manners?'

'Mor… morning, Mum. Mum, I've been calling you since yesterday,' she say.

'Really? I've been busy. What happen, you need to ask me more questions to help you find Ian?' She look at me strange, as if she don't know how to reply. 'Dat's not what you make your full-time business now?'

'No, Mum,' she say, standing behind me by the kitchen door. 'That's not why I'm here.'

'Oh? I know is not just me you come an' see.'

'It's Papa,' she say.

'Yes. What happen to him now?'

'He… he's died, Mum.'

I turn around, not sure if I hear her right.

'I've been trying to call you,' she say, quiet an' slow like she too tired to talk.

'What – what you say? Joe? Joe *die*?'

She nod her head an' sit down.

A loud humming start in my ears. 'What? But—?'

'No one could get hold of you.' She start to cry.

I sit down beside her. 'But how? How dis happen?'

'He… he was having a panendoscopy…' She talking an' crying at the same time. 'Then—'

'A pan… what?'

'A procedure.' She pull a tissue from her pocket an' wipe her nose. 'He couldn't swallow his food. They had to check… they put the thing down his throat and… they tried to revive him, but—' She shake her head.

I caa even fully understand all of what Yvette is saying. 'When? Since when dis happen?'

'Yesterday. I've been calling. Auntie Lucille said she'd called. Don't you check your answerphone, Mum?' She wipe her face.

For the past few days, I don't call nobody an' make sure nobody, especially dat Cedric, caa call me. One time alone, I force myself to go to the gym. 'You mean to say, Joe die?'

She nod her head an' sniff. 'He had cancer, Mum.' Her voice still quiet.

'Cancer?' I rest back in my seat, looking at Yvette.

'Uh-huh.' She nod. 'In his lungs, it had spread—'

'Cancer, Yvette? Joe had cancer an' you never tell me?'

'He didn't want everyone to know.'

'Everyone? Ahh. But Elsa did know. Dat was why… Oh, I see now. Dat was her reason for coming here… To tell me.'

'She didn't find out from me, Mum. She… she already knew before I told her.'

'Joe had cancer an' you never tell me, Yvette? An' now you come to tell me he die? Auntie know?'

'Yes. They came to Papa's last night. He was attacked and stabbed, Mum and you made it clear that you didn't want to see him. You didn't even ask me to wish him better.' She stand up. Her eyes fix on me now. 'What's going on with you, Mum?'

I pull up the collar on my gown. It's two days since I take a real bath. 'I just wake.'

'But why haven't you been answering your phone?' She go to the passage. 'You've unplugged the phone?' she shout. 'No wonder. And you complain?'

'I did just want some peace in my head,' I say, although I wasn't sure if she hear me.

'Why would you unplug your phone? I need to call Auntie,' she say, when she come back in the kitchen. 'Let her know I got hold of you.'

Yvette leave, talking about Bel an' going to Joe house. I go back to my bedroom, hardly seeing, tears fulling up my eyes.

I sit in front of the dresser an' look straight ahead of me without seeing, pull open the dresser drawer an' take out my wedding ring. I hold it for a while, then slide it back on my finger.

The first time I did take it off was early in our marriage. A Saturday, when we did plan to go to one of the dances at Freemont Street. But when the day reach, Joe tell me he must go down to the club an' expect me to come too. When I tell him I'm not coming, he tell me to go to the dance then, an' enjoy myself.

I was blue vex. I tell him I had enough of his blasted domino club. Like is only God can come before it.

I did pack a few things in a bag, planning to go stay at Auntie, then I pull the ring from my finger an' throw it after him.

'Dat don't stop you from being my wife,' he say.

'But you can never put me before dat frigging club?'

'Come with me den, Doli,' he say, an' start telling me about he have responsibilities – the club relying on him. So I not relying on him too?

Joe dead?

It was his sickness Elsa did come here to tell me about. Elsa. She did have a heart, after all.

I lie down in my bed an' let the phone ring.

Chapter Thirty-Two

Yvette

Tonight was the fourth of the nine nights. And when Miss Belvina walked in, I was sure Mum would be right behind her, but she wasn't.

'You seen Doli at all?' she asked me, looking round, frowning.

I told her I hadn't seen nor heard from Mum since I'd told her Papa'd died.

'You don't find that strange?' she said.

I shrugged, saddened that Mum's resentment towards Papa was too deep to allow her to show her face at not even one of his wakes. It was common courtesy. A way of showing respect. They'd been apart for a long time, but they were still married, for goodness' sake. I'd even seen the ring on her finger now and again. And he was my dad. Where was her support for me?

'She might come later,' Miss Belvina said. I wanted to believe her, but suspected she was only trying to make me feel better.

I introduced her to some of Papa's friends. She offered to help so I took her to the kitchen to meet Miss Elsa. Spicy scents were escaping from the kitchen and people were dotted around the room in conversation, while the tender voice of Jim Reeves murmured, 'Distant Drums' from the two speakers on the floor.

As with the past three nights, Mr Bobotte and most of the other men were engrossed in a domino game, which included the necessary ingredient of making aggressive threats to their opponents on how they were going to 'deal' with them. In the middle of all this was drinking and laughter. I imagined Papa sitting amongst them, hurling his own threats and challenges at members of the opposing team, with that mischievous twinkle appearing in his eyes when he was about to win.

The man who'd introduced himself to me and Pe as Nathan on the first night, stood up, animated as he leaned over the table. 'This one,' he said, with robust vigour, 'is for Joe! Game finish.' And he slammed his last domino down with such force it startled me.

They burst into loud chatter and laughter after that and, again, I imagined Papa sitting at the table with them, taking his turn to shuffle the tiles and everyone selecting their set of six. With this game finished though, some people left the table.

I called Mr Bobotte aside and asked if he wanted anything from Papa's personal things. 'You know,' I said. 'Something to remember him by.'

'Dat would be nice,' he said.

'Tell the others too. They might want to take one of his trophies or medals,' I said.

'He... he had a hat – a black one he didn't wear too often,' Mr Bobotte said. 'Dat is what I would like. Although now I'm thinking about it, it might not fit dis big head I have.' He rubbed the bald patch surrounded by the greying curls on his head.

'I'm sure Papa would be happy for you to have it,' I said.

This wake was a social gathering and these people may not have loved Papa the way I did, but they were helping to shorten the evenings I would otherwise have spent sinking in grief.

Chapter Thirty-Three

Doli

As I hear the gate open, I get up from my bed an' peep through the side of the curtain. When I see is him, I rest my back on the wall, biding my time for when he leave.

I did call him, two days after he come here.

'I want to ask you not to call me anymore,' I did tell him.

His voice change straight away. 'Oh, I'm so sorry,' he say. 'I shouldn't have—'

'No, is not dat,' I tell him, because I didn't want to hear him go over the thing I'm trying to put out of my mind.

'It's probably best to talk,' he say.

I tell him I would rather we didn't an' he say, 'Okay.' So, I trust we did reach an agreement.

It's over a week now I don't pick up the phone when he call an' don't call him either. In my books, dat has to be sufficient for a person to know you don't want dem.

'Doli!' the man start shouting through my letterbox.

'You are a big woman, Doli,' Bel tell me a few days ago, when she did come to try an' convince me to go an' pay my respects at one of the wakes Yvette was holding for Joe. 'This kind of hiding you doing is for teenagers. Children.'

But Bel don't understand. I just caa face it. All those people dat would be by Joe waiting to pass judgement on me. An' now dis Cedric coming to my house making noise outside my door.

Go away, Cedric. Go away. I close my eyes waiting for my wish to come true.

'Doli?' he shouting again.

I walk light like a ballerina to the top of the stairs.

'Doli. You're in there, aren't you?'

I hear Bel in my ears again. I am not a chile. I walk downstairs, stand by the door an' say, 'What is it, Cedric?'

'Can we talk? I don't have to come in. Just open the door slightly. You don't even have to see or look at me.' He lower his voice. 'I'm sure you don't want people hearing me shouting through your letterbox. And I don't either.'

I look up at the ceiling as if I was expecting to get some direction from dere, then I let a heavy breath out, unlock the door an' open it a little.

'Thank God,' he say.

I stay behind the door so I caa see him, neither he me, an' I hold the handle in my hand.

'Can I come in?' he ask.

'But you—'

'Okay. Okay,' he say. 'I know what I said. I'll keep to my word. Doli... Doli.' He like he forget what he want to say. 'I... I know it's only been a short while since we've met, but you're really affecting me. I mean, I'd... I think the best thing would be to discuss, you know, face to face, but... what's made you decide to not see or speak to me anymore, Doli?'

When he realise I was not going to answer he say, 'Maybe you feel bad about what happened the other night, but I certainly enjoyed it. Thought you did too... but there's nothing I want more in the world right now than to get to know you better, Doli.'

I don't say nothing, but inside, I feel my heart beating fast, fast, fast, as if a mad dog is chasing after me.

'Doli? I've fallen for you,' he say.

I quickly close the door an' pull back up the clip.

Chapter Thirty-Four

Yvette

Organising Papa's funeral kept me focused on practicalities. Papa wouldn't have wanted too much fuss, but as far as I was concerned, everything had to be done nicely. Help from Pe, Miss Elsa and Miss Belvina made it easier. Miss Elsa had stuck by me with dressing Papa's body. I'd never handled a corpse before, and the experience was one I hope I'll never have to go through again, but in the end, it was satisfying. I'd done right by Papa.

The final decisions were about wreaths, corsages, hymns, times – and fees had to be paid, of course.

Two weeks had passed and I still hadn't heard from Mum.

'You mean to say, she don't come to not one of de Nine-Nights?' Auntie Lucille had asked me when I told her, last week.

I told her I'd been to Mum's yesterday. Her lights were on, but she hadn't opened the door. And she must have unplugged her phone again.

'What could be wrong with Doli, onh?' Auntie said.

'Honestly, Auntie, I don't know what else to do. Miss Belvina thinks she's depressed.'

'Dee-pressed?' Auntie said, her brows lifting as she leaned back and rolled her eyes. 'Don't worry, *ich mwen*.' She touched my arm. 'I will make sure she open her door.'

Being able to leave the problem with Auntie was a huge relief. The funeral was in two days. I wasn't going to chase after Mum anymore, nor try to convince her to come.

*

I arrived at Auntie's house the evening before the funeral to find Mum sitting at her kitchen table with a cup of tea in her hand.

'Mum?' I said.

'Hello, Yvette,' she responded, without looking at me.

'I tell her she sleeping here with us tonight,' Auntie said. 'Tomorrow we must look like a fam'ly.'

I walked around the table so I could see her face. 'Where've you been hiding?'

'Hiding?' she said. 'If I was hiding, I would not be here.'

Her face looked tired and dry, like a neglected plant. Papa's death would have shaken her, but surely not bring her down like this.

'So you're coming to—?'

'Of course,' she said, like nothing could keep her away.

I left her with Auntie and went to my room.

At five thirty I was wide awake and freezing cold under the extra blanket I'd asked Auntie for last night. I moved about as quietly as I could. My first mission was to slip into the front room to put the heating on, but the sound of low mumbling as I passed Mum's door made me stop and put my ear close to it. Was she talking to herself, or reciting a prayer? I started backing away, but stumbled.

'Shhh.' Uncle was behind me, in his dressing gown, a cup in his hand, a finger pressed against his lips. He moved the finger and pointed downwards. I followed him on tiptoes, praying Mum wouldn't open her door.

'Coffee?' he asked, when we got to the kitchen.

'Yes, please,' I said, slowly getting over my embarrassment of him catching me snooping on Mum.

'You get up early?'

'Yeah.' I nodded. 'Mum's up too,' I said, sitting down.

'De three of us,' Uncle said.

'I wonder what's going on with her.'

'Everybody have their troubles. You don't necessarily have to turn theirs into yours.'

I wanted to ask him what his were, but I wasn't sure how he'd take it. 'Sounded like she was praying,' I said, rubbing the tops of my arms.

'Dat's a good thing. Prayers.'

'If it helps, I suppose.'

'I have to take dis up for Luce,' he said, pouring hot water from the kettle into a brown teapot. 'Your coffee is dere.'

'Uncle?' I said, as he was leaving. 'Can you put the heating on, please? I'm freezing.'

'I had just finish doing dat when you bunks me.'

Within a few minutes, he was back. 'Your auntie on de phone,' he said.

'Who?'

'Agnes. Your Auntie Agnes want to say hello. Quick.'

I rushed past him.

'Okay,' I heard Mum saying, before I got to the top of the stairs. 'Yes… of course. Look, she here,' and she handed me the phone.

'Hi, Auntie,' I said, 'How are you? I called you, but—'

'I know you all busy getting ready for, you know, but I just wanted to say a quick hello an' dat I hope everything goes okay, which I am sure it will.'

'I – I got a lett—'

'I can't stay, Yvie, money running out already. We will talk again soon. Take good care, eh?'

And she was gone, leaving me standing on the landing with the receiver in my hand.

'Auntie? Auntie Luc—?' I called.

'She in de bathroom.' Uncle's voice came from above me.

I sat on the top of the stairs waiting.

'Is Auntie Agnes still in Trinidad?' I said, standing up, when Auntie Lucille appeared.

'I believe so. I… I don't have time for Agnes an' her stupidness, chasing after dat chile. Calling people so early in de morning, when dey busy preparing to go to a funeral an' she herself should be sleeping. Let me go an' drink my tea, you hear. Check on your mudder – see if she all right for me. An' stop worrying about Agnes. Agnes good for herself.' And Auntie started back to her and Uncle's bedroom.

I guessed Auntie Agnes was bound to have stopped worrying, now that she was actually in Trinidad with Dionne.

I didn't feel much like eating myself, but as a temporary distraction from family tiffs and thoughts of having to say my last good-bye to Papa, checked if anyone wanted toast or something else to eat.

Chapter Thirty-Five

Yvette

'Everybody ready?' Uncle shouted through the house.

I went to check on Mum and found her sitting on her bed in her underwear.

'Auntie sent me to see if you need any help,' I said, standing in the doorway.

'So you all think I cannot dress myself?'

'Everyone else is ready. And we can't be late.'

'An' you think I don't know dat?' she snapped, and turned to give me that same disapproving look she'd given me when she came down for breakfast earlier in her nightgown.

She could see, though, that apart from my handbag and shoes, I was ready. She stood up, in her matching black bra and knickers, got her dress off the hanger, pulled the zip down and stepped into it. Her body looked toned and healthy. I hoped mine would be like that when I got to her age.

'Here, let me,' I said, but as I was pulling the zip up, a couple of pins dropped out of her hair.

'Oh, shucks,' she said, when one of her curls fell down the side of her face.

'Don't worry. I'll fix it.'

After that, she let me arrange her grey, veiled hat stylishly on her head, then I left her to finish her make-up.

*

At the first sight of the hearse with the red, purple and white flowers round Papa's coffin, my throat closed. A bubble expanded in my chest. I stood still, hoping it would pass. Tears pooled in my eyes, blurring my view of the two men, dressed in pitch-black suits, matching ties and white shirts, coming towards us.

Auntie Lucille and Uncle were sitting opposite me and Mum in the limo. I sat staring at Papa's picture on the funeral pamphlet I'd picked up from the seat when I got in.

He looked dignified and handsome in the Caribbean-style shirt-jacket buttoned up to his neck. It was one of three pictures Miss Elsa had given me to choose from; all taken when he was accepting awards on behalf of the club.

'It's a good picture,' Uncle Anthony said. While I was studying Papa's face, Uncle had been studying mine. I tucked the booklet in my handbag and gave him a feeble smile, then glanced at Auntie Lucille fussing over her shoes.

Uncle cracked his window open. He wasn't the only one needing air. In line with custom, we would be driving to Papa's flat first, where we'd meet the other two limos carrying Miss Elsa, Jackie and the rest of Papa's closest friends, and their wives.

Through the window an Asian woman, her head wrapped snugly in a white scarf, was pushing a buggy with one hand while trying to hold on to a child struggling to keep up, in their rush for the pelican lights. Further along, a young black boy was walking with a mobile phone to his ear. The November wind was blowing, making the Pakistani-style trousers an Asian man was wearing balloon out around his legs.

When we arrived outside Papa's flats, Mr Bobotte was standing next to one of the limos, looking up towards Papa's window. Inquisitive people were hanging around, no doubt wondering whose funeral it might be.

I took a deep breath and brought my window further down to greet Mr Bobotte, who'd started making his way towards us.

'We ready,' he said, his hands in his pockets, eyes wet – from the wind, or from what he was feeling inside.

We were on the move again, with the limo gliding towards the Catholic church Miss Elsa had recommended for the service. She'd made the initial arrangements with the priest, Father Fowler, and I'd met with him later to confirm things.

The traffic started to build up. Our procession, led by the hearse carrying Papa's coffin, followed by two limos and the string of other vehicles snaking their way to the church, was creating congestion. As we got closer, mourners on foot began prodding each other to move along. The hearse was coming. A woman stumbled as she mounted the pavement in her fancy heels.

In no time, the undertakers were helping Mr Bobotte, Mr Frederick and some faces I recognised from the Nine-Nights, to lift the coffin onto their shoulders so they could carry it into the church.

The image of Papa trapped inside that narrow silver box panicked me. *He's not alive*, I reminded myself. Mum, Uncle, Auntie and I walked slowly behind the coffin-bearers into the packed church. This was really happening.

The bearers put Papa's coffin down on a stand below the pulpit and I led the way to our seats on the front pew to our right.

'Hang in there.' Pe's unexpected voice whispered in my right ear. I turned. Addae was sitting next to her. He pursed his lips and gave me a nod of encouragement.

Ahead of us on the pulpit, Father Fowler was trying to adjust the microphone. His long, purple, black and green robe made him look even more garden-gnomish than the last time I'd seen him.

'Welcome everyone,' he said, in a high-pitched voice.

Hushing sounds gave way to silence. I stared blankly ahead.

'We are here,' Father Fowler continued, 'not so much to mourn, but to celebrate the life of Joseph Kenneth Francis…'

Papa's name sent my gaze back to the pulpit. Father Fowler seemed to be floating to make way for Miss Elsa to do the first reading.

My gaze returned to Papa's coffin, and I slipped into a vacant space again.

'Joe – Joseph…' I heard. My mind tipped back into the service. '… has been taken…' Mr Bobotte was in the pulpit now, pulling a handkerchief from his pocket. '… was born in… married Dolina…' A moan came from Mum's direction. 'Joe first started working with me in 1970, but we was friends long before dat…' Mr Bobotte continued.

I drifted again until Pe whispered: 'It's you,' in my ear. 'Your turn.'

I found my folded sheet of paper, breathed deeply then eased past Mum, Auntie and Uncle. On my way, I noticed the wreath I'd ordered for Papa. Green leaves outlined the letters 'P A P A'. White lilies filled the inside of each letter. The double-six domino wreath with two sections of six white dots of flowers between a faint white line across the middle, also caught my eyes. I kept moving.

A mass of eyes looked up at me in the pulpit. All these people. Sitting, standing. All here for Papa. Tears were about to blind me. I sniffed. This had to be done right. I straightened up, cleared my throat, cast my gaze to the back of the church and exhaled.

'It's heartening,' I started, though that wasn't a planned part of my eulogy, 'to see that my father touched so many lives. Thank you.'

I took a deep breath and started to read.

'I was five years old when I first met Papa. I'd met him before that, of course, as a baby, but I can't remember that…'

The crowd chuckled. Precious days of my childhood with Papa rushed through me. The words on the page were blurry. I blinked, wiped my eyes, cleared my throat and continued.

'As a child, in St Lucia, I had always looked forward to meeting my parents in England. I was happy when I met Papa. He was the one who kept Tim-Tim and other childhood stories from home alive; proverbs and riddles like, "Hanging water? – Coconut, of course".'

A quiet laughter filled the church.

'I remember one day, when I told him I'd make him proud by coming top in my English test, he told me: "Don't do well to make me feel proud, *ich mwen*, make yourself proud."

'This man who some of you knew as a staunch and passionate domino player – chairman of the Flyers Domino Club – or as a good friend, was so much more than that to me. He was as tall as the sky and as lovable as anyone could ever be. He was everything good, with some little disappointments, of course, wrapped in love for me. The bond we had can never be broken. Not even in death.'

Holding back tears was affecting my voice. I continued.

'He touched my life in so many meaningful ways. I miss you, Papa. Remember,' I paused. '"Don't mind how bird vex, it caa vex with tree." You'll always be my tree, Papa. We'll meet again, when the time it right. Rest in peace, Papa.'

Mutterings came from below. I sniffed again and picked up my sheet of paper.

The organ was already playing before I got back to my seat. I swallowed. Another hurdle over.

Voices started filling the church. 'O Lord my God… in awesome wonder… How great Thou art…'

Each word amplified my grief. I had to hold up.

Father Fowler's sermon claimed that Papa was alive in heaven, without worries, free of disease, renewed in Christ.

I wanted to believe that.

Two altar boys were walking around the church swinging a censer that made a clicking sound with each puff of incense it dispersed into the air. There was another prayer, then an invitation for people to come forward to say their last goodbye to Papa.

'You not coming?' Auntie Lucille leaned past Uncle to prod me.

I shook my head. I'd said my goodbye to Papa's body at the chapel of rest, after dressing him.

After Mum, Auntie and Uncle had gone to say their goodbyes, Pe appeared beside me.

'You okay?' Her arm was around my shoulder.

'Mmm.' I nodded.

A howl echoed through the church, changing the previous rhythm of whispers and quiet sobs to a hushed panic.

Mine and Pe's eyes met. I stood up to see what was going on.

'*Bondyé.*' Mum was screaming. 'Joe? Joe? Why Joe? Why? *Bondyé.*'

Everyone's attention was on the area where Papa's coffin was.

I rushed across to find Mum bent over, clutching her stomach with an unsteady Auntie and Uncle doing their best to hold her up. I tried to relieve them, but Mum started throwing her fists at me, resisting every move I made to touch her.

'You did not tell me… not tell me,' she was shouting. 'My own daughter, an' you—'

'I've got her.' I looked up into Aaron's face. He held on to Mum, almost lifting her off the ground as he walked her back to her seat. A tap on my shoulder. I turned. Someone handed Mum's hat to me.

There was no sign of Aaron when I returned to my seat, but Miss Belvina appeared at the end of the pew in a grey-and-white suit.

'Doli,' she called quietly to Mum, who was now sitting next to Uncle, looking grim-faced and resolute. Uncle tapped her and pointed Miss Belvina out to her. 'Come,' Miss Belvina said, waving her hand. Mum got up and left with her best friend's arm around her.

I started wishing she hadn't come, causing a spectacle at Papa's funeral. Why was she lashing out at me? Did she think she had had a right to know what Papa didn't want all and sundry to know? She hadn't even had the decency to come to a single one of the Nine-Nights. It's always got to be about Doli. Doli. Doli. Doli.

Everyone was back in their seats, having walked around the coffin, some bursting into tears, others looking regretful and sad. Father Fowler gave another short sermon, asking God to receive Papa into heaven and to bless the congregation. The organ opened up again for 'Amazing Grace' and it was time for Papa's coffin to be carried out.

'Where Doli?' Auntie ask Uncle as we stood up.

He spoke quietly in her ear.

'But we was all together,' Auntie was saying, shuffling along the pew to follow the coffin.

'She's with Miss Belvina,' I told her. 'It's better.'

'But—' Auntie started.

Uncle whispered in her ear again. She raised her head and mumbled.

This time, following the hearse was like seeing a precious delivery to its rightful place. Our convoy of cars, vans and coaches meandered out of Bow, through Mile End and on to Manor Park Cemetery, where we drove through the large black gates, along narrow tarmac roads lined with silver birches and pine trees shielding what had to be thousands of graves.

By the time we got out of the car, they'd already taken Papa's coffin from the hearse and the bearers were in place. This was it. We were putting Papa's body in the ground.

The sun was peeking out as we followed the lead up to a grassy slope and onto a large area with a fresh allotment of graves. Two were without headstones. The flowers on them were drooping.

We continued along a path where the grass was worn down, no doubt by foot-traffic like ours, and stopped in front of an open grave with fake grass along its edge and planks of wood across the hole. Tall trees, and a shorter one with clusters of white flowers resembling snowflakes, blocked our view of the road to our left.

Papa's coffin was placed over the hole. His final resting place. Father Fowler, who'd appeared like magic, was looking over our heads as if mentally urging the stragglers to hurry along. A couple of minutes later the grave was surrounded.

'Where your mudder?' Auntie asked.

I looked around. 'Don't know,' I said. I didn't care either.

Mr Bobotte and Jackie joined Father Fowler in asking the graveside mourners for hush, which they responded to, and the burial part of Papa's funeral began.

'We gather here,' Father Fowler began, 'to commit the body of our brother, Joseph. Let us offer our silent prayers for Joe.'

I bowed my head, heard the shuffling of more people arriving, and couldn't think of a single prayer to say for Papa.

'Almighty and ever-living God,' Father Fowler began again, '...perpetual light shine... May he...'

'Blessed be the name of the Lord,' the mourners responded, making the sign of the cross.

The fake grass was pulled away. Papa's coffin was being lowered down.

'The Lord's my shepherd...', the mourners began to sing.

'Come,' Auntie said, and she led me to the mound of soil that would cover Papa's coffin. Fill up his grave.

I followed Auntie's lead, picking up a few lumps of soil to throw onto Papa's coffin after they'd lowered it.

Despite the loud singing, with Jackie shouting each line of 'Amazing Grace' to guide the singers along, I could still hear the unnerving, scratchy sound coming from the hoist lowering Papa's body into the hole. I started to shake.

Auntie guided me towards the grave and I turned away after dropping my handful of soil into the hole. Then, *slam*. A spade full of soil dropped on top of Papa's coffin. *Slam*, came another. The ground started to move. *Slam*. Another and another. Was this really happening? Thick soil being thrown on top of Papa's body. My heart – everything behind my ribs – contracted.

'… how sweet…' voices were singing.

I shuffled closer to the grave and looked down. The coffin was hardly visible. Papa was gone. Gone with all hopes of second chances. His life was over and I was slipping, growing limp. 'Papa,' I shouted, trying to get even closer.

'It's okay. It's okay,' Miss Elsa said, turning me around. I buried my sobs in her chest.

'I'll never see him again,' I said, sobbing. Pe appeared and led me away.

'You can come here any time you like and talk to him,' she said. 'And he'll hear you.'

'He won't.'

'You'll see,' she said.

We sat on a bench under a huge yew tree, my face partially hidden from the view of the graveside ahead of us. Tears wouldn't stop coming.

'How is she?' Aaron's voice was above my head.

'It's okay,' Pe said.

'Yvie?' I felt his hand on my back, but couldn't look at him.

'I'm fine,' I said, my face still hidden.

'You sure?' he said.

'Don't worry. I'll make sure… she'll be fine,' Pe said. 'Your mum…'

I sat up. Aaron was walking back towards his mother, and Auntie and Uncle were coming our way.

'I cannot stand up no more,' I heard Auntie say. 'Dese shoes…'

'Dey almost finish,' Uncle said. He and Auntie sat on another bench close by.

When nearly everyone was gone, we got up and went back to the graveside. I wiped my eyes some more.

The rough mound of dirt had been transferred to a neat oblong, covering the length of Papa's coffin. Me, Pe, Miss Elsa, Jackie and a couple of other women from the domino club helped to arrange the wreaths and bright bouquets people had brought, over Papa's grave.

Chapter Thirty-Six

Doli

I drag myself out from my seat an' my body start to shiver.

'I know you need something to warm you up,' Bel say, once we step inside the house. 'You have anything strong?'

I tell her to check the cabinet.

'Right. I putting the kettle on and giving you five minutes for you to get your arse back down here, Dolina Francis. You hear me? No more of that hide-and-seek business you take up with lately.'

I go upstairs, look at my bed an' all I feel to do is put on my nightie an' get under my blankets. I take off the funeral clothes, throw dem on the side an' find a ole tracksuit to put on. Everything have me so mix up.

When I reach downstairs, I find Bel in the sitting room, her foot up on the long sofa, a glass in her hand.

'Come on, let's take a drink for your departed husband. I made you a cup of coffee.' An' she point to the cup on the side table with half a bottle of Mount Gay rum next to it.

'Since when you start to drink like dat?' I ask her, as I sit down.

'Since I decide to start truly living.'

I give her a sideways look. 'Huh.' An' pick up my cup.

'And I put a coupla drops of rum in your coffee.'

I was about to put the cup back down, when she say: 'Come on, Doli, it will help to warm and relax you. God knows you need some of that. I know your ex-husband just die, but something else going on with you?'

'I'm not myself, these days,' I tell her.

She ask when last I go to class. I tell her a while ago.

'I know, because I went there last week and there was no sign of you, after you told me you were going.'

She drink from her glass an' make up a face. 'You know this is the first time I ever drink rum straight?'

'Why you never say you want chaser?' I say, then get up an' bring her a tin of coke from the kitchen.

'Ice. You have ice?' She look up at me an' is then I notice how bright her lipstick is an' how much it suit her high complexion.

'So, Doli, tell me,' Bel say, when I come back with the ice, 'what's really going on with you?'

'Things,' I tell her. 'A lot of things, but as the Father tell me a couple of days ago, only the Almighty can judge.'

'So you start back at church now?'

'You could say dat.'

'But what is it the Almighty have to judge you for?'

I drink more of the coffee. Dere are things in my life I don't have the strength to talk about with anyone, but I say, 'My sins. Mistakes.'

'Who on earth don't have those?' She drink the remainder of the rum in her glass an' burst open the can of coke. 'Pass the bottle,' she say. I hand it to her. 'Well?'

I don't say anything.

'So you really don't want to talk?' Bel say.

I still don't answer.

'Okay,' she say, an' take a sip from her fresh drink. 'Let me give you my news then, since it look like the constipation in your mouth is preventing you from talking. I have met a lovely man. And you are the one I have to thank for it.'

'Me?' I almost spill coffee down my front as I sit up to look at her.

'Yes, because guess where I meet him?'

I still looking at her.

'In the gym when I was looking for you. And tomorrow night he taking me to the pictures.'

I feel happy for Bel an' almost start crying again, as I watch her eyes brighten with excitement.

'You still seeing that man – the Antiguan?'

'No. Not really,' I say, quietly, afraid to move my mind on to Cedric.

'How you mean? Is either you seeing him or you not seeing him.'

'It… it didn't work out.' I drink the remainder of my coffee an' put the cup down.

'That nice gentlemanly man? What happen?'

'Things just didn't work out.'

'You give him a piece?'

'Not really.'

'How you mean, "Not really"? Come on, Doli, is me you talking to. Yes or no?'

'I… I find out all his teeth don't belong to him.'

'What?'

'The shock – the way things happened, make me feel too embarrassed. Bad.'

'How you mean?' Bel like she want to laugh. Not sure if I joking or serious.

I was in two minds whether to tell her, but I tell her anyway about how things happen the night Cedric was here.

'You mean all er this happen right here on this sofa?' She point, move her bottom an' look down on the sofa, as though she expect to see some evidence. 'He good?'

'Uh-huh. He good.' I nod, smile an' a little shame catch me again.

'So why? Because you see his false teeth you don't want to see him, or you 'fraid the sex will be too good?'

She teasing me now, but hearing her talk about Cedric like dis make me feel more shame.

'I... I don't know, Bel. The sex thing, it happened too soon an' as for the teeth – oh God. Dat so surprise me.'

'Doli, at our time of life, not all of us can say we have all of our teeth. We're not all as fortunate as you. I myself have two crowns. An' if the ting was nice, what's the problem? You are a big woman and him a big man. Come on, girl. I refuse to drink alone,' she say, an' lean over to splash a little more rum in my cup.

Chapter Thirty-Seven

Yvette

I'd spent the earlier part of the morning finishing off writing thank-you cards to some of the people who'd sent wreaths and helped out with Papa's wake and funeral. I'd also sieved through the carrier bag of personal papers I'd taken from Papa's flat, created a pile for dumping, another for 'not sure', and a third I'd put in an envelope to give to Mum. We hadn't spoken since the funeral but today, whether she opened her door to me or not, I was going to hand at least some of her duties over to her.

Miss Elsa had taken responsibility for letting the people from a local charity into Papa's flat to take his unwanted stuff. I'd kept what was left of his trophies and medals. I couldn't throw them away. Sorting Papa's papers out had brought on more tears. Each episode felt more cleansing than the last.

I left the house. The sun being out made the cold more bearable. A black cab pulled up a couple of cars behind mine. I walked past it. Seconds later, I heard someone shout, 'Ruthie?', stopping me dead in my tracks. I turned around. A slender woman wearing a beige mac was standing on the pavement.

'Pattie?'

'That's me.' She smiled, stooped slightly then straightened up again. 'Yes.' Her voice rose into a high-pitched squeak. 'Me.'

I walked towards her, giddy with disbelief.

'Why didn't you let me know exactly when you were coming?' I said, embracing her and the nutmeggy scent she was carrying. 'Come. Let's go in.' I took the handle of her case.

'I was praying you would be home,' she said, following me into the house, 'and I wouldn't have to make the taxi put me to sit down somewhere to wait until you got home, or go and find somewhere else to stay.'

'I meant to contact you,' I said. 'But things got—'

'Don't worry. It's not your fault. It's me who should have let you know,' she said. 'But it looks like you were going out.'

I told her I had been going to drop an envelope off at my mother's. 'I wouldn't have been long.'

'I don't know how you all manage to live in this kind of cold,' she said, standing in the hallway and squeezing one hand alternately with the other.

'You get used to it,' I said, smiling inside. I led her into the sitting room. 'I'll make you a hot drink.'

'Hot? No. Not for me,' she said, hovering by the sofa. 'I only drink cold.'

'So how am I going to get you warmed up?'

'First let me use your bathroom.'

I pointed the toilet out to her and while she was gone, rushed downstairs to turn the heating up and looked around to make sure the place looked decent. I couldn't believe Pattie was actually here. In my house. Was this real? I tried to recall everything she'd said in her letter.

'I've been holding this pee for so long,' she came downstairs saying. 'I prefer to stay away from public bathrooms. But,' her voice went up by a couple of decibels, 'look at you, Ruthie!' She started sizing me up.

'And you. Pretty as ever,' I said, admiring how her two single cornrows highlighted her cheekbones. 'And nobody calls me

Ruthie anymore. Not even Auntie Agnes. It's been Yvette for the last thirty-odd years.'

'Right. Like me. Everybody knows me as Dionne now. But it's so good to see you,' she said. We hugged again. 'Sorry about the nutmeg oil.' She fanned the air in front of her face. 'I know it makes me smell like an old lady, but I'm suffering from a stiff shoulder. Health before vanity, eh?' She giggled and stirred up an old girlish memory of how we used to be.

'Of course. You want something to eat? I could make you a room-temperature drink—?'

'Room temperature?' She giggled again. 'Maybe later. You said you were going to see your mother.'

Her St Lucian accent had become intertwined with the sing-song Trinidadian twang, similar to Miss Belvina's. Dionne had developed a whole new accent. Living in the sun and, no doubt, her diet, had given her milky-toffee-coloured skin that smooth, invisible-foundation look.

'It can wait,' I said, leading her into the front room. 'I can't believe you're actually here. Here in the flesh.'

'I don't want to stop you from doing your business. As long as you don't mind dragging me with you,' she said.

I hesitated. 'You sure you're not too tired from that long drive from the airport?'

'Tired? Girl, I'm so vex with myself. I slept through most of that long drive here and missed so much sightseeing because of that.'

She was reaching for the mac she'd peeled off and left on the banister. The clothes she was wearing weren't made for this kind of weather. I offered her one of my coats. 'If you don't mind,' she said.

'Temperature's not the best today.'

'I notice,' she said. 'Even with sun.'

As I was getting the coat from the cupboard under the stairs, Aaron texted me.

How you doing today? I miss you. Please call.

His texts had been coming at least three times a day since the funeral. I'd been ignoring them mainly. I wasn't ready to deal with any of that relationship stuff.

Will call, I texted back.

'Everything okay?' Dionne asked. She'd seen me putting my phone away.

'Yeah. Sure you're not hungry or anything?'

'No. Come on,' she said, pulling the coat on. 'Oh, yes. Now this feels good.'

She wriggled her body like she was nestling into a cosy space and grinned.

'We sharing clothes again?' she said.

'You remember?'

'Of course.'

I smiled with her, but her response had nudged at the hurt she'd caused me, and added more questions to the list building up in my head. Despite that, I was happy to see her; to have her here next to me.

'So how've you been?' I asked, as we pulled away, the car engine sounding loud in the cold air. 'I hear you're married – and have a lovely daughter.'

'Yes. Yes to both.'

'And you?'

'No and no to both,' I said.

'You not hasty like me.'

'You mean haven't had your luck.'

'Luck? Luck, you call it?' She laughed. 'You like living here?' she asked.

'You mean the country or the area?' I said, moving up a gear.

'Both.'

'The country's not great – weather's crap most of the time. But the area I live in is okay for me. There's a large enough black community, which I feel at home in, most of the time. Around that is a nice mix. We've got a good market where we can get our green bananas, yams – mangoes too, in the summer.'

'Oh. Fresh?'

'Well, as fresh as possible.'

'You all have a lot of Indian people here,' Dionne said, as we crossed Roman Road.

'Yeah. People tend to live where there are others like them,' I said. 'When Mum first came, they went to where their own people and family lived too. When you're in a foreign country, you usually head for where there are others like yourself.'

'Of course. I see,' Dionne said, turning to look at the different shops and people we passed en route. 'You… you have some kind of job around food, right?'

'Dietician,' I said.

'That sounds fascinating. Studying food, advising people on what they should or shouldn't eat.'

'There's more to it than that,' I said. 'Sometimes the problems are psychological.'

'Oh. That sounds very involved.'

'It has a lot to do with people's relationship with food.'

'Relationship? Real complex.'

'Yours must be complex and interesting as well.'

'Oh, yes. Sad too and sometimes, just complex.'

I parked the car a few doors away from Mum's house, but left the engine running to help keep the car warm.

'I won't be long,' I said, as I got out.

I walked briskly up the road. My plan was to drop the envelope through Mum's letterbox and sneak away. And everything was going as planned until I was about to shut her gate behind me. I heard knocking and looked up. She was standing at her bedroom window waving. *Damn.* The relief I'd felt after dropping the envelope in the letterbox changed to despair. I gave a polite wave back and continued trying to shut the gate. Then I realised she wasn't waving. She was beckoning me to come back. My chest rose with the deep intake of air. I exhaled and walked grudgingly back to her door. I wasn't in any mood for a reprimand or an argument.

She was wearing her purple dressing gown. 'Morning, Mum,' I said. The smell of burnt toast flitted past onto the street.

'Good morning,' she said, her eyes falling briefly on the envelope in her hand, then shifting back to me again. 'I… I was going to call. What is dis?' She lifted the envelope closer to her face.

'Papa's papers,' I said. 'You're still his wife, so they belong to you.'

Her shoulder-length hair was closer to its natural state: wavy with strands of grey. It looked like she hadn't put a comb through it since the funeral.

'You don't want to come inside?' she said.

'I'm in a bit of a rush.' I glanced behind me.

'I… I have to talk to you,' she said, sheepishly.

'Someone's waiting for me in the car,' I said, trying not to make the dark rings under her eyes and her soft, depressed tone any of my business.

'Who?'

'A friend.' I glanced over my shoulder again, picturing Dionne sitting alone in the car.

'I wanted to tell you sorry,' she said.

'For what?' I could think of many things she should be wanting to say sorry for.

'For… for how I behaved in the church. What I said – it wasn't right. I really don't know what happen to me. But… but you say you have a frien' waiting for you.' She ran her hand along the side of her head, like she was wiping it.

'Mum, look,' I said. 'I'll come back later. Is that okay?'

It wasn't just her behaviour in church she had to apologise for. She'd given me no support with Papa's death or funeral.

'All right,' she said, touching her hair again.

She hadn't moved from the doorway when I was shutting the gate. I rushed back to the car, planning to call Miss Belvina to ask whether she could check on Mum. I couldn't do anything right now. I had a surprise visitor.

'Everything all right?' Dionne asked, when I got back to the car.

'To be honest,' I said. 'I'm not sure.' I tugged at my seat belt. 'I'll check on her later.'

'It would be nice to meet her,' Dionne said.

'Oh. Oh, sorry. I didn't realise.'

'It's okay. Another time.'

Mum wasn't looking her best and I don't know why I was worrying about her after the way she's behaved towards me since Papa died, but I was. She was my mother, no matter what. Going back would save me from feeling I had to check on her later or tomorrow, and a fresh face might cheer her up. 'Come on, then,' I said, releasing my seat belt.

'You sure?'

I was brimming with doubt, but 'Yeah,' I said.

*

'You come back? Why – who is?' Mum leaned sideways to get a better view of Dionne, standing behind me.

'This is Dionne, Mum,' I told her. 'The girl… cousin I was brought up with in St Lucia.'

'You are the chile Agnes was—'

Dionne edged closer. 'Yes,' she said. 'It's nice to meet you, Miss—'

'Well, come in, come in,' Mum said, and led us into the front room. 'The kettle just boil.'

'Dionne doesn't – you got anything cold?' I told Mum.

'Well, yes,' she said.

'You have a nice home, Miss Doli,' Dionne said, though her eyes were mainly on Mum.

'I… I wasn't expecting company,' Mum said. 'Otherwise I would have fix myself up.'

'You look fine to me,' Dionne responded.

She didn't know how well turned out my mother always was.

Dionne was hovering in the doorway. I left Mum offering her a seat and headed for the kitchen.

As I poured lime juice into a glass, I imagined Dionne being engrossed in her surroundings. Taking in the black-and-white picture of a beaming Mum holding her wedding bouquet, and an ancient, enlarged graduation picture of me, curly permed hair hanging down the sides of my face. Stark contrast to the natural hairstyles I wore now.

When I got back to the front room, Mum was gone. Dionne lifted her eyes off Mum's display of pictures on the Formica-and-glass cabinet and took the drink from me. 'Miss Doli went upstairs. She said she needed to freshen up.'

Bringing Dionne in had had some good effect, then.

I sat down briefly, watching Dionne's eyes travel around the room. 'Won't be a minute,' I said. 'I'll just see what she's up to.'

Mum's bedroom door was open. 'Mum?' I knocked lightly on it.

'Come. Come,' she said.

'You coming—?'

'What you make of all dis?'

I wasn't sure if she was referring to Dionne's arrival or the state of her room. It was stuffy. Her bed unmade. There was a towel thrown on the back of a chair, cups on her bedside tables, clothes hanging on her wardrobe door and another pile on the floor. Was Mum okay?

'The girl. Where she come from?'

'Dionne? Trinidad. She's only visiting,' I said.

She started searching through her wardrobe. I assumed, for something to put on. 'At you she staying?' she asked.

'Yes. Anyway, we're not stopping.'

'Everything going all right?'

'I'm managing,' I said. 'What about you?'

'Okay,' she said, pulling open one of the dressing-table drawers.

I sat on the edge of the bed and explained that I'd been through Papa's papers, which was why I'd brought the envelope round.

'An' you was just going to drop it in my letterbox an' go?'

She dragged a pair of tracksuit bottoms and a top from the drawer, threw them on the bed behind her, then took off her dressing gown, revealing her snug body dressed in green knickers and a stretchy bra top.

'I didn't want to disturb you,' I said. 'Anyway, I wasn't sure you'd want to see me after… Thought you might still be annoyed with me,' I said, shuffling.

'I already tell you I'm sorry,' she said, pulling the zip on her tracksuit top up to her neck.

I told her I'd be sorting out Papa's flat before handing it back to the council. 'Did you want anything of Papa's – a memento or—? I've got a few of his—'

'Me? No. No.' She sat on the bed looking at me. 'So,' she said, 'you finish with all of dat Ian business now?'

'I haven't been pushing it,' I said. I hadn't been in touch with Rob Payne since he called me at one of the Nine-Nights. 'But we're still looking.'

'You mean you caa see dere is no use in you wasting your time with dat now? I… I'm sure you have to pay these people to do all of dis…' – she waved a hand around – 'dis nonsense.'

'It was Papa's wish,' I said. 'I'm just sorry I let him down. I'd hoped to find something out before he—'

'So what he care about it now? You caa let sleeping dogs lie?' Mum said.

'What's it to you whether I find him or not, anyway? Don't tell me you're still trying to punish Papa. He's dead, Mum.'

This was a good time to leave. This conversation was stirring up bad feelings I was trying to get over. Dionne, my visitor, was waiting downstairs.

'Punish Joe?' Twisted lines gathered on her forehead. 'I simply do not see the sense in searching for… for the man. He would never be interested in getting in touch with Joe.'

'How do you know that?' A thought struck me. 'Wait a minute,' I said. 'Are you hiding something – something you know about Ian, from me?'

'Of course not.' She turned away.

I stood up so I could see her face. 'Did you—? You and Ian had some kind of a friendship on the ship, didn't you?'

'Why? What would make you say dat?'

'I'm not stupid.'

A sound came from downstairs. She stilled herself to listen.

'Hello?' Dionne shouted up.

I edged out of the bedroom.

'We'll have to talk about this,' I said quietly, then started making my way down. 'Let's go, Dionne.'

Mum followed me to the top of the stairs.

'Goodbye, Miss Doli,' Dionne said, looking up at Mum. 'Hope to see you again. The drink was nice.'

'Yes. Okay. Bye. Goodbye,' Mum replied.

'You all right?' Dionne asked, when we got to the car.

I told her I was, though I was sure she'd detected I wasn't being totally upfront.

'Miss… your mum seems like a nice lady.'

'She's okay,' I said. 'Most of the time.'

'Something happen to upset you?'

'I'll be okay,' I said.

I'd lost all desire for chit-chat and couldn't stop thinking about the conversation I'd just had with Mum – the look I'd caught on her face when I asked her about Ian. She was hiding something.

By the time we got home, I was in a slightly better mood. Plus, I was keen to reconnect with Dionne, find out what was going on with her. Why she had contacted me after so many years. Why was she really here?

'You must be hungry,' I told her, as I took my coat off, anticipation building up in me.

'I could take a little something,' she said, 'but not that fish and chips I hear you English people like so much.'

'That's Friday night "tea",' I said, smiling.

'Oh. Okay. Wrong day, wrong time, eh?' She laughed. 'Just joking, eh. Chips is fine.'

She went off to wash her hands, as I started preparing some food to eat.

'I spoke to Auntie Agnes a couple of weeks ago,' I said, when she came back. 'She was in Trinidad with you, wasn't she?'

'The old witch might have been in Trinidad, yes,' Dionne said, sitting down. 'But not with me.'

My eyes couldn't open any wider, with the look I gave her. There was such venom, resentment and spite in her tone. Auntie Agnes? A witch? She'd brought her up, sent her to university. Loved her.

Maybe Auntie Lucille was right about Dionne being ungrateful.

'She should be back in St Lucia. If she hasn't followed me here,' Dionne said. 'I hope my letter wasn't too confusing.'

'Well, it was a bit.'

I slipped a knife through a tomato and tried to dismiss thoughts about how close I'd come to telling Auntie Agnes about Dionne's letter.

'Are you and Auntie going through some kind of… you know?' I asked.

'Girl,' she tutted, 'much more than that.' I turned to see her tilting her head to the side. 'You want help with anything?'

I told her, no. The chips were already in the oven with some veggie sausages, and I was about to add the tomatoes. I'd had some porridge earlier and wasn't that hungry, but I'd have a little with her so she wouldn't feel uncomfortable eating on her own, with me looking at her.

'I promise, I will tell you everything,' she said, and asked if she could first use my phone to make a quick overseas call.

'Of course,' I said. There was a phone in the kitchen, but I presumed she'd want some privacy, so directed her to the line in the front room.

The food was ready and on the table when she came back.

'So come on,' I said, after we were seated. 'Tell me. You and Auntie had a falling out?'

Dionne leaned across the table. Her deep black eyes met mine. 'It's a long story, eh?' she said.

I held her gaze. 'Go on.'

She picked up her fork and cut through one of the sausages. 'I've had issues with Auntie Agnes for a long while now—'

'Oh, really?'

'But at the wedding—'

'Auntie's wedding? You were there?'

'Uh-huh.' She nodded.

I gulped and exhaled. 'But she told me it was a quiet thing.'

'Well, it was, kinda,' Dionne said, shrugging. 'She told me that some of Leonce's family was coming and begged me to come to represent hers.'

'But we have relatives in—'

'You don't know Auntie's pulled herself away from all of her family up in Desruisseaux? In fact, she avoids any part of the island where she knows there's family that might expose her for the hypocrite she is.'

I swallowed and glared at Dionne. Why would she talk about Auntie Agnes in that way?

'At the time you left,' she continued, ignoring the disapproving look I'd given her, 'I suppose we were too young to realise there was hardly any family visiting us. Over the years, that just got worse. You were not there anymore and the only family that was left for me was Auntie Agnes.'

Mum was always accusing Auntie Agnes of thinking she was better than others, especially because she moved up north where most of the well-to-do people live.

When I'd visited her a few years ago, she was always too busy with church work to go with me on the odd trip to relatives. And despite what some of the family might think or say, to me Auntie Agnes's case was understandable. She'd had a right to move, if she felt it was going to be better for her and for us. It was simple social mobility. But my thoughts were stuck now on Auntie choosing – no, insisting – on Dionne coming to the wedding, but not even telling me about it until it was all over.

'Let me tell you,' Dionne was keen to continue.

'Okay.'

'The strangest thing happened at that wedding, girl.'

I sprinkled a few drops of tomato sauce on my plate.

'I noticed these two women. One was older – around Auntie Agnes's age. The other younger – in her fifties, I'm sure. They were talking and looking at me. When my eyes caught theirs, the older one looked away. The younger one smiled. I smiled back. But I felt kinda uncomfortable. You know?'

'Mmm.'

Dionne stabbed a few chips with her fork. 'Finally,' she said, 'the younger one came and sat beside me. Introduced herself, said her name was Rosina. It turned out she was a distant cousin to Leonce. But as nice as this lady was, she couldn't stop asking me questions.

'Questions? Like what?'

'First it was about the picture Auntie Agnes has of you and me on the bureau in her front room.'

'What picture's that?' I tried to think back.

'You might not remember it. We were still small, around seven or eight months, wearing clothes made from the same material with little red flowers and white lace on the hem. We looked so cute. Like twins.'

A distant look fell on her face. She smiled, then returned to the present again. 'This Miss Rosina asked which one was me, in the picture. I told her. Then she wanted to know who the other baby was.

'Me?'

'Uh-huh.' Dionne popped a chip in her mouth. 'Then how long I had been living in Trinidad and if I have family there; where you were and if you had family there.'

I tried to concentrate, hooking on to Dionne's every word. What did all of this have to do with Auntie Agnes? Or anything else, come to that?

'I didn't make much of it at that time,' she continued. 'I had only come to St Lucia for three days. But, girl, two days after I arrived back in Trinidad – don't ask me where Miss Rosina got my number – the lady called me, all the way from Canada. And this time, she came straight out and ask how old I was and if Joseph Francis is my father.'

I straightened up, dropped my fork on the plate and took in a gulp of air.

'Papa?'

'Yes,' Dionne said. 'After that, I couldn't stop thinking about her questions – everything the woman had told me.'

'Like what? What else did she tell you?'

'She said she had a child, a daughter, for him. For Joseph Francis.'

'Papa? My papa?' I pointed at my chest.

Dionne gave two slow nods. 'She said, the baby was not even four months old – not long christened – when her grandmother took it away. Her breast milk had started to dry up soon after she'd given birth. Her grandmother said it was a sign.'

'For what? To take her baby away?'

'Yes. Give it to somebody she knew could give it better care – a better life.'

'How could she let someone take her baby away like that?'

'They were poor people,' Dionne said, 'and you know how things used to be. Her grandma was boss. Anyway, according to her, at the time, she didn't know who the old lady took her baby to, but she trusted her enough to know that she wouldn't leave her gran-baby with just anybody.'

'So who was this person?' My mind was racing. I was sure I'd worked it out, but needed to hear Dionne confirm it.

'Auntie Agnes, of course.' Dionne put a piece of tomato in her mouth and paused to chew.

I'd lost all interest in eating.

'Next thing you know' – Dionne swallowed – 'Miss Rosina got shipped to Canada. Her grandmother died and took that important piece of information with her.'

This was a hell of a story Dionne was telling me. 'But I don't understand,' I said. 'Why did this Miss Rosina woman think her baby was you?'

'She wasn't sure, not just from the picture. Remember as children, how people used to say we looked alike and we could pass as sisters?'

'Uh-huh.' We used to let people believe we were sisters all the time. I wasn't totally convinced about that resemblance thing now, but the warm feelings of our childhood together were floating back to me. I sighed. 'So you're saying Papa was your father too?' It was an outlandish question, but it was the conclusion coming to me. 'You're my sister? This child Papa didn't know about?'

'No.' Dionne leaned across the table. 'The child Mr Joe didn't know about isn't me. It's you.'

*

'Don't be stupid,' I said, straightening my back. 'I know who my mother and father are. I've been here with them for the last thirty-whatever years.' Dionne's story was laughable.

She looked me square in the face. 'Me and Miss Rosina went and confronted Auntie Agnes.'

'What d'you mean?'

'According to Miss Rosina, apart from Auntie Agnes, there was only one other person who knew who Miss Rosina's grandmother – the old lady – had taken the baby to.'

'Who? Who was that?'

'The baby's godmother. She had travelled with the old lady that night, waited by the road while the old lady handed the baby over. Rosina's grandmother had made her promise to never tell, but when she saw Miss Rosina back in St Lucia, after so many years, she felt it was a sin not to tell her.

'Auntie Agnes was denying it at first, when we confronted her. But she realised that now everything would be in the open. Everyone, including Leonce, would know. She couldn't hide it anymore. Girl, the thing almost sent her crazy. She had to confess.'

Dionne sat back in her seat.

'So…? Did she say? Which… who the baby was?'

Dionne nodded. 'You. You, Yvette.'

'No. Don't. That's rubbish,' I said, pushing my chair back. 'That can't be, Dionne.' I stood up. 'No. I know my parents – my family. And Papa didn't have any other children. I was the only one. He would have said if he had any more.'

'He didn't know,' she said, emphatically. 'He left the country before he even knew the girl he'd been with was pregnant. And, yes, we could say she, Miss Rosina, should have tried harder to find him and her child, but she said her grandmother blocked her, then so much time had passed it felt impossible.'

'This can't be,' I said, pacing from table to sink and back. Dionne was out of her head. 'Not me.'

'I know there has to be more than one Joseph Francis in the world,' she continued, 'but in St Lucia? And he is from Bexon, right?'

I walked towards her. 'And… and this… this Miss Rosina's claiming to be my mother? From a picture? A – a story?' I shouted.

'It's not just a story, Ruthie.'

'My name's Yvette!' I shouted again, looking down at her.

'And it's just like you, too – after all those years of… of deciding you don't want to know me, or have any contact with me, to come all this way to land that kind of shit on me.'

'You think I would do that?'

'Why not?'

'I'm not that kind of person.'

'Says you,' I said, pointing at her.

Dionne took a long, shuddering breath. "I found it hard to believe her at first. You left St Lucia as a child. Maybe you've forgotten how old people hold on to secrets. And I probably would not have given Miss Rosina the opportunity to convince me, if I had known my own parents.'

What the hell was Dionne saying?

'You don't know how much I wished it was the reverse – that this nice lady would have turned out to be the mother I have wondered about for so many years! That she had found me – her daughter. Auntie Agnes had me believing that my mother and father were Guyanese who'd come to live in St Lucia. She said they'd left me with her to go to Venezuela and had never made contact since. But as I got older, all what she was saying didn't seem to fit into place. There was a lot of missing information and I could see she wasn't comfortable when I tried to quiz her about it. You know how many trips I have made to Venezuela, trying to find my mother or father? Walking round trying to see some kind of resemblance of me in people in shops, on the buses, in the streets?' Her voice softened, then rose again. 'Huh. Why you think I took my scholarship and went to study in Trinidad? To be close by to Venezuela – just in case.'

'But we're cousins,' I said, desperate to maintain the link I still wanted with her.

'You must know by now that's not really true,' Dionne blurted out.

'Yes, but… We were like cousins… sisters.'

'Yes. Like. But for me, as I got older, never sure.'

As children we'd understood that both Dionne's parents and mine were away. That wasn't unusual. Lots of parents left their children with close friends or family to go overseas. The difference, we'd both accepted then, was that I was in touch with my parents, but Dionne wasn't with hers.

'Our blood connections never really bothered me, to be honest,' I said. Ultimately, whether by blood or adoption, I saw her as my cousin – close enough to be a sister to me, in fact.

'Anyway, to be sure,' Dionne continued, 'Miss Rosina and myself had a DNA test, and she isn't my mother.'

'Not being your mother doesn't mean she's mine,' I spat out.

'Can't you see it all makes sense, Ruthie – I mean, Yvette?'

'So when? When did you do this DNA test?' I said.

'A few weeks ago.'

I needed evidence for some truth in what she was saying. 'Show me. Show me. Where is it – the results?' I said.

'I have it upstairs. And in my emails.'

She rushed upstairs and returned in less than two minutes with a couple of sheets of paper. I sat down, deciphering the information that confirmed what Dionne had said about her and this Miss Rosina's test.

'I'm sorry,' she said, sitting back down. 'I really am. I couldn't think of a better way for me to tell you. You think I would come all this way if I didn't believe all of this was true?'

'No, you wouldn't, would you?' I got up and walked away from the table. This crazy story Dionne was trying to land on me, set a fire up in me. Broke the dam of pent-up resentment and pain she'd caused by cutting me out of her life all those years ago, tossing me aside. Making me feel dispensed with. Now, after years of turning her back on me, she was here insisting, claiming the mother I've always known to be mine was really hers. I walked back to the table and faced her.

'You wouldn't have come all this way just to see me, would you? You haven't wanted to know me since… since – God, how long? But suddenly, you believe you've discovered some hidden secret that could make you feel better about yourself, and you're… you're ready to travel the earth to let me know that – coming all this way to mess up my life. Well, don't bother! I know who I am and no one can take that away from me.'

'Yvette!' Dionne looked stricken. 'It's not like that. I did not come here to mess things up at all—!'

'But all of this stuff – this DNA stuff – is about *you*. Not me. It doesn't have anything to do with me. How do I know if you and this Miss Rosina haven't colluded on… on some sick joke for you to get at me,' I said, looking at her. 'You could both be suffering from some sort of personality disorder for all I know. Where are her contact details? I need to speak to her.'

'Yvette, please. You are welcome to her contact details, but I think you need to calm down.'

Her words riled me even more.

'Calm down?' I glared at her. Who the hell was she to tell me to calm down? She was the one who'd come here disrupting my already busy head space with her crap.

'The bottom line is,' she continued, 'we have to have DNA tests with Joseph Francis. I believe he's our father. Yours *and* mine.'

'Oh. Oh, really?' I sneered.

'Can't you see?'

I refused to.

'If I am lying or having some kind of joke on you, as you say, there will be no harm in all of us having tests. It will prove everything!

'I just don't understand,' she continued, 'you saying you're not interested in knowing who you really are. Not even now that doubts have been planted? You telling me you would seriously want to continue living the rest of your life not knowing who your real parents are?

'I have lived with it ever since I have known myself. Now I see the opportunity to find out the truth. Who my mother and father really are. And I don't know about you, but I want to take it. If—'

'Papa's dead.' I spat the words out like blobs of bitter aloes. Tears filled my eyes.

'What?'

'We buried him last Friday. Didn't Auntie Agnes tell you?'

'Oh, sh— God, I didn't once think he might not be alive. Oh, no. So you're in mourning? God, I'm sorry.' She slid her plate to the side.

I sniffed and started clearing the table. She offered to help, but I told her it was fine. I wished she'd get out of my sight. Evaporate out of my house.

'So, how did he die?' she asked.

I squirted washing-up liquid onto the sponge then told her about the lung cancer, the events that led to Papa's death. All matter-of-factly.

'That must have hurt you, eh?'

'He was my father,' I said. 'I loved him.'

'Mmm.'

I felt calmer after that and suggested we sit in the front room. 'It's more comfortable there.'

We took our drinks with us. I sat on the large sofa and she took the floor.

'I know you're finding this hard to take in,' she said, once we'd settled. 'I did as well, but you'll see – we have both been fooled into believing we were each other. You are the real Dionne and I am Yvette. Your parents – at least your mother, is really mine.'

My tongue sat in my mouth like a lump of cloth. I wanted this story to go away.

Dionne was rattling on: 'I'm sure, once you've completed the tests, you'll see that Miss Rosina is your rightful mother. And I'll bet money too, that we share the same father.' She looked at me, 'But you know the most hurtful thing?'

I swallowed. 'What?'

'Auntie Agnes, that *conniving* woman, must have made the switch well before she sent you to England. Remember when she tried to get us to start using what she insisted was our real names. Remember? She even insisted everyone called us Yvette and Dionne.'

Dionne sounded so sure of herself.

'We'll have to tell Miss Doli, you know that?'

I didn't answer.

'We can do it together, if you like. Go and see her and tell her.'

I shrugged.

'We could take legal action against Auntie Agnes too for what she'd done, you know,' she continued, then paused. 'But it looks like I've come and added to your grieving. That makes me feel terrible.' She dropped her head and stared at the carpet.

We sat in silence for a while, then she said: 'What was he like, your – Papa? You mind if I call him that?'

I swallowed again and tried to redirect my thoughts. 'He… he loved to socialise, his dominoes… but his life, to me, was a bit of a mess. Not in a horrible way. In a sad way.'

'He wasn't happy?'

I took a sip from my drink. 'I don't suppose he was. I know he tried to be the best he could've been for me, but if I'm honest – and I'd never admit it to him – it wasn't enough.'

'I remember you telling me, in your letters, how nice he was.'

'He was, especially when I was a child.'

I told her how he tried to keep in touch with me when he and Mum finished; how he came to visit me when I was studying in Birmingham, even though his main reason for being in the city was for a big domino competition.

'So why did they split up – him and… Miss Doli?'

I shrugged. 'Mum wasn't into what he was into,' I said. 'She didn't want to share him with the domino club. Before he left, there were constant arguments when she'd tell him to leave. Then when he did, she was so pissed off. It was like he'd insulted her. Papa hated arguments.'

'And neither of them got married again?'

'No. Papa had casual things after that. And don't ask me anything about Mum's love life because she keeps that so hidden, you'd think she was trained by the CIA.'

We giggled. I was trying to relax, wishing this – this meeting with Dionne had come under different circumstances. Without the crazy question marks. A visit that was simply about us repairing the rift in our relationship. Then she said: 'You think we would be able to get any of his hair, or even blood, from somewhere?'

'What… what for?' I glared at her. 'For God's sake, Dionne,' I snapped. 'Do you know what all of this means to me? How it's affecting me? My life? I've just buried my father. Yes. *My* father. You turn up trying to convince me that my mother isn't my mother and now you want my father's blood. To prove what, that he isn't my father either?'

'No. No, Yvette. I'm sorry,' she said, walking on her knees to reach me. 'I'm not trying to prove anything like that. All I want is the truth and DNA tests are the only way we can prove anything, for either of us.'

'Maybe I don't want proof,' I said. 'Maybe I just want things to stay as they are – were, before you came.'

'Oh, God. I'm so sorry. You… you want me to go?'

I took a deep breath in and exhaled. 'No,' I said. As painful as it was, there was still a lot to talk about, things to resolve.

'I'm sorry,' she said, again. 'I know you might feel like I'm rushing everything, but I only have a few days here and I don't want to go back with nothing.'

'We cleaned his flat from top to bottom soon after he died,' I said. 'And cleared it out to hand it back to the council.'

'You cleared everything? Didn't keep anything?'

'Nothing that would have his blood or hair.'

'You sure?'

'What d'you mean? Of course I'm sure.'

My words – something, seemed to have clipped her enthusiasm. Her voice became sullen. 'Your health service is not likely to be interested in doing it for us, but there's a company that operates on the internet. They only need a hair sample.'

'Papa's hair?'

'Yes. And ours. I hope you don't mind, but I have arranged for the sample bags to be sent here.'

'What?'

It came to me again. As much as I yearned for that old reconnection with Dionne, her real purpose for being here was to find her parents. I felt pushed away again.

She stood up, brushed the back of her trousers lightly with her hand, and said: 'I have a few things to catch up on,' then she went upstairs.

I was in the kitchen cleaning up after cooking, when a tired-looking Dionne ambled in wearing a long, brown dress and thick mohair cardigan, her head tied in a floral scarf.

'You're up,' I said.

'Mmmm.' She covered her yawn. 'Good evening.' Her voice was slow and rugged.

'I didn't expect to fall into that kinda sleep,' she said.

'You must have been tired,' I said. 'I've cooked.'

'Oh, I hope you didn't do that just for me.'

'It's no problem.'

She got herself a glass of water and sat down.

I wiped my hands and sat opposite her. 'Why did you stop replying to my letters?' I said.

'I…' A distant look fell into her eyes. Her expression hardened. 'I started hating you for leaving,' she said.

'Hate me?' Her words brought tears to my eyes. 'I didn't want to go, leave you or Auntie. You knew that. And I thought our letters… I didn't have a choice—'

'I know. I know all of that, but you have to understand that, after you left, it was like part of me was missing. I mean, for as long as I could remember, before that, we were hardly apart. Then—'

'I missed you too, you know.' She looked at me, registering my tone of voice. 'Especially on that bloody long ship journey with a bunch of strangers.'

'But I was the one left behind,' she said. 'Before that, I always had someone beside me – to hold me up. Suddenly – whoosh.' She swiped a hand through the air. 'You were gone. We had already moved far from Desruisseaux. Everybody was calling me Dionne, instead of the Pattie I was used to. I felt so alone. I had no one. And nothing could replace you. Not even your letters. But you? You were fine. Far, far away with your mother and father.'

'You knew I really didn't want to go, Dionne. You knew that. It—' The pain was choking me.

'I know. It wasn't your fault,' she said, 'but when you're a child, things don't always add up. You don't understand certain things, feelings and by the time I started to make sense of things, it was too late to go back and put things right with you.'

'But it wasn't,' I said. 'I never stopped loving you or wanting you in my life, Dionne. In those early days, I would have dug a tunnel that would take me straight back to you and Auntie, if I could. When you stopped writing, it was like death. I had a sister, then I didn't.'

'The pain was too much,' she said, after a pause. 'But I suppose we were so young, with no say at all in what happened to us, where big people decide to take or send us. Then Auntie Agnes started behaving like I was her prize possession.' She indicated with her fingers to put inverted commas around the last two words. 'It was as if this one child she had left had to make up for the one she had to give back. And with everything else—? I couldn't take it. I had to leave. Put some distance between me and her.'

'And me?'

'I can only say I'm sorry,' she said.

'Oh, Dionne,' I said, standing up and walking towards her. We put our arms around each other then parted, each wiping our eyes and sniffing.

'But you seem to have done very well for yourself,' I said, sitting back down.

'Well.' She sniffed again. I handed her a piece of kitchen paper from the roll on the table. 'Stacy is lovely, but the marriage thing? That's not too hot.'

'I take it Auntie doesn't know that. She's always going on about how nice your husband is and how great everything is with you.'

'She would like to believe she knows everything that's going on in my life, but she doesn't really. Until I found out about what she did to us, we used to talk regularly, but we haven't been that close for...' She paused and raised her eyebrows. 'I don't know how long.'

I was finding it hard to believe. Auntie Agnes had never had anything unkind to say about Dionne. She'd put her right up there on a pedestal. Never let on that there was anything amiss in their relationship.

'I've felt like I'm a disappointment to her,' I said. 'Thirty-eight. No husband. No children.'

'You care what she thinks? Everything in time.'

'I don't have much of that left,' I said. 'Knock, knock, knocking on forty's door,' I said, recalling Randy Crawford's sweet, sad lyrics. Only, she had been knocking on heaven's door.

'You must have a special man, though. Good-looking girl like you.' Dionne wriggled like when she'd put my coat on earlier.

'I did, or thought I did.' She leaned in towards me, as if anticipating hearing more. 'But that's a long story,' I said.

'So what's his name?'

'Aaron.'

'You were together long?'

'Three and a half years,' I said, 'but he doesn't want children.'

'No? Lord, I don't think I know one man who doesn't want children,' she said. 'I know plenty who will have them, then leave them to the mother or somebody else to bring up.'

'Mmm. I know some of those too,' I said. 'How long are you here for?'

'Ten days.'

'Ten days? Why such a short time?'

'Girl, if you know the amount of work I have waiting for me to finish in the next two weeks alone! Ten days is all I can squeeze in. In fact, there's some work I need to finish tonight.'

She explained that she was a new partner in a law firm. Expectations were high.

'Computer's up in the front room, if you need it,' I said.

'I know. I saw it.'

'Password's "Angel".'

'Angel?' she said.

'It's what Papa used to call me.'

Dionne and I got through almost two bottles of wine that night, while filling each other in on our lives. Our conversation incited me to get acting on things. There were questions that needed to be answered.

The next morning, while Dionne slept, after some jammy toast, coffee and a couple of paracetamols, I got cracking on trying to establish how I could go about getting a DNA test. Dionne was right – there was only one private company offering the postal service she'd signed up for, but they weren't even based in the UK.

I felt a strong urge to call Auntie Agnes, but they'd be fast asleep over there, plus I wasn't sure whether she was back in St

Lucia or still in Trinidad. I hoped Dionne would sleep on for a while because I planned to visit Auntie Lucille. I hadn't seen her nor Uncle since the funeral and she was likely to know where I could get hold of Auntie Agnes.

Chapter Thirty-Eight

Yvette

'Eh-eh, morning, *ich mwen*,' Auntie Lucille said.

'Morning, Auntie,' I said, wiping my feet on the doormat. 'Auntie, I need to talk to you.' I stepped inside.

'You know?' she said, her voice low and unusually cheery.

'Pardon, Auntie. Know what?'

Her face brightened, eyes widened. 'Agnes here. She surprise us.'

'Auntie Agnes? Here?' I said, hanging up my coat. My strong urge to speak to her was quickly turning to fear.

'Upstairs,' Auntie Lucielle said. 'Agnes?' she shouted over her shoulder. 'Look, somebody here to see you.'

I'd spoken often to Auntie Agnes, but it was over ten years since I'd seen her, so, like Auntie Lucille, I was supposed to be excited – overjoyed with the idea of being with her. I hadn't totally bought Dionne's story, but every organ behind my ribcage felt clumped together, balled up in my chest. Dionne's words: 'If she hasn't followed me here', repeated in my head. Auntie Agnes *had* followed her here. What did that mean?

'Yvie?' Auntie Agnes's voice came from above us. 'I am up here.'

'Go. Go,' Auntie Lucille said, tapping my arm. 'She in your room.'

This was my chance to get confirmation of Dionne's story: confront Auntie Agnes, like she said she and this Miss Rosina had. Get the truth from her mouth.

'Come too, please, Auntie,' I said, looking at Auntie Lucille. 'Please.' I couldn't face it alone.

Auntie Lucille gave me a questioning look. I nudged her forward and moved aside so she could lead.

'I hear the funeral went well,' Auntie Agnes was saying, as we reached the top of the stairs. Thoughts of Dionne's story made me want to turn around and leave. But my need to disprove her propelled me up the stairs and straight into Auntie Agnes's embrace.

'It's so good to see you,' she said.

I shuffled out of her soapy scent. 'Dionne's at my house,' I said, backing away. She was standing the furthest in the room, by the wardrobe. Auntie Lucille stood between us, looking surprised at what I'd said.

'Dat chile is here?' she said, looking at her niece, Auntie Agnes, who lowered her bottom onto the bed, her gaze on the wardrobe in front of her.

'She came yesterday,' I said. 'Is what she's told me true?' Auntie Agnes's didn't moved. 'That you sent the wrong child to England… to your sister?' My heart was beating like I was in the thrust of a morning run.

Auntie Lucille gave Auntie Agnes, then me, a puzzled look.

'Is it true?' I said, my eyes locked on Auntie Agnes as I came further into the room. 'Did you swap our names, our identities – make me take Dionne's real name? Have you fooled all of us? Mum, me, Papa? Am I really a… a child… some old lady gave to you?'

Auntie Lucille leaned towards her niece. 'Ag – Agnes? What is going on?'

'Tell us, Auntie Agnes,' I said. 'I need to hear the truth.'

What I wanted to hear her say was that everything Dionne had told me was a big lie – a mistake. That Dionne was sick. Unstable

– we had to get her some help. But the look on Auntie Agnes's face was the same one Dionne used to wear when, as children, we'd been caught snacking on a forbidden paste of condensed milk and sugar. I held my breath, petrified of her answer.

'I am sorry, *doudou*,' Auntie Agnes said, her voice barely a whisper.

Dread from what she was about to say froze me.

Auntie Lucille sat down next to her niece. 'Agnes?' she said.

'I… I… You all don't understand,' Auntie Agnes said, in a fragile voice that rattled me.

'Then make us. Make us understand,' I shouted, my fears giving way to anger.

Auntie Agnes's hands sat limp in her lap. 'I was on my own after Mama passed,' she said. 'It would have been my time now to go to Englan', but I didn't truly want to. Didn't see the sense. I loved St Lucia. Helping in the church made me feel good an' I had plenty of seamstress work. Then when Doli told me she wouldn't be able to do her classes, work an' take care of the baby, I didn't see any reason why she shouldn't send the baby to me. I didn't have a man an' didn't see a time when dat would happen. The baby was my niece after all. She arrived, an' in no time, was everything to me. In fact' – the side of her mouth trembled as she turned to me and smiled – 'only five months old, she was, you know… As soon as I set eyes on her, I decided to call her Pattie – I had always liked dat name.'

I was sinking.

'Agnes?' Auntie Lucille said, as if she was trying to wake her.

'Not long after dat,' Auntie Agnes continued, 'I had just finished putting my Pattie to sleep when I heard a sof' knock on my door. A ole lady was dere, her head tied in a *mouchwè*, colours like Mama used to wear. Her eyes were bright an' wide open, in the dark. She pushed the parcel she was holding into my chest. "You taking care of one of Joe chile, you can take care of de nex'",' she told me. Her voice was quiet, as though I was the only one she wanted to hear her.'

'Me?' I said, my voice pained and shallow.

Auntie Agnes nodded.

I wanted to die.

'Eh-eh.' Auntie Lucille shuddered and swayed from side to side.

I was a nobody? A giveaway? Insignificant? I looked away.

'Before I could say anything,' she continued, as if she was in a confessional box, 'the ole lady turned an' in no time she was gone. I took the parcel inside an unwrapped it. Look at my blessings, I said to myself. I had twins.'

The respect I had for her dissolved. Hurt fed the rage brewing inside me. 'You're downright wicked,' I screeched, facing her. 'You've messed up our lives. You realise that?'

'I knew dat one day Doli would make a claim for her chile,' Auntie Agnes continued, as if I hadn't spoken.

'You had no right,' I shouted.

'You,' she said, silencing me, 'was a lovely chile in your own way. According to the ole lady, you was Joe's chile – my Pattie's sister. My love for you would grow, but for my Pattie – I could see Mama in her.'

'All these years, you've been conning us, had us all living a lie. Making me feel like I was special… I felt *you* were special.' I staggered back towards the door.

'But how you could have de heart to… Agnes? Doli know about dis?' Auntie Lucille said.

'When Doli asked me to send her chile, Yvette, back for her—'

'*Bondyé*,' Auntie Lucille mumbled.

'I started to pray for God's help – his forgiveness.'

'Eh-eh, Agnes? Don't put God in dat.' Auntie Lucille shook her head. 'Uh-uh.'

Auntie Agnes glanced at her aunt, but continued. 'My Pattie was just a couple of months older dan the baby the ole lady gave me. An' the resemblance between the two of dem was dere. I didn't have to lose my Pattie. All I had to do was send a chile with the name Yvette Angelina Francis to Doli an' Joe an' keep my Pattie. I had their papers. Nobody would ever know. As long as dey carried the name.'

I leaned against the wall by the door, wilting, her words crushing me. My body slid down the wall, stopping when my bottom hit the floor. Dionne was right. I wasn't Yvette Angelina Francis. I pulled my knees up to my chest and squeezed my eyes shut to blot out the pain. How could this be? Who the hell was I? Who was my mother? Father? Real family?

'What is going on dere?' Uncle Anthony's voice shouted from behind the door.

'Jes now, Anthony,' Auntie Lucille shouted. 'Jes now.'

I looked across the room, tears mudding my view.

'I gave the both of you everything I could,' Auntie Agnes said.

'Listen to yourself,' I hissed. 'You're evil.'

'Everything…' she continued.

'But you mean to tell me,' Auntie Lucille said, 'Doli could not see dat de chile you send for her was not de same one she did send for you?'

Did Auntie Lucille not know? Her niece, Doli, wasn't that attentive.

'But you didn't have de right—' Auntie Lucille continued.

'Luce?' Uncle shouted again.

'Jes now,' Auntie Lucille shouted back as she waddled to the door.

Uncle's feet appeared next to mine.

'What…?' His voice was loud and rising. 'What is going on?'

Auntie Agnes stood up. 'I am sorry. God will forgive me. You – all of you, must find it in yourself to forgive me.' She came closer and stooped next to me.

She was only three years older than Mum, but the darkness and crumpled skin round her eyes said different. The sadness embedded in there showed her torment.

I despised her.

'Don't touch me,' I said, flinching and leaning away from the hand she put out to me. 'I don't even know you.'

She fell backwards onto the floor. 'I still see you – both of you – as my children,' she said.

'Well, we're not,' I shouted, standing up. 'Not me. Not Dionne. You're despicable and not me, Dionne nor God will ever forgive you for what you've done.'

'Why the hell somebody cannot tell me what is going on?' Uncle shouted, glaring at the three of us.

'Ask her,' I said, pointing to Auntie Agnes. 'Glad I'm not really part of this frigging crazy family.'

My world was crashing. I pushed past Uncle in the doorway and rushed out.

The cold hit me. I realised I'd forgotten my coat. But no way was I going back for it. My mind was all jumbled. I felt stranded. Adrift. Who was I? Where did I belong? The questions wouldn't stop coming.

My phone vibrated in my bag. I answered without checking who it was.

'Yvie?' Aaron's voice sent me further off-balance. 'Please don't hang up, Yvie,' he said. 'Where are you?'

'It's not a good time, Aaron,' I said, in a throaty voice.

'Why is it never a good time, Yvie? I need to see you. I can come to you.'

'Not now, please, Aaron,' I said. 'Really.' Tears were threatening to start again. My head was pounding.

'I'm leaving now.'

'I'm not at home.'

'Well—'

'I… I'll come to you,' I said.

Anger, bundled with confusion, took control. Sent me driving like a maniac through the back streets from Bow to Islington, cutting through amber lights, dismissing people at zebra crossings. I wanted nothing more than to believe this was all a big misunderstanding: Dionne arriving, what she'd told me, Auntie Agnes's story that tied up perfectly with hers – all of it was simply a nasty, horrible joke. Reality would set in and I'd realise that none of it had happened. That was what I wanted to believe.

I tried to compose myself before reaching Aaron's front door, but the red and swollen eyes looking back at me in the rear-view mirror reaffirmed everything. This wasn't a dream, a delusional thought in anyone's head. It was real and I couldn't will it away.

'You crying?' Aaron said, as soon as he saw me.

'I can't stay long,' I said, already feeling this was a mistake.

'In a bad space, huh?' he said.

'Mmm.'

He took my arm and led me into his living room. Thoughts of the last time I was here slipped into my mind. Why was I here?

'What is it?' Aaron said. 'Missing your paps?'

I shook my head. 'Not that.'

'Come. Sit down. It's not me, is it? Because I'd never do anything to purposely hurt you, Yvette.'

I started crying again.

'And I'm sorry about everything,' he said, kneeling in front of me.

'It's not... not just you. Not Pa...' I rummaged through my bag for a fresh tissue. 'It's – I've just found out, I'm not really... not... not Yvette.' I burst into tears, my face in my hands.

'What? Yvette? Say that again?'

'I'm... I'm some child that was given to my aunt in St Lucia by an old lady, when... when I was a tiny baby.'

'What? You're not making sense, Yvie,' he said. 'Start again. I'll get you a drink.'

'No. No,' I said, turning my lips into my mouth to stop myself from crying.

'I'll get you some water.'

While he was gone I blew my nose and took a few deep breaths.

'Take your time,' he said, kneeling in front of me again. 'What's going on?'

I started with Dionne's letter, told him about her showing up, what she'd said and Auntie Agnes's confirmation of it.

'Who the hell am I?' I said. 'I've been living my life as someone else. Celebrating the wrong birthday. My God. It's crazy. I don't belong, Aaron! I don't belong in... in this family. Don't belong anywhere.'

'Wait. Wait a minute, Yvette. Everyone belongs somewhere. And you are you. No matter what.'

'Where, though? Where's my family? I've been using a fake name, got a fake Mum... family. My... my identity's a fake.'

'Yvette,' Aaron said, after a long pause. 'I can't tell you that the adjustments you'll have to make – if this turns out to be true – are gonna be a walk in the park, but no matter what, you're still you. The intelligent, gorgeous, wonderful person that I, and loads of other people, know and love. And I'll bet money your pap's blood runs through your veins.'

He peeled my hand from my face like he was moving one delicate layer from another and tried to meet my eyes. But I kept my gaze on the floor.

'Things will eventually fall into place. I'll still love you for who you are. Hey. Listen,' he said, 'if your mum's not really your biological mum, I can feel better about her checking me out. Remember that day in the kitchen?' He chuckled, shaking his head. 'That was a little too weird.'

I couldn't help smiling.

His arms made a snug ring around me. 'It's going to be fine,' he said, moving back slightly to hold my face between his hands. 'I love you,' he said.

His full lips were on and off mine, as his fingers wiped the tears off my cheeks. 'I miss you,' he said.

'It's so horrible,' I said. 'A mess.' I burst into tears again.

He got off the floor and sat next to me. 'It'll be okay,' he said. 'You'll see.'

A warmth was spreading from his body into mine. His arm felt firm and secure around me. I was in a safe space.

'Why don't you stay?' he said. 'Just for proper company tonight. We can talk.'

Dionne came to my mind. She'd be up by now.

'I can't,' I said. 'Dionne's at home. I hadn't planned to be away for this long.'

'Call her. Tell her you'll be delayed.'

But I didn't. I didn't want to call. Tension was easing out of me as he caressed my back. I turned and relaxed into him and welcomed the cushioning feel of his lips on mine again.

His hand was under my cardigan, stroking the tip of my nipples. I wanted to forget all of the problems between us. I wanted to go back to the way things were. Me and him loving each other, Papa alive, and I was who I'd known myself to be: Yvette Angelina Francis, daughter of Joseph and Dolina Francis. Parents, who despite their differences and questionable ways, loved and cared about me.

He'd unbuttoned my cardigan. I helped him pull it off, together with the jersey top I was wearing underneath. Kneeling down in front of me, he dropped fluffy kisses on my chest. I moaned, uncontrollably as he teased my nipple and gasped when he cocooned one in his warm mouth. I reached for his crotch, but like a tease, his mouth was on the move again, planting moist kisses over my chest and tummy. He continued down, kissing the tops of my thighs, and melted me completely when his lips reached between my legs.

'Ahhh… wait… 'I'm not on the pi—'

'It's all right,' he said, quick and quiet like he didn't want any distractions. 'I'm not letting you go.'

My phone was ringing in my bag. As soon as I opened my eyes, it stopped. The wooden Maasai was lying on his side, across the floor. The lower half of my body was trapped under Aaron's heavy thigh. His arm was flopped across my chest. *Shit.* What had I done?

'Mmm… where you going?' he said, half-asleep.

'Toilet,' I said quietly. Waking him might mean having to unpack stuff – like what had just happened.

'But come straight back.' His body went limp again.

I picked up my things and tiptoed out to get dressed. Checked my phone. The missed call was from my house.

I crept back into the front room, stooped down next to Aaron and whispered, 'I've got to go.'

He opened his eyes, squinting slightly. 'Why?' he said, as if it was unthinkable.

'I told you, Dionne—'

He propped himself up on his elbows and took a quick glance around.

'She'll be wondering where I am. I can't leave her there all on her own like that,' I said.

'I'll come with you.' He made to get up.

'No. It's best you don't. Not today. I'll call you later.'

'Promise?'

I leaned closer and gave him a full kiss on the mouth.

'Come on,' he said, trying to draw me closer.

'I can't,' I said, and stood up to avoid toppling down on him. 'I'll call.'

Chapter Thirty-Nine

Yvette

The scent of Aaron's aftershave was lingering under my nose until I pushed open my front door. It was definitely fish. The first voice I heard was Mum's, then Dionne shouted: 'We have a visitor.'

'What're you doing here?' I asked Mum.

There were two used plates and cutlery on the side table. My front room smelt like an unaired kitchen.

Mum stood up. 'You think Agnes could do a thing like dat?'

I looked down at Dionne sitting on the floor. 'You've told her,' I said.

'Uh-huh.' She nodded.

'I cannot believe it. I just caa—' Mum said, coming towards me. 'Agnes? Agnes do a thing like dat?'

'Miss Doli bought us some West Indian food,' Dionne said, picking herself up off the floor and grabbing the plates. 'We left some for you. Let me go and wash these out. You want me to bring yours?'

'I'm okay,' I said, as she slipped past me, leaving a trace of nutmeg.

'I just come here to talk to you,' Mum said. 'An'… an' the young lady tell me… My God, how… how dis could happen? An' neither me nor Joe suspect anything. You believe it? You think it's true?'

'It all seems so,' I said, my tone dull and listless.

'We have to…' She trailed off. 'What you think we should do?'

I shrugged. A craving for my own company made me turn to leave the room.

'I know I did wrong,' Mum said, touching my arm, 'not telling you about me an' Ian. Dat is what I come here to explain, but—'

I was fully aware that she had arrived in England pregnant. She and Papa had told me that story loads of times. And, until now, I'd only seen the romance in it.

'Come an' sit down, *ich mwen*,' she said, tugging at my arm.

I followed her to the settee, though it was one of the last places I wanted to be. With her, and Dionne – her real daughter – and me, the misplaced one.

'Imagine,' Mum lowered her voice, 'if you did make the mistake I made on dat boat... I...'

'So you and Ian were—?'

'I should never have let him encourage me to drink,' Mum said, shaking her head. 'I wasn't experienced in any of those things. I... I don't even remember...'

Unplanned sex happens all the time. Mum wouldn't be the first. She was young, no special boyfriend – but unprotected with two men?

'Dis Dionne,' her voice drew me back to my doomed dilemma, 'seems a nice girl, but you are the only chile I know as my daughter. The only daughter I know. I cannot... cannot change my feelings towards you, just like dat. I was talking with her – Dionne – about dat thing, the tests she say people can take to prove who their mother or father is. An' I agree, it's a good idea.'

Dionne entered the room with a plate of food on a tray. Me and Mum looked up at her.

'Green fig and mackerel,' she said, handing it to me, then finding a space on the floor between me and Mum. 'Nice, with not too much pepper.'

The herby fishy smell started circling again.

I glanced at the tray on my lap. 'I've seen Auntie Agnes,' I said.

'Eh-eh. She's here? You see her?' Mum said, sliding her bottom to the edge of her seat.

I nodded. 'And you were right,' I told Dionne.

'What she say?' Mum said, edging further off her seat. '*Vyé ipokwit-la.* The old hypocrite. What she have to say for herself – dat Agnes?'

'How sorry she is and how we must forgive her.'

'I suspected she would follow me,' Dionne said.

'Only God can forgive her,' Mum said.

'She believes He already has,' I said, staring at the food on my plate.

'What Auntie an' Uncle say?' Mum asked.

I swallowed some saliva to moisten my throat. 'He wasn't there until later,' I said, and put the fork down.

'Well. Well. My own sister can do dat to me? When Agnes turn to be so… so…? You mean to tell me, she couldn't find one man in the whole of St Lucia to give her a chile?'

'I'm not sure if she did it because of that,' I said.

'So why? What could provoke her to do a thing like dat?'

'Maybe she was lonely,' I said, quietly.

'Or crazy,' Dionne butted in.

'Well… well … well. Agnes hide dat side of her good.'

'Deceitful beyond belief,' Dionne added.

'God only knows,' Mum said.

After a crumbled silence, Mum sighed, picked her handbag up and took out her keys.

Me and Dionne looked at her.

'It's getting late,' she said, and stood up. 'Let me know when you all want me to come an' give dat sample, eh?' Her eyes slid from me to Dionne.

I followed her to the front door, stepped out with her and took her arm.

'You better tell Dionne about what happened on the ship,' I said, quietly. 'Otherwise, I'll have to. She's going to find out if Papa wasn't her father.'

She looked at me, statue-like. Her lower lip quivered and she bent her head. 'Good night,' she said and walked away.

'She's okay?' Dionne asked, when I went back in.

'Mmm.' I nodded.

'I've been meaning to give you this,' she said, and handed me a small, brown envelope. 'Miss Rosina asked me to give it to you.'

I took it from her and went upstairs.

Chapter Forty

Doli

My involvement with Ian on the boat is not something I feel proud to talk about. Man an' woman business is not something big people should have to discuss with children. Yvette is asking for too much from me. An' as much as dat girl, Dionne, seem nice, I am still not sure I believe Yvette isn't mine. The chile I did send down for Agnes to take care of for me.

Mama must be turning circles in her grave to find out what Agnes do. Agnes, my big sister, always quiet... shy – more shy than me, an' close, close, close to Mama. How she can do dat to me? Agnes dat everybody, especially me, believe to be so kind, was always helping me out; somebody I did always trust.

Frien's can never take the place of fam'ly, Mama used to tell us. Mama, it looks like you was wrong. I see Bel care about me more than my own sister. We talk a lot since Joe funeral an' dat make me see how I let myself go. I didn't even fully recognise my own place. Rinse clothes amongst dirty. The bathroom look like nobody don't live dere. *Bondyé*. I couldn't tell when I last open a window in the house.

I make a list of the things I agree with Bel I have to do to keep from drowning in the deep, dirty water I feel trying to pull me down.

'It'z you?' Cedric say, when he hear my voice. His own sound like he have a bunch of tissue paper push inside of his mouth.

'I phone to say sorry for… for the way I behaved. I… I didn't understand myself.'

'Thaz's okay,' he say.

'But what… what happen to your voice?'

'Hot feeling ma bez,' he say.

'The flu?'

'Norr. Ah had zome dentol wok done yeserday. Huts to talk.'

'Oh… oh. I… I didn't realise. I'm so sorry.'

Cedric, who could always find something to say about something, was silent.

'Well, I better let you rest,' I say. 'Take care, eh?'

'Mmm. Hanks for calling.'

Before I could put down the phone I feel to punish myself. Bel was right, I was ready to let Cedric go for something dat had nothing to do with the kind of man he is. The man had problems with his teeth.

'Give an' take,' Bel tell me is what life is all about. I know dat. I have to learn to do more giving, an' taking people for who dey are, like dey have to take me.

Joe die already, so I cannot have a conversation with him, but I hope I will be able to make Yvette understand.

Chapter Forty-One

Yvette

I was brushing my teeth, the next morning, when I heard Dionne going down the stairs, then the front door shutting. I rushed to my bedroom window. She was getting into Mum's car.

In that short time, they were already bonding. And why shouldn't they? Mum, the mother I believed was mine, really belonged to her, didn't she? Not me.

The envelope Dionne gave me last night from Miss Rosina was sitting unopened in the bottom drawer of my dresser with Papa's bundle of 'not sure' documents. I'd been too scared to open it.

I braced myself, as if I was about to receive a verdict, got the letter out and sat on the bed to read it.

My dearest daughter, it started.

As I write this letter to you, I wish I could see you face-to-face, to hold you to my chest and smell you, like I did when you were a baby. I know you are a grown woman now, but I can still see your little feet, hands and little round face before Gwamama took you away.

I loved your father, Joe, very much. He was my first and I trusted him, but things happen in life and we cannot always be in control.

You have two sisters, Rhonie and Layla. Like me, they are very excited to meet you.

I know you must have doubts, but I remember everything about you, including your birthmark. It's a dark shape like a small almond at the back of your right knee. That cannot change.

My God. I dropped the letter, went quickly to the mirror to confirm what I already knew. How else could she know that? Could someone have told her?

I picked the letter back up.

There is so much more to explain than I can say here.
My number is at the top of this letter. Please write and send me yours so that we can talk.

With so much love, your mother, Rosina.

'Rosina.' I said her name out loud. Was she truly my mother? And sisters? I have sisters? The idea of her, of them, what she'd said, added another layer of complications, things to unravel; to dig out of this box full of stuff I'd have to understand, accept and come to terms with.

I put the letter back in the drawer.

I was due back in to work on Wednesday, but that wasn't likely to happen. Not now. I made some coffee and turned my phone on. There was a missed call from Pe and three from Aaron. Both had also texted: Pe confirming our plans to meet for lunch later. And Aaron wanted us to meet for a drink when he finished work.

After calling Brenda to extend my leave, I vacuumed the stairs and landing, and put a load in the washing machine, the whole time rereading the letter from my supposed mother in my head. Occasionally, touching the birthmark behind my knee.

*

'Sorry I'm late,' Pe said, settling into a chair opposite me. I'd watched her manoeuvre her hips between the tables to get to where I was sitting, in our favourite Turkish eating spot.

'You look happy,' I said.

'They're gonna pay half of the fee for the Masters.' She rocked her head from side to side, beaming. 'If I get in.'

'That's great. Course you'll get in.'

I was happy to see the excitement in her eyes. She deserved this.

We selected our usual. Me: sea bream and salad. Her: chicken kebab.

'So?' she said, leaning across the table towards me, as soon as the waitress turned her back.

I updated her and saw some of the calmness and joy she'd brought to the table seep away.

'So, she's your sister?' Pe said, sitting upright.

'If it turns out that Papa's her dad.'

'DNA tests would confirm everything, but that can take ages, can't it?'

'Dionne already arranged for us to do it privately – even before she arrived,' I said.

Pe put both her palms on the table and stared at me. 'She's some kind of woman,' she said.

'Damn presumptuous, you mean.'

I told her about the birthmark.

She swallowed. 'Makes it all the more likely, doesn't it? That you are the one – the lady's child.'

'Mmm.' I hadn't been able to convince myself of that yet.

Our meals arrived.

'You gonna contact her, then?' she asked, dragging the chunks of chicken off the skewer and onto her rice.

'Miss Rosina? Yeah. At some point.' I pushed the food around on my plate. 'I just wish things could go back to…'

'Before she came? Dionne?'

'Before she sent that bloody letter.'

What about Aaron?' she said, I sensed she was trying to change the subject.

'Well, I did tell him I wasn't on the pill anymore – at least, I tried to.'

'The mind was strong, but the body weak?'

'It'll be okay,' I said.

'Like last time?' She raised her eyebrows and gave me one of her bulging-eyes stares.

'That was different,' I said, determined not to let the conversation move to the time when, six months into my relationship with Aaron, we'd messed about without a condom and I'd ended up pregnant.

Pe had helped me find a private clinic, driven me there to have the termination then, fifteen minutes later, driven me back home because I'd changed my mind. Three weeks after that, I was in A&E with period pains and not pregnant anymore. After an overnight stay and D&C, I was back home again. And I'd never told Aaron about it.

'Whatever happens,' Pe said, looking up as a couple walked by our table, 'you won't be alone – in managing everything.'

Alone was exactly how I was feeling – panicky, too, since my life was feeling more and more like a busted tyre with multiple punctures.

'I'm supposed to be meeting him later,' I said. 'He wants to talk.'

'Talking's good.' Pe took her napkin off her lap and wiped her mouth.

'Yeah, so is talking to Addae about the course.' I tapped her hand.

'That? I will. I will,' she said, laughing. 'Your thing with Aaron's different.'

'I can't get past him – you know, Aaron, chasing after that invisible ex of his. After so long. Can't help wondering what his real reason was for doing that.'

'But she's dead, Yvie, and if he was still hung up on her you wouldn't have been having the kind of relationship you've been having for the last how many years. You believe what he's told you, don't you?'

'I don't know.' I shrugged.

'He could've told you he was only away working. That would be perfectly plausible, wouldn't it? He didn't have to tell you about going to find a woman and possible child. And you can't fault him for caring – about the child, I mean.'

I'd considered all those points Pe was making. And she was right.

'Oh, before I forget,' I said, wiping my hands. I handed Pe a bag containing two books I'd bought from the multicultural bookshop near work. 'For my Temi.'

'Ooo.' She peeked inside. 'Aw, thanks, Yvie. I'm sure he'll love these. Thanks.'

'Tell him I sent it with a kiss.'

'You need to stop spending your money on my son like this,' she said.

'Who else would I spend it on?' I smiled.

Arriving home to an empty house, revived thoughts of what Mum and Dionne could be up to without me. My mind was on Rob Payne's PI Services when she returned.

'You've been shopping,' I said. She was standing on the doorstep with carrier bags hanging from both hands.

'Yes, I have.' She sounded pleased with herself. 'I should have told you last night. Miss Doli offered to take me to the stores today,' she said.

'Yeah. I could have given you the spare key in case I wasn't in when you got back.'

'I didn't want to trouble you.' She headed for the stairs. 'And I thought it might be good if I was out of your way for a while. Let me put these upstairs.' She lifted one of her arms in front of her. 'Stacy will be so excited when she sees the lovely things I've bought for her.'

'You busy?' She came back down a few minutes later.

I told her no. I'd been checking my emails.

She sat on the sofa behind me. 'I've been thinking – and talking with Miss Doli,' she said.

I turned so I could see her.

'Since you have already cleared Pa... Papa's apartment, so we cannot get anything that would help us from there, you think we could check if the hospital still has any of his blood? They must have taken some.'

'Papa's blood?'

'Or tissue, you know.'

Before I could work out a response the doorbell rang. It was Aaron. 'Oh, hi,' I said. I didn't think he'd just turn up. 'Come in.' But he didn't come any further than the inside doormat.

Dionne's presence was like a prod in my back. I introduced them.

'Nice to meet you,' she said.

'You too.' Aaron nodded. 'Hope you enjoy your stay.'

Me too,' Dionne said and thanked him, smiling.

Then he turned to me. 'Ready?'

'I...'

'Just have a good time,' Dionne said. 'I have plenty to do.'

I grabbed my bag and coat and followed Aaron out.

The mixture of his aftershave with the leather in his new estate car slightly overpowered me.

'You okay?' he asked, before driving off.

'Just, I wasn't expecting you,' I said.

I had agreed for us to go out later, agreed we needed to talk, but we hadn't arranged a time. Him turning up like that hadn't given me a chance to even check my hair or put on some lip gloss.

'How are you?' I said, cracking the window open.

'Not bad.'

'So, d'you think she looks like me?' I said, examining my face in the visor mirror.

Aaron shoved a Motown tape into the player and turned the volume down. 'Likenesses are easy to find if you're looking for them.'

'What d'you mean? You didn't see any?'

'I don't know, Yvie. I didn't look that close.'

'So it didn't stand out to you?'

'Not really.'

'So where we going?' I asked. He was taking the back streets to avoid the Friday night traffic.

'A Jamaican pub up in Shoreditch. Nothing fancy, but I know the guy who owns it.'

We parked around the corner and went swiftly through the drizzle to the pub which was, to me, bordering on shabby. It was tucked under a railway bridge and with the smell, look and feel of any other English pub I'd been to with work colleagues. The big difference here was being greeted by the unmistakable voice of Gregory Isaacs singing 'Night Nurse'.

Aaron held my elbow lightly, guiding me further in. 'Red wine?' he said, turning to me with raised eyebrows.

I was busy assessing the place. 'Yes. Yes, please,' I said. English pubs generally weren't my thing. Apart from the unpleasant smell of beer, they had an atmosphere that made me feel out of place. But this one had a good mixture of people and the music helped.

'We'll go downstairs. It's quieter,' he said, then faced the bar.

I couldn't see any stairs, so loitered close behind him. It reminded me of our first date, when we met up at a trendy wine bar near Liverpool Street and I decided this new man ticked all the right boxes.

Now, I was taking in his familiar stance, broad shoulders, thick arms, waves in his short-cut hair.

'They've only got Merlot,' he turned and said.

'That's fine.'

I followed him around to an area leading to 'downstairs'. The only other people there were a couple of guys at a table looking at wide sheets of paper that could have been building plans. The music was faint. Aaron chose a table away from them and put my glass down next to his usual Guinness. He took his jacket off, rubbed his hands together then sat down opposite me.

I pulled my arms out of my coat sleeves and took a sip of my wine.

'So how are things?' he said.

'Still messy. You know.'

'Mmm.' He took a gulp of his drink and looked around, like the place was new to him. 'It's all right, isn't it? This little place.'

'It's okay.'

'If he spruces it up here and there, it could be a good little venture.'

'Mmm.' My eyes also took in the room, the dark wooden tables and chairs. 'Music's nice.'

'So what's going on?' He leaned in, his elbows on the table, one hand covering the other under his chin.

'I told you last night,' I said, looking right at him, part of me not wanting to think about it.

'If there's anything I can do to help, I'm more than willing.'

His enquiring eyes were all over my face. His lips so appealing. I shifted my gaze to an empty space past his shoulder.

'Yvette,' he said.

'Yeah?'

'I said, I want to help. You listening?'

'How?' I looked at him.

'I... I don't know. In every way... whatever. I want things to go back to how they were between us, before—'

'You ran off?' I said.

'That was something I needed to do. I've told you that,' he said. 'I've done it now. It's over. Time to move on.'

'Where are we moving on to, though, Aaron? Because I don't want what we had anymore.'

'What... what d'you mean?' He frowned.

'This is part of the problem,' I said, sitting upright. 'Where we were was good, but not good enough for me. I need more than what we had or have, Aaron. Do you think you can give me that?'

He took another sip of his drink. 'Yvette.' He glanced over both his shoulders as if he needed to be sure no one was listening, pulled his chair closer to the table and leaned further in. 'I love you, Yvette,' he said, 'and I want you in my life. It's clear you have a lot going on right now, with your dad, this cousin or sister of yours showing up, and everything, but I want to be part of that – to help you... help—'

'I don't need you feeling sorry for me, Aaron.' I tried to stifle the break in my voice.

'You're not hearing me, Yvette, man,' he said. 'This is not...' – he looked over his right shoulder again and lowered his voice – '...

pitying, Yvette. I'm trying to understand and help you, like any other person who… who cares about you would.'

His obvious frustration was making the table wobble. 'I know my rushing off to Holland hasn't helped and I'm sorry for that, but can't we put all of that behind us now?'

'Haven't you heard me, Aaron?'

'Yes. So… so what is this "more" that you want?'

'Don't pretend we haven't discussed it before. You know exactly what I want.'

He took a deep breath, glanced at the other side of the room, then looked at me again. 'A child? Children? You sure that's what you really want?'

I looked him square in the face. 'I've wanted it long enough to know.'

'Yvette,' he said, sounding slightly calmer, 'I'm not gonna lie, I've been thinking about it much more in the last few days since—'

I frowned and threw a look at him.

'Look, Aaron,' I said. 'I'll be thirty-nine next year and will already be classed as a geriatric mother, even if I had a child right now. I might have already missed my chance for having any, full stop, but I'm not prepared to continue in this relationship with you and not having a child simply because you don't want one. That scenario doesn't take what *I* want into account.'

'Isn't that part of it? I mean, if you think you're too old to have children, why not just embrace it? Wouldn't that be liberating? The freedom?'

I turned to avoid him seeing the pain his words were causing me.

'There are lots of women nowadays who don't have children – some of them through choice,' he said.

'As you well know, I'm not one of them. This conversation's over, Aaron.' I reached for my coat on the back of my chair.

'But—'

'I'm tired.' I pushed my chair back.

'Yvette? I do want to make this work for us – for you too, but it's not that straightforward for me.'

There was an honesty in the way he spoke and the innocence on his face made me wish I could hold it between my hands and kiss him. I loved him and wished things could be different. Yes, I wanted a child, maybe two, but also, knowing exactly who I really was – getting to the truth – was gnawing at me now, too. I had to be ready to face necessary changes coming my way: the end of this relationship, who I really was biologically. I had to be able to hold up and not allow myself to collapse.

'Where d'you wanna go?' Aaron asked when we got in the car.

'Home, of course.'

'Right. What happens now?'

'What you have in mind for your life is incompatible with mine, so we part,' I said, trying hard not to cry.

'We could carry on talking at mine,' he said.

'Aaron, I have a lot of crap going on right now. Crap I need to sort out.' My voice had changed. If I didn't stop talking, I'd start crying, so I shut up and tried to focus on the plans Mum, Dionne and I had for confirming who I really was.

He knew better than to continue the conversation, so I settled into a tear-suppressing journey with the odd 'feel-good' song from his Motown's greatest hits deflecting my mood.

'How much do I owe you?' I said, when we got to my house.

'For what?'

'The PI – Rob Payne,' I said. 'You've given him some kind of deposit.'

'I can't remember, Yvette. It doesn't matter.'

'It was for my father,' I said. 'I want to pay you back. Please give me an amount.'

'I said—'

'Please, I have to do this.' My cheque book and pen were already in my hand.

'Okay. Okay… make it fifty pounds,' he said.

'That's all?' I said. It didn't sound right. I quickly wrote the cheque for one hundred.

'You don't need to do that,' he said.

I left it on my seat.

It was so quiet when I got in, I assumed Dionne was asleep, but as soon as I slipped my nightie over my head, there was a faint knock on my bedroom door.

'Yvette?'

What did she want? I was angry with the fucking world again. 'Yes?' I said.

Her head was tied in that same scarf of hers and she was wearing what I presumed was one of her recent purchases: a pair of brushed cotton floral pyjamas.

'Everything all right?' she said.

I told her it was, but it didn't sound convincing, not even to me.

'I wanted you to know that the sample bags should be arriving on Thursday,' she said.

'Oh… oh. Okay.'

'And I hope this will not upset you, but would you be able to contact the hospital Papa was in to just confirm whether they have any samples of his blood or something left?'

'Okay,' I said.

'You'll be able to do it tomorrow?'

'Should do.' I sat on the bed. This was all weighing me down.

'So, how was your date with your hunk of a man?' she said, her tone suddenly more jovial.

'Oh, it's properly over now.' My voice was flat.

'I'm so sorry.'

'It's for the best – long term.'

'I'm really sorry about everything you know, Yvette.'

'It's not all your doing,' I said. 'You only came to bring the truth.'

'But you sure you want to finish with Aaron? He seems a nice guy.'

'I want to be a mother,' I said. 'I have a lot of love to give to a baby – a child. I know age isn't on my side, but I'm more than ready to be a mother. And I think I'd be a good one.'

'Of course.' She sighed. 'I don't know about here, but it's not easy to find a good man, girl.'

'Don't I know that.' It was my turn to sigh.

'There's a lot of possibilities for a beautiful, intelligent woman like you.'

'The possibilities I want don't seem to be on offer,' I said. I was at a senior level at work, with a salary good enough to cover my bills and save. I wasn't in any hurry to get further up the greasy pole. There was plenty of space in my heart and in my life for having my own family. Children, husband or living-in partner. Staying with Aaron on his terms would have meant me carrying on suppressing my longing for that, or giving the desire up altogether.

'D'you think we'll turn out to be sisters?' I said.

'Pretty sure.'

So Mum still hadn't told her about Ian.

'Who does your Stacy look like?'

'Stacy?' Dionne's face brightened. 'It's hard to say. She smiled. 'She's cute – that I do know.' Dionne giggled.

'What's she like?'

'Fun. She's a fun, fun girl. She loves to draw. That child draws everything she sees – even what she imagines. She's real special.'

'Does she know about me?'

'Uh-huh.' Dionne nodded. 'She even wanted to come with me, but this wasn't the right time, plus there's school. You will definitely meet her one day.'

'That would be nice,' I said, after a short pause.

'I'm sorry I had to add more troubles to your life. I come at the wrong time, eh?'

She wasn't wrong, but when would have been the right time?

Chapter Forty-Two

Yvette

The strands of grey had disappeared from Mum's hair and her lipstick and powder were back. But the level of conversation between the three of us, as we put our samples of hair into our individually labelled plastic bags, suggested that everyone's thoughts were as entangled as mine.

'I caa stop,' Mum said, after Dionne finished sealing her bag. There was a fresh breeziness about her. 'I have a frien' to visit. You all take care, eh? We'll talk later.' She rubbed my arm in a way she'd never done before and rushed to the front door.

Mum was gone and all of our sample bags were sealed, except for the empty one meant for Papa.

'It's such a shame – so bad Papa has died,' Dionne said.

I wasn't sure if those were words of sympathy from her to me or personal disappointment relating to Papa's DNA. Mum still hadn't told her there was a possibility that he might not be her father.

After Dionne left for the post office, I called Rob Payne to see how things were progressing with the search. He said he'd be in touch soon.

It rained heavily for the rest of the day. I tried calling Mr Sutton's secretary to see if she knew whether the hospital might have any blood samples belonging to Papa, but no one answered the phone. After checking with the main switchboard, I found out his secretary was off work for a few days. I told them my query and they referred me to the microbiology department, who said the request would have to be put in writing by Papa's next of kin.

Dionne looked deflated, when I updated her. 'I was hoping to get further than this when I decided to make this trip.'

She hadn't banked on Papa not being here. We agreed to ask Mum about writing the letter. 'But I'll be long gone,' she said, 'by the time they check all of that.'

Back upstairs, while responding to texts from Miss Elsa and Miss Bel, asking how I was, I felt the tingling of cramps. With all that was happening, I'd pushed that particular concern to the bottom of the list. A period would mean one less thing for me to worry about.

I called Miss Elsa. I owed her a big thank-you for overseeing the clearance of Papa's flat.

'It's no problem at all, darling,' she said. 'We did find a couple of old pictures that had fallen behind the wardrobe. I have them here for you.'

Hearing her voice made me long for Papa and the friendship me and her had developed because of him.

'I've got a surprise visitor from Trinidad,' I told her, without going into details. We agreed we'd get together as soon as I had more time to myself.

It was six in the morning when I opened my eyes. I made some coffee, then checked my emails.

There was one from Brenda about work, but I skipped that to move on to the one from Rob Payne's PI Services. They'd found Ian Douglas. The news sent a charge through me. It was too early to call them now, but they'd be open by the time I'd showered and got dressed.

'I take it you've received the email,' Rob Payne said, after Inez put me through.

'Yes. It's great,' I said. 'But you didn't give his address or telephone number.'

Rob Payne advised me that he'd put some documents in the post, but could let me have Ian Douglas's contact details now, if I wanted.

Ian Douglas was living in Hertfordshire. Writing his address down gave me a bout of satisfaction and relief, mingled with dread.

'I can't thank you enough,' I said.

'Your payment's good enough – and recommendations, of course,' Rob Payne said. I imagined him secretly puffed up with pride that he had a satisfied client.

'What is it?' I said. 'The bill.'

'Oh, that's already been taken care of.'

'But… by… by whom?'

'Aaron, of course. We gave him a special rate and he insisted on finalising it. It is okay, isn't it?'

Damn. 'Oh, I'll sort it out with him,' I said.

'Best of luck with contacting Mr Douglas,' Rob Payne said. I'd declined his offer to do that for me. 'And, before I forget – sympathies again for your dad's passing and sorry we didn't get to finish the job before – you know.'

'Okay. Thank you,' I said.

'And, er… tread carefully when making contact with Mr Douglas. You don't know what you might be walking into.'

'They've found him,' I said to Dionne, who'd walked in as I cut the call. She was dressed like she had somewhere to go. 'Ian Douglas,' I said, responding to her puzzled look. 'The man I told you Papa asked me to find for him.'

'Oh, that's good,' she said. 'I'm pleased for you. I'm going to do some sightseeing with Miss Doli today.'

'Mum?'

'I didn't really come here for that, but then I thought why not? I'm here. You want to come?'

'No. No. You go ahead,' I said, and took the piece of paper I'd written Ian Douglas's contact details on. 'You might as well. I'm sure you'll enjoy it.'

'She's on her way.'

I gave her the spare key and hoped part of Mum's plan today would include telling her about Ian.

As I prepared to leave the house, I thought about Papa. If he'd been alive, how would he have felt to know I'd found Ian? Would he have wanted to come to meet him with me?

'You didn't kill him, Papa. He's alive,' I said out loud. 'He's alive.'

King's Cross Station was bubbling with people, most dragging travel bags and some pushing buggies. Small groups gathered under train timetable boards. Whistles were blown, giving the all clear for trains to depart, while face-to-face and a few mobile phone conversations, interrupted by overhead announcements, filled the air. The added ingredients of food-on-the-go: burgers, chips, toast, teas and coffees weaved through the to-ing and fro-ing, confusing my senses. I forced myself to focus, bought my ticket and boarded the train. As we moved off, I tried to block out the chatter and movements in the carriage and concentrated instead on the view through the window next to me.

The city gave way to suburbia, then large areas of grassland dotted with creamy blobs of sheep and black-and-white cows.

Living in London can make you forget how beautiful and pleasing to the eyes some parts of England are. But the perceived calm and safety are deceptive, at least to people looking like me. I was expected to integrate – lose myself in Englishness, like Brenda – or accept the isolation, strange stares and comments from white people reminding you that you were 'a foreigner' who didn't belong here.

All Papa had asked me to do was to find out whether Ian was dead or alive and, according to the PI services, he was alive. So, why was I making this trip? Wouldn't that information alone have satisfied Papa? But what if it wasn't the right Ian Douglas? What if the PI services had made a mistake? I had to see for myself. Meet him. Ask a few questions. I could have waited for Mum to tell Dionne about her and Ian before coming. Dionne might have had more to gain from making this trip than me. Mum might not be brave enough to tell her, but I had to know whether Ian or Papa was Dionne's dad.

Rows of relatively new houses with neat little front and back gardens signalled that we were close to the end of the forty-five-minute journey to Letchworth.

The map indicated that Ian Douglas's house was only a bus ride away from the station and since it wasn't that cold, bussing it might be more pleasant than getting a cab. There were some non-white faces around, but not so many that I'd forget I was in unfamiliar territory. I got off the bus three stops after the town, followed the directions I'd highlighted on the map, and found myself in a crescent of semi-detached houses made of orangey bricks. In front of them was a patch of manicured grass with three metal, antique-looking benches on it. Despite the tree stuck between each semi, the place had a sterile and unwelcoming feel.

I walked up the path leading to Ian's door and put my map away before ringing the bell.

'Hello? Yes?' came a voice from behind the white metal door. It opened with the safety chain on. 'Can I help you?' the woman said, in an accent I couldn't place.

'Good afternoon,' I said, and told her my name. 'I'm looking for a Mr Ian Douglas.'

'And you are from—?' she said, her eyes examining me through the tiny gap in the doorway.

'Er… London,' I said.

'And where do you know him from?'

'I… I don't personally,' I said, 'but my mother and father know… knew him. They travelled here from the Caribbean together – on the same ship. It's a long story.'

'Oh.'

'If you let me in, I can explain.' This wasn't going right.

'As a matter of fact, he's not here at the moment,' the woman said. 'He won't be back for a few days.'

'Oh,' I said again. I hadn't prepared myself well enough for this.

'Why didn't you call before coming?'

'I… I tried,' I lied, 'but there was no answer.'

'Well, you should've keep trying.'

'Yes,' I said, feeling disappointed and stupid.

'What did you say your name was again?' she said.

'Yvette. Yvette Francis,' I said, reminding myself that wasn't necessarily correct.

She asked me to wait, closed the door and came back with a piece of paper and pencil, which she handed to me through the narrow gap in the doorway.

'Write your details down for me,' she said. 'I will give it to Ian when he returns and ask him to call you.'

'Thank you,' I said.

The door clicked shut as soon as I handed the information to her. But, halfway up the road, when I turned to check where the sound of footsteps was coming from, I saw the woman walking briskly towards me. I waited for her.

'I'm sorry,' she said, when she got closer, panting as the wind played with bits of her silky, greying hair. 'I hope you didn't think I was being rude. Come. Come with me.'

She led me back to the grassy area in front of the house. 'I didn't ask why you came,' she said, trying to tuck in a bunch of hair blowing across her cheek. She was Afro-Indian like Miss Belvina. Mum, and her generation, were likely to call her a *dougla*.

'It's a bit complicated,' I said.

'I'm his sister, Geraldine,' she said. 'One has to be careful these days. But you seem like a nice girl. All the way from London, you say you've come?'

'Yes.' I nodded.

'Why don't we go inside?'

Geraldine showed me into a cosy front room where a real log fire was burning, and offered me a seat on a comfy sofa, then some tea, which I declined until she said she was going to have some.

There were pictures of people I assumed were family and friends. The one that caught my eye was directly above the fireplace. A confident-looking man, sitting on a chair, wearing a dark suit. I got up to scrutinise his features: soft, friendly brown eyes, like Geraldine's; his nose widened towards the tip and his warm smile showed a hint of teeth. His short haircut looked like a shadow over his head.

'Oh, that's our Ian,' Geraldine said, coming back into the room with a tray. 'I hope a regular brew is okay. It's what we like.'

I told her that would be fine and while we drank our tea she told me that Ian was currently in hospital.

'Oh. I hope it's nothing serious,' I said.

'It's a regular thing, especially lately,' she said.

I discovered she was his only sister, a retired nurse who came to England in her late teens.

'The reason why I've come is…' I wasn't sure where to start. 'Your brother… Ian, was involved with someone on the boat trip to England.'

'Oh, yes?' She raised her eyebrows and took a sip of her tea.

'I think they have a child,' I said quietly.

'What?' She almost dropped her cup. She paused and said, 'It's you? The child is you?'

'I'm not sure. There's another person, the same age as me. Dionne. It could be either one of us.'

'My God.' Geraldine held a hand on the side of her face. 'But how did this happen? How could it?'

'One of us, whom I believed was me, was sent back home as a baby.'

'Home?'

'St Lucia, where my parents are from.'

Geraldine's shocked expression softened into one of empathy. 'Okay,' she said.

'Well, this baby, which could be me, and Dionne – the other person – were taken care of by the same woman in St Lucia until I was nearly five and was sent back here.' It felt weird. Detached. A little disloyal, referring to Auntie Agnes as simply a woman. 'She, the woman, has confessed to swapping us,' I continued. 'What we're trying to do now it find out which one of us is which – who our real parents are.'

'God,' she said. 'Sounds messy. So this child would be my—'

'Niece,' I said. 'Your niece.'

'My God,' she said. 'I gave up on motherhood so long ago. And have long accepted that I would never be anybody's auntie, either.'

I felt her emptiness and tried hard not to slip into her apparent space of acceptance.

'You're in a difficult situation,' she said. 'You both.'

'Yes,' I said, and I explained about the tests.

'Our Ian used to come across as being quite a player, you know, especially during his heyday. But no little nieces or nephews have come as a result. A niece...' she said, her voice lowering as if she was thinking out loud. 'What joy it would be to discover a niece.' She paused. Her eyes were glistening. 'But I would need to ask him first. I couldn't just—'

'I understand,' I said, though a part of me wished she'd pop upstairs, come back, hand me a sample of her brother's hair and send me merrily on my way.

'My father – the man I've always known as my father – said no one had seen your brother since the night before they docked,' I said. 'It niggled at him for years, but Papa had no way of contacting him.'

Her voice became quiet again. 'He's epileptic, our Ian.'

I was glad to hear her confirm it.

'That day, when the ship arrived, the good friend I had sent to pick him up turned up at my house without him and with the frightening news that my brother had been taken to the hospital. Imagine my panic.'

'God,' I said.

She had a hand on her chest. I felt sorry to force her to relive the whole experience.

'But everything turned out as well as could be expected, in the end. He still has his episodes – has difficulty walking at times, but he's not doing too badly.'

'Oh, good,' I said.

'Listen, just leave things with me. Oh, but that would mean you having to make another trip, assuming he agrees.'

I was a bit wary that she might find me over-presumptuous, but told her I had the sample bag with me. 'I was hoping he'd be here,' I said, about to reach into my bag.

'Of course. Yes. I can put the sample straight in, if he agrees.'

'And send it off,' I said.

All she'd have to do was write his name on the stick-on label. The postage was already paid. The results would go to Dionne.

She took the bag from me, agreeing it would speed things up. I couldn't stop thanking her.

'We are helping each other,' she said.

The look of desperation I caught in her eyes made me hope it would be Dionne who'd turn out to belong in this family. Geraldine was a bit too close to the childless woman I feared I might end up being.

Dionne wasn't back when I got home. I wrote out a cheque for four hundred and fifty pounds to send to Aaron for what I hoped would cover the rest of Rob Payne's fees.

Chapter Forty-Three

Yvette

I stared at the phone for a few seconds before answering it.

'Is that Yvette?' It was Geraldine.

The last few days had been full of ifs and buts: trying to guess what Ian Douglas might decide; what influence his sister might have on him.

I held my breath for a second. 'Yes, Geraldine.' I exhaled. My wait for this call was over. 'How are you?'

'Not too bad at all.'

'Have you told him?'

'Ian? Yes,' she said. 'He's with me now and would like to talk to you, if you don't mind.'

I told her I didn't and in no time a smooth, formal-sounding voice said: 'Hello?'

'Is this Ian – Mr Douglas?' I said.

'Yes. Yes. You are Joe's daughter?'

'You remember him?'

'Of course.'

Papa's story of his altercation with this man replayed in my mind. Papa and him as young men.

'I hear he's passed.'

'Yes.'

'I'm sorry to hear that. I never got to see him or anyone else after that silly business – that silly fight of ours. I was acting stupid, looking for a challenge, and I got one.'

'He was sorry about… for what happened between you and him on the ship. He hadn't forgotten you. That's why he asked me to find you. We hoped I would before he—'

'So, he and Doli got married then?'

'Yes.'

'And how is she?'

'She… she's okay. I suppose Geraldine's told you about the possibility that you might have a child with her?'

His tone lifted. 'Yes. That's what I understand. I must say, the whole thing sounded too bizarre at first.' He cleared his throat. 'Quite unexpected. It was such a long time ago. And yes, Doli and myself did get close. I mean, she was a very beautiful woman – guess she still is. I've thought about her at odd times. So full of… just nice to be around. My plan was for us to stay in touch, of course, but this stupid… mix-up with Joe, and the damn epilepsy, turned everything upside down.'

'I'm sorry,' I said. It all sounded very sad.

'Oh, don't be.' He livened his tone again. 'A father, eh? And I find out all thanks to Joe setting you to finding me? So, he didn't dislike me that much after all.'

'He wanted to know if you were okay, after the fight.'

'Mmm,' Ian Douglas said. 'Well, I've talked it all over with Deanie. We agreed tests would be the right way to go.'

'Oh, that's fantastic,' I said. I'd lived up to my promise to Papa to find Ian Douglas and was pleased he was alive. Papa would have been too.

'We all need to be sure,' Ian Douglas continued. 'Though it would be a lot to start fathering a child at my tender old age.' The lowering of his voice, when saying the last three words, made me imagine him smiling in some shy kind of way. I wished I could have seen this man that Papa couldn't put behind him. The man my supposed mother had found so irresistible.

'Let me put Deanie back on,' he said.

'The sample's right here,' Geraldine said. 'I'm going to send it off as we agreed, and save you another trip. I'll send it express, too.'

'You sure?' I said, although that question should have been directed at myself. I was putting a lot of trust in someone I hardly knew. 'Thank you so much.'

'As long as you or Di—?'

'Dionne,' I said.

'Yes. As long as you let me know,' she continued, 'as soon as you get the results.'

I assured her that we would.

Chapter Forty-Four

Yvette

Me, Mum and Dionne had asked for the individual DNA test results to be emailed to each person separately, and we'd arranged to be together when we read them. So Mum arrived at seven in the morning with me and Dionne, still in our night clothes, huddled around the computer. I was at the keyboard.

The coded numbers and letters my eyes first skimmed over were part of the analysis, but irrelevant to me at this point. It was what was written below in plain English that had me frozen. I took a deep breath and released it slowly, as I read:

Dolina Morella Francis is excluded as the biological mother of Yvette Angelina Francis. Probability of maternity is 0%.

Over the last few days, I'd had enough discussions and time to think and consider everything so was pretty sure what the results would be. But seeing it written on the screen in bold black letters hit me with such a destabilising force, I had to read it again. Then, what I wanted was to press a button, make a wish – find a way to erase the whole situation. But DNA does not lie. Miss Rosina. Dionne. No one was trying to trick me.

'Mum's your mother,' I said to Dionne, my breathing shallow.

'Let me see,' she said, poking me in the back. 'Let me check mine. Please. Let me see.' Her voice went into that squeak of hers.

I drifted over to the armchair by the window, truth bleeding into me.

'You are my mother,' Dionne was saying. 'I have found my mother.'

I was in my house. My home. But I didn't feel like I belonged there. I saw myself walking out, going to find the place – the family I belonged to. I'd been an unknown fraud; wearing Cinderella's slippers, and passing as her. But the truth had finally smacked me in the face.

Dionne's glittery eyes met mine. Her euphoria obvious from her smile, but I couldn't share her joy.

'If,' Dionne said, still holding my gaze, 'the hospital has samples of—'

Mum was sitting on the sofa behind Dionne, her hand over her mouth.

'You've got to tell her about Ian,' I said.

Dionne got up, walked to the middle of the room, threw a glance at me, then towards Mum.

'Ian?' Dionne said.

Mum's voice fell to a near whisper. 'Come an' sit down,' she said. 'Dere… dere's something I have to tell you.'

Dionne frowned, flashed me a look and sat next to Mum. 'What? What is it?'

'Yvette already know,' Mum said.

Dionne turned her gaze to me again.

'You… I got pregnant with you on the boat coming to Englan'.'

'What?' Dionne said.

'Well, you see…' Mum gave me a pleading look. 'Me an' Ian did get friendly on the boat.'

'Friendly? You mean you and him – Ian? That same—'

'Yes, she had sex with both Papa and Ian on the ship coming over here,' I said, bluntly.

The muscles in Dionne's face tightened. 'Miss Doli?' she said, looking back at Mum. 'What you saying?'

'She's saying your father could be Ian or Papa,' I said.

Dionne stared at her confirmed biological mother.

'It's true,' Mum said, looking away. 'I didn't want to tell you, if it wasn't necessary. But Yvette—'

'You didn't think I needed to know? After everything?' Dionne's raised voice forced Mum to look at her again.

'I didn't want to cause you—'

'So Joseph Francis might not be my father?'

'I… I don't believe,' Mum said, lowering her head, 'dat… dat Ian is your father.'

'But he could be,' Dionne said. 'And you…' She gave me an accusing look. Her bottom lip started to curl as her eyes brimmed with tears. 'Didn't you say you found him?'

'Yes, and I went to… to look for him, but—'

'You find him? Ian?' Mum said, standing up. 'You see him?'

Dionne's eyes stayed fixed on me. 'Why didn't you take me with you, if—?'

'I didn't see him,' I said. 'And we don't know if he is your real father.'

'Oh, God. This is a whole heap of madness,' Dionne said.

'But I got a sample of his hair,' I said.

Dionne turned sharply towards me.

'It went off yesterday, to the same DNA company.'

'How you manage to do that?' Dionne said.

'I just did,' I said.

'You did that? For me?'

I nodded.

'Really?'

She came towards me. I stood up and she wrapped her arms around me. 'Thank you,' she said, quietly, in my ear.

Chapter Forty-Five

Doli

I bide my time long enough, telling myself it don't make sense going to see my sister unless something good will come out of it, but the feelings I was carrying started to burn like pepper inside me.

'Where Agnes?' I ask Uncle.

'Eh-eh. Doli?' he say.

I step inside an' drop my bag on the floor. 'Agnes?' I shout out. I see her skinny arse on the landing outside Yvette old bedroom.

'Who is dat?' she say. Her voice sounding as innocent as ever while she moving backwards to go in the room.

'Yes. Hide. Is best you hide. You…? Call yourself a sister?' I say, stamping up the stairs.

Before she could get away, I catch hold of her jumper.

'Dol – let me… let me explain,' she say.

I grab her arm, hold it tight, push her up against the wardrobe an' trap her dere, the smell of soap powder on her clothes suffocating me.

'Explain,' I say, 'why you try to steal my chile from me? Who the hell you think you are?' I jab her with my knee. 'God?'

'I… I never had your luck, Doli,' she cry.

Her head come up in my face as she struggling to get away. I grab a piece of her hair.

'Luck? My luck?'

'Doli, please,' she scream, an' lift her arm for protection. 'Every man wanted you. You had a husban'… plenty opportunity to have more chil— Doli! Stop. Please.' She twisting an' turning.

'So is for you I have my chile?' I get another chance an' give her one elbow in her face.

'Lucille?' I hear Uncle shouting.

'*Vyé ipokwit.* Old hypocrite. Sly mongoose, you,' I say, an' push her against the wardrobe.

She crying, putting her hands over her face, but the more she cry the more I want to beat her arse.

'For you I make my baby?'

I lift up my hand, my fist set tight, ready to land on her again when Uncle grab me.

'Dat's enough. Enough, Doli.' Uncle start to pull me out of the room.

'What right—?' I say, pushing against him so I can land another blow anywhere on Agnes. 'No right—'

Uncle drag me to the top of the stairs.

'She sorry,' Auntie shout.

'It's me dat's sorry,' I say. Water fulling up my eyes. 'Sorry I did ever trust my own sister with my chile.'

'Bring her down, Anthony,' Auntie shout again.

'All dis fighting not going to change anything,' Uncle say.

'Why? Why you all protecting her?' I say, when Auntie reach the landing. 'She is the… the devil himself.'

'Everybody entitled to some forgiveness,' Uncle say, quietly, as if his voice lose its strength.

'No matter what, she is your sister. Fam'ly,' Auntie say, standing by the bedroom door.

'I leave all of you for God,' I say, an' stomp back downstairs, my heart drumming, blood running hot in my veins.

*

I sit in my car. Part of me is dead. Another part feel to kill. Everything in my life need fixing. I vex with the world, an' more vex with myself. I start to drive, still planning on how I going to get a chance to batter dat Agnes again. How Auntie an' Uncle can protect her like dat, I will never know. Who in dis world can I trust? Not Agnes, not Auntie, not Uncle. Dey make a ring to protect Agnes, when she is the one dat do the wrong. Now because of her everything turn upside down.

'What happen to you?' Bel say, when she see me.

I tell her how I fight with Agnes.

'You? You fight her?' she said. 'You?'

I look at the two nails I break. 'I am no better a mother than Joe was a father,' I tell her, while we sit in her kitchen, busy making tea.

'What? What you mean by that?'

'How many women would not recognise their own chile? My own chile dat come from inside me, Bel.'

Bel put a cup of tea in front of me on the table an' sit down. 'Your husband didn't suspect anything, either,' she say.

'Bel, I didn't really want to have a chile, when I was pregnant with Yvette,' I say, quietly. 'Not the way it did happen. I believed Englan' would give me opportunities, choices; a chance to be able to decide which way my life will go.'

'Doli, everybody come here looking for better – better than they had back home. Most of us didn't get it.'

'Maybe I didn't love my baby enough,' I tell Bel. 'If I did, I would have paid more attention… recognise something. Anything, even small.' I take in some air an' release.

'Not every woman wants to have children, Doli. You know that. We take what we get and try to make it work. Isn't that what you tried to do?'

I listening, but cannot find any words to respond.

'All those things that just come to light,' Bel say, 'are sad, painful for everybody involved, but there is nothing you can do about what has already happened. All any of you can do now is try to fix what you can.'

'Fix? Dat can ever fix?'

'Little by little, maybe.'

'You think I am a good person, Bel?'

'Of course. You are my closest friend, Doli. How could you not be a good person?'

As she say dat, I think again about how I was about to turn my back on Cedric because of the shock to see his mouth without all of his teeth. An' how much shame I did feel after he explain to me dat he did lose some of his teeth due to a electric shock dat throw him across a room. It's months now the dentist trying to fix it.

'At least now the truth is out,' Bel say.

'Bel, I didn't even know – remember – anything special about my baby, to help me recognise her when she come back to me.'

'Neither did Joe.'

'But who was nursing an' mostly changing her, Bel? Not me?'

If I could have get closer to my own chile before sending her to St Lucia, I might have been able to see a difference in the one Agnes send back to me.

I leave Bel. An' on my way back home pull up by the church.

Dere was a dance on our final night on the ship. Me an' Moira left the other girls in the hall to go an' the use the toilet. While we freshening up our lipstick, I realised one of my earrings missing.

Moira look around with me to see if we find it, but it wasn't anywhere we could see. I tell her I going back to the room to put on a different pair. Although I was hoping to find it on my way.

I had almost reach the stairs when I hear a voice from behind me.

'Why you moving so fast?'

I turn an' see is Ian, who did always have a way of showing up when you don't expect him.

'I don't have time,' I tell him, an' continued walking.

Before you know it, he beside me. 'Girl, you know you leaving a trail of your sweetness behind you?' he said.

'Is dat so?' I replied.

'I have something I want to share with you. I think you'll like it,' he say.

I stop an' look at him. 'Share with me?' I had a hand on my hip to let him know I am not in no pappyshow with him. 'Ian, you like too much playing, you hear?' I tell him. I chups an' continue on my way.

'Wait, wait. Don't take it like that,' he say. 'I know what you thinking, but is not that – not that at all.'

'What is wrong with you?' I tell him, when I reach the cabin an' find him right behind me.

He laugh.

'Move yourself,' I say, trying not to let my eyes linger on his because I already feel dem rolling over every part of me. I open the door.

'Let me show you, nuh?' he say.

'What?'

'I'm sure you going to like what I have here in my pocket,' he say, 'but I can't reveal it out here.'

'Where is it?' I ask him.

He tap on the right side of his chest an' smile.

'Hurry up. Show me,' I tell him. 'It's only you an' me here.'

'That's too risky,' he say, an' point with his head to my room.

I know it was wrong to allow him to come inside the room, but dere was… like the devil controlling me.

'Show me,' I say, once we get inside. I see is a bottle he have, so I let him know I am not a drinker.

'But you will like this one,' he say. 'It sweet – like you.'

'You see you?' I laugh, an' feel my inside start to sof'en.

'Believe me,' he say. 'You never taste nothing like it. Come on,' an' he remind me dat dis is our last night. 'Tomorrow, we reaching England.'

It was time to experience new things.

'Ah, you see? You see how you like it?' he say, after I take a taste. He tell me the drink name is madeira an' his eyes start to move all over me. 'This is your first taste of freedom. Here's to freedom.' He hold the bottle up in front of him, drink some an' offer me some more. I start to feel good.

'Freedom,' I say, an' swallow. Dere was no Mama, no Agnes. Nobody from the village to pass judgement or point any fingers at me.

My head, my whole body, like it start to float. I don't know if is the boat or my body rocking. Rocking but not afraid to fall. The touching, rubbing an' lips touching lips give me such nice feelings. Everything did feel so nice.

The next morning, somebody was calling 'Doli' an' shaking me. 'Wake up, girl. We reaching Englan'.'

'Eh-eh,' Moira say, when I come out from under the blanket. 'Somebody was too tired to even put on nightie, last night.' An she give me a little wink dat tell me my secret was hers.

I open the car door an' walk towards the church. Only the side door was open. I step inside an' as I dip my finger in the holy water to make the sign of the cross, I see the priest going in his side of the confession box.

I enter the other door an' kneel down.

'Bless me, Father, for I have sinned…'

Chapter Forty-Six

Yvette

Life had to go on, the world and time keep moving, but I wasn't ready to be without Dionne's presence in my house, my life. Her arrival had broken the frame of everything I knew about myself into smithereens; transformed the storm my life had been in into a full-blown hurricane, but having her here helped to steady me.

She had to go back to her life. This was something else I had to accept. Sadness drenched me as I looked at her blue suitcase by the front door.

She pushed her bottom lip up and sighed. 'I suppose I'm ready.'

As I saw her to the taxi, I wanted to ask again if I could at least come to the airport with her, but me and Mum had spent the last twenty-four hours doing that. Dionne was adamant. She wanted to go alone.

Last night, she and I agreed to keep the names we'd lived with since Auntie Agnes sent me to England. We wouldn't take legal action against Auntie Agnes either. It wasn't worth it.

Dionne had arranged for the DNA test for her and Ian Douglas to come directly to me. She'd find that easier to manage.

'Just make sure you contact me straightaway, eh?' she said.

I promised I would and took a deep breath as we looked at each other. The girl, now woman, who'd been so much like a part of me – the sister, the cousin – I'd had, then lost. Had I found her again? Was the love she had for me as alive as the love I had for her?

She opened her arms. 'I wish I could stay longer,' she said, hugging me. I held her. The last time we had parted like this we were children. Then, I was the one leaving and our relationship had crumbled.

'We won't lose touch again,' she said, as if she was reading my mind. 'I will make sure of that.'

'Come on, children,' Mum said.

We came slowly apart, holding hands, eyes still on each other.

'Contact Miss Rosina,' Dionne said. 'You will like her. She's nice. And, Miss Doli—' I dropped Dionne's hand as she turned to Mum.

'Mmm.' Mum nodded and pursed her lips.

'Mum?' Dionne said. 'We'll meet again?'

Mum gave another nod. Holding back her words and feelings made the colour rise in her face. She opened her arms to Dionne for the longest hug I'd ever seen her give anyone.

It was early, and I'd hoped that Mum would stay, at least to have a cup of tea, after we waved Dionne off, but she said she had to go.

'I'm preparing a special lunch for a frien'.'

'Oh,' I said.

'His name is Cedric.' The glint in her eyes said more than the half-smile she gave me. 'You'll soon get to meet him,' she said, and skipped off to her car.

I went upstairs and stood for a moment in Dionne's room. Her scent hadn't left – not the nutmeg oil she'd arrived with, but the Angel perfume I gave her, along with the paints and drawing pencils for Stacy. The pleasure I got from seeing Dionne's face light up when I presented them to her came back to me.

'I'll never stop wearing this,' she'd said, sniffing her wrist. 'And Stacy will love these. Thank you, Yvie.'

I faced my reflection in the mirror on the inside of the wardrobe door she'd left open. A close look confirmed that except for the darkish shadow tiredness had stamped around my eyes, nothing was different, at least not outwardly. We can't deny genetics, but it's life experiences – all of them – that has made me into the person I am today.

'What does she look like?' I recalled asking Dionne, the night when she'd handed me the envelope from my mother. 'Rosina. Miss Rosina?'

'Pretty. She's real pretty. Kind of like our – your complexion. Not dark. Not light. About your height, and her voice – it's so gentle, soft – makes me feel so at ease.'

I tried to picture my biological mother as Dionne described. Which parts of her had I inherited?

Chapter Forty-Seven

Yvette

It was almost ten o'clock before I dragged myself out of bed the next day. When I got downstairs there were three envelopes on my doormat. I picked them up.

One was addressed to Mum, and the Royal London Hospital stamp on the front told me exactly what it was likely to be. As Papa's official next of kin, confirmation of whether they had any samples that might have Papa's DNA in it would have to go directly to Mum, but she'd suggested I gave my address.

'You are the best person to handle dis. Not me,' she'd said.

I hadn't stopped being hopeful the hospital would have some kind of samples belonging to Papa. I dropped the other two envelopes on the floor and stood as if in suspended animation, staring at the important one still in my hand.

The first line alone told me. They had nothing which could be used for DNA testing on Papa.

I rang Dionne straight away.

'At least we tried,' she said, when I relayed the news, but the intense disappointment was in her voice.

I'd been back at work for almost two weeks and was trying not to get too caught up in the scares of job losses from the pending restructuring, so I shut myself up in my office for a desk lunch.

I bit into my sandwich – and put it down promptly, as an email from the DNA company dropped into my inbox.

Clicking on it to open it, I covered my mouth and brought my eyes closer to the screen. 'Huh?'

Dionne wasn't my sister, after all. Ian Douglas was her father.

I sat back in my seat, my arms flopped by my side, then rushed out to get an international telephone card.

'My God. I can't believe it,' Dionne said.

The line went quiet, then I heard a sniff that made me imagine Dionne's bottom lip curling, her wiping her eyes.

'It… it doesn't change anything between me' – the tremble in her voice subsided – 'and you. You are my sister. I don't care what any DNA test has to say about it. I can never repay you for finding him.'

'Is someone with you?' I said.

'Stacy's asleep, but – no. I'm not alone.'

It was quiet again, but only briefly.

'I'm sorry,' she said, 'I… I just – I need some time to – I'll call you back.'

I forwarded the email to her straight away, together with Geraldine and Ian Douglas's contact details. *Please let them know ASAP*, I told her. *I'll let you tell Mum.*

Chapter Forty-Eight

Doli

After dat day Yvette force me to give Dionne the idea dat Ian might be her father, I pray I would never have to talk about dis again. But the chile almost put me in hospital when she call me from Trinidad an' tell me is he, Ian, dat's her father.

'I have the results here in front of me,' she tell me.

'But…' I tell her, 'I… I was so sure. I am so sorry.'

True, I was friendly with Joe as well as Ian on the voyage to Englan', but with Joe I had my eyes wide open. It wasn't just something dat happened. Joe was tender an' loving, understanding it was my first time.

'I'm just glad I can finally stop wondering who my mother an' father are. Why they left me like that. Didn't care about me.'

I wasn't sure what to say to the chile. Yvette is who I always see as my chile an' I don't know if dat can ever change. Now it feel like is two daughters I have. One I bring up as mine, love, feel close to; an' the other, a little baby dat did come out of me. A nice chile.

'I know I might never be as close to you and to him like… like I would have wanted, but he seems happy about finding me too,' she say. 'Him and his sister.'

'His sister?'

'Yes. Auntie Deanie. We had a long conversation over the telephone.'

'Dat's good. I'm glad,' I tell her.

'Neither one of you brought me up,' Dionne say. 'So there is a lot we'll never have. But I thank God for making things happen to allow me to find the both of you.'

Her words make something collapse inside me. 'I am sorry for causing you so much... so much confusion an' hurt,' I say. 'I myself still trying to work things out.'

'We all are,' she say.

My own papa died when I was very young. People used to tell me I was his favourite. Agnes was Mama's, but dere was no questions about who our mother or father was. I grow up knowing full well who my fam'ly on mother an' father side was.

'I wish things was different... better,' I say.

'It wasn't all your doing,' Dionne say, but I know the parts I played in all of dis. What both me an' Agnes do cause pain an' confusion to a lot of people. Neither of us are without sin. Still, I don't know if I could ever forgive her.

I finish talking to Dionne, an' remember the day Auntie Lucille did force me to confess.

'So Doli,' Auntie Lucille said, after she call me to her room. The smell from the paraffin heater was making me feel like I was seasick again. 'When last you see your menses?'

'Two... two months ago, Auntie,' I say.

'So Irene send you here to me pregnant?'

'No. No, Auntie. No.' I start to tremble. 'It... hap – happened on the boat, Auntie.'

'On the boat?' Auntie lift up her head from the pile of rinse clothes she was folding. 'Doli,' she say, 'you cannot raise a chile here on your own. Englan' is not like back home when some-body – your mudder, sister, cousin or so – will be dere to give you a hand. You know both me an' Anthony working. Who is de father?'

I dropped my eyes. 'Joe – Joseph Francis, Auntie.' The name just spring from my mouth.

'From where?'

'Bexon, Auntie.'

I was expecting her to curse an' call me all kinds of names, tell me how she was going to write an' tell Mama everything, but she say: 'Anthony have a few contacts. We will try to find dis Joseph Francis – Joe, you say dey call him?'

'Yes, Auntie.'

'Anthony will do what he can to find him an'… an'… we will see.'

I continued spending every morning an' night kneeling by my bed, praying with the rosary Mama did make sure I didn't leave St Lucia without. Yet still my periods didn't come.

But Uncle did find Joe an' he had come to see me.

'So?' he said. His wide eyes was fixed on me. His complexion didn't look as dark as I remembered an' I wondered if people back home were right when dey say the English cole does make people skin come lighter.

'Joe… you… you know on the boat, when we… when… you know. The thing dat happen on the boat between us—'

'What?'

'Dat night, Joe, when you an' me… Joe, I'm pregnant,' I tell him.

'For me?'

'How you can ask me dat?' I said, an' tears come to my eyes.

'Jesus Christ. You pregnant?' He start walking up an' down Auntie an' Uncle room.

'You said dis would not happen – I would not get pregnant, Joe.'

'You pregnant?'

'Sit down, please, Joe. You confusing my head.'

He sit down.

'So what you think I should do?' I did ask him.

'Do?'

'About dis baby, Joe.'

'I… I don't… I don't know, Doli.' His voice turn funny.

A couple of weeks later, he ask me to come an' live with him. He say his chile must have a father.

All those years, I was busy showing Yvette what a disappointment Joe was an' vex because she couldn't see it. But what about me? I have been a disappointment to her too, in so many ways. I wasn't ready for children when I get pregnant an' maybe I had no right having any but, when you find yourself pregnant, you pregnant an' carry your chile.

The marriage I had with Joe was not what I had expected. Wanted. An' I couldn't find it in my heart to forgive him for not being the man I did want him to be. To be by my side more. Now, I have to let all of dat go.

Nothing never stays in the dark for ever, Mama used to say. She was right. I had buried the fact dat either Ian or Joe could be the father of the chile I was carrying so deep inside my head, I almost forget it was dere. I thank God dat I do not have to face Joe with the truth an' already make arrangements to give all of what he leave to Yvette, his rightful chile.

Chapter Forty-Nine

Yvette

I knew I was pregnant even before the results from the pregnancy testing kit. That tingling of cramps hadn't amounted to anything. I didn't tell anyone though, except for Papa, when I made my usual Sunday visit to his grave. Part of me was scared I might have another miscarriage. As the days went by with no signs of that happening, my confidence mushroomed into a quiet joy and hope.

'God, I'm happy for you, Yvette. Who would believe all of this could happen, eh?' Dionne said, when I rang to tell her the news about my pregnancy and to confirmed to her that my DNA results proved Miss Rosina was my real mum. 'Things will work out fine.'

'Mmm,' I said.

Talking with my new mother reaffirmed that only Papa could be my real and biological father. Death had taken him physically, but my love for him will die with me.

Mum told me about Auntie Lucille and Uncle leaving for St Lucia with Auntie Agnes. They were going to see about building on land they have in Vieux Fort. Plus, according to Mum, neither Auntie nor Uncle felt Auntie Agnes was fit to make the return trip alone, and she'd be lucky if her new husband stayed with her after finding out about all of this. Imagine Auntie Agnes, ending up marrying a distant cousin of mine. That's almost laughable.

One day, I might understand why she did what she did. Right now, I can only see it as cruel and selfish. Thinking she could fool everyone, including herself.

They'd tried to call me, but I couldn't face speaking to them, especially Auntie Agnes. The love I'd had for that woman was now a slow, dwindling pain.

Christmas didn't feel like Christmas without Auntie and Uncle. Me and Mum spent the day with Miss Bel and her family, plus Cedric and Raymond, Mum and Miss Bel's new men. I got on well with Miss Bel's daughter, Michelle, who was making a career change from kitchen assistant to professional chef. Her attempt at the Caribbean Christmas black cake was passable, but didn't have that *je ne sais quoi* Auntie Lucille's had.

'It need a little more rum an' essence, but she has a lot of years ahead to fix it,' Mum whispered to me, after our first tasting.

A new closeness has grown between me and Mum. Funny how it came after finding out she wasn't my biological mother. She'll always be my mum in the emotional sense – she's the one who brought me up. Guess it's the same for her.

Pe insisted on me joining her and some of Addae's family for New Year and while she and I took stock of the previous year, I told her about the baby.

'I knew it,' she said. 'That's why you've had this… this kind of calm… okayness about you. And the tiny little weight gain—?'

I hadn't realised any of that was showing.

'You told Aaron yet?'

'Is there any point?' I said.

'What d'you mean? After all of this? He has a right to know, Yvette. I don't have to tell you that.'

I didn't answer. I'd managed to avoid any contact with him over the last few weeks, but I knew what I had to do.

'What if he says he doesn't want to know – doesn't want any baby? Child.'

'Well, you know you're fully equipped to take care of your child, but you know, just as I do, that having two loving parents has to be better than having one.'

'I don't want my baby being rejected.'

'He or she won't be.'

'Well, not by me.' I rubbed my little hump and smiled.

'So it's gonna be a pregnant lady for my chief bridesmaid then,' Pe said, her tone more lifted.

'What?' A light sparked in me. 'You and Addae?' I grinned. 'At last! Please tell me you've told him about the course.'

She nodded. 'He's okay about it.'

'Told you he would be. Getting married. Wow.'

'Yes, we've agreed. His mother says she won't leave until we do.'

'Yippee.' I clapped my hands. 'And you want me to be your chief?'

'Who else? You'll be the only bridesmaid, in fact,' she said. 'It's just gonna be the registry office, but we're gonna do some serious partying after. I'm leaving the organising of that to her too. Keep her busy.'

'Congratulations.' I hugged her.

'To you too.' She rubbed my arm. 'It's great to have you back. I've been feeling like since that Dionne left, she's taken a piece of my bosom friend with her.'

I told her it wasn't like that. 'It's not been easy adjusting to everything.'

'I know.' Pe reminded me she'd had her big loss as a child. 'I haven't forgotten how much it hurt, not being able to have my mum because she was sealed up in a grave. Constantly wishing for a real family I belonged to. But, Yvie, think about it. At least you were raised with people who made you feel loved. You didn't feel like you were an outsider – the one everybody knew didn't belong.'

'Feel a bit like that now,' I said. 'Struggling to make the facts feel real. But more than anything, Pe, it's the deception. The lies that hurt the most.'

'I know,' she said.

'Especially from those you trusted, loved and you felt loved you in return. That's frigging disturbing.'

'Don't forget you've got me. I'm here and love you no matter what.' She chuckled and gave me a hug. 'So when's the baby due?'

'August.'

'Summer baby.'

I nodded.

'You sure you're all right?'

'Mmm. I'm getting there,' I said.

I've questioned so many things over the last six months. Weaved through sleepless nights filled with fretting, anger and grief. Who was I before Dionne arrived? Who am I now? The people close to me, who are they? Were? How have they affected my life, my personality? What's more important now? What should I shed, and what should I hold on to?

The pain all of this has brought hasn't completely left. Tears come easily to me and at unexpected moments. The genes I've inherited, minus physical scars, have created the me I see in the mirror, my outside. But what about my personality? How far have those genes influenced that? My views, the way I see life – the world?

It's easy to agree with Mum and Dionne that what Auntie Agnes did to us was beyond forgiveness, but thinking it through,

I'm glad I was the one she sent to England, because I wouldn't want to change the Yvette I am today.

The top-heavy daffodils were bopping their yellow heads at me as I stood embracing the fresh January air. I dropped the rubbish in the outside bin and went back in, washed and creamed my hands, then picked up the phone in the living room. It was time.

'Aaron, it's me,' I said, on hearing his voice.

'Yvie? You okay?'

'Yeah. I'm fine. I wanted to tell you that I'm pregnant.'

'What?'

The line went quiet.

'You still there?' I said.

'You saying you're pregnant? For me?'

'Who else, Aaron?' I stroke my tummy.

'My God. I'm going to be a father?'

'Yes.'

'We'll need to talk. Can… can I come over now?'

'Of course.' I put the phone down, smiling.

Being pregnant is the best thing that's come out of the last six months for me. I wish Papa was here to share the joy. Still, there'll be more than enough love in my child's life, especially from me.

'And, Baby?' I tapped lightly on my tummy. 'There'll be no secrets about who you are.'

A Letter from Steffanie

Dear reader,

I want to say a huge thank you for choosing to read *This Other Island*. If you did enjoy it, and want to keep up to date with all my latest releases, just sign up at the following link. Your email address will never be shared and you can unsubscribe at any time.

www.bookouture.com/steffanie-edward

The theme of identity wasn't part of the plan when I started writing this novel, but I wasn't surprised when it muscled its way in because it's an area I have always been interested in. I hope the journeys Yvette, Doli, Joe, Dionne and the rest of the characters have taken you on was captivating and, like me, you were able to enter their world, crying and laughing with them along the way.

I hope you loved *This Other Island* and if you did, I would be very grateful if you could write a review. I'd love to hear what you think, and it makes such a difference helping new readers to discover one of my books for the first time.

I love hearing from my readers – you can get in touch on my Facebook page, through Twitter, Goodreads or my website.

Thanks,
Steffanie

 Steffanie-Edward-101943815246620

 @EdwardsaEdward

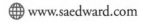 www.saedward.com

Acknowledgements

I would like to thank my mother, Patricia Edward, who planted the seed for this story when she told me about her trip from St Lucia to England on the ship, *Bianca C* in 1960. Thank you too, to Uncle Eddie (Maurice Edward 25.3.35 to 10.2.94) – memories of you helped me create one of my key characters.

Heartfelt thanks to my friends and family, especially my children Marvyn and Shikila, for always encouraging and believing in me.

Esmena Doyley, thank you for being there and for the Jamaican star earrings you gave me to remind me that I am a star.

A huge thank you to my beta readers, Audley Stewart, who never grew tired of reading my drafts, Linda Cadogan, who stepped in at short notice, and Nigel Cooper with his special eye for detail. My husband, Tee, for his encouragement, grammar and linguistic advice and late-night pep talks.

Special appreciation to Debi Alper, for your support and encouragement, especially when I was at my lowest. You went over and above your call of duty at Jericho Writers and have been an invaluable mentor to me.

Thank you to my editor, Isobel Akenhead, without whom this book might not have been published by Bookouture. Thanks also to the rest of the Bookouture team for helping to take this novel through to final publication.

I am grateful to everyone who has helped me in the completion of this novel.